Unexpectedly You

Boston Boys
Book 1

Felicity Snow

Acknowledgments

Thank you to my amazing street team for all of your support in getting the word out about Alex and Bentley's story! And thank you to my amazing beta readers, Hawthorne Gray, Sarra Lancey, Amanda Martin, and Erin Nelson. And of course, my editor Jen Sharon.

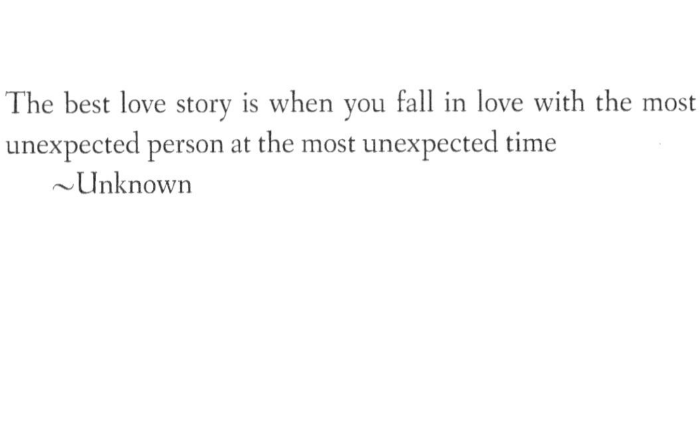

The best love story is when you fall in love with the most unexpected person at the most unexpected time
    ~Unknown

Chapter One

Alex

I give myself one last look in the mirror of my visor and make sure my dark hair is as stylishly tousled as it was when I left my apartment before grabbing the oversized stuffed penguin on my passenger seat and climbing out of my car. It's February in Massachusetts, so it's a bit nippy as I make my way up to the apartment building where I'm picking up my date. But since I've dealt with sub zero temperatures my entire life, I find myself only doing a brisk walk, rather than a full on run as I clomp through the snow and up the stairs, opening the front door and shivering as it closes behind me. I make my way up another set of stairs to the second floor and look for apartment 2D, which is where my date said she lived. We've only been out twice after meeting and chatting on Tinder. I've enjoyed being with her and we agreed to go out again tonight, and she wanted me to pick her up, so she gave me her address.

Her apartment building is nice, not super high end but not a dive either, and only about a ten minute drive from mine. The gray carpet in the hallway is clean and there's artwork of flowers decorating the beige colored walls, along with decorative off-white sconces providing warm light and an inviting environment. It seems relatively quiet as I stop in front of her door and let out a breath before knocking. I was supposed to be here at seven thirty, and I'm just a couple of minutes late.

I start when I hear a voice from the other side of the door that is most definitely not Stacy's. "Just a minute!" It's rich and smoky, with a southern drawl, and when the door opens a moment later I'm staring at a man with golden skin and bright blue eyes, his hair up in a messy bun, a few of the blond and brown strands having fallen loose and framing his handsome face.

"Can I help you?" he asks, a bit timidly as he wipes his hands on a towel. His eyes move from me to the oversized plush penguin in my arms before he meets my gaze again, looking as confused as I feel. He's a bit bigger than me, broader, more muscular, and a few inches taller than my own five eleven.

"Uh," I stammer. "I'm looking for Stacy. I must have the wrong apartment."

He blinks. "This is the right apartment, but she's not home right now." His gaze lands on the penguin again. "Who are you?"

"Her date?" I say it like it's a question even though I don't mean to. I swear I see him flinch, and his face goes slightly pale.

"Her date?" he repeats, his voice so soft I barely hear it.

"Yeah, uh, are you her brother?" I ask hopefully.

He clears his throat, his cheeks flushed now. "No, I'm her boyfriend."

My eyes widen and I swallow, taking a step back. "Shit, man I'm sorry. I swear she never said she had a boyfriend. I didn't, I mean, I wouldn't. It was only twice, and nothing happened, I swear. I...shit, I should go." I turn to walk away but then realize I'm still holding the rather large stuffed penguin and I sure don't want it now, and I'm not giving it to Stacy. I turn back to him. "I'll uh, I'll just leave this here and you can do whatever you want to with it." I take a couple of hesitant steps forward like I'm approaching a rabid animal and set it down outside the door.

"Sorry, again," I stammer, before hightailing it out of there.

Fuck, what a mess. The guy looked awful hearing me say I was here to pick up his fucking girlfriend, and I wonder if I'm the first guy she's cheated on him with. God, I'm really glad I'm not the type to fuck on a first date because I would feel ten times worse if I'd slept with her.

So, little miss Stacy is a two-timing bitch. Good to know. I take my phone out of my pocket to text her. Instead though, I see that I have a text from her that I must have gotten on my way here.

Stacy: Hey, change of plans, can you pick me up from work instead? I'm running late.

Me: Yeah, no. I won't be picking you up at all

Stacy: Wtf?

Me: Yeah, see the problem is, if I wanted to take you out anywhere, I would need to get permission from YOUR BOYFRIEND!

Stacy: Bentley is there?

Me: Yeah, sure. I didn't ask his name but let's just say neither of us were expecting the other. That's a fucking shitty thing to do, fyi. To him and me. Next time you cheat, leave me out of it. That guy deserves way better than you and I don't deserve to be used in whatever sick game you're playing

Stacy: Fuck you, you don't know anything about him or me

I don't bother to reply, just block her number. No way I'm dealing with that shit.

I sigh as I set my phone down and pull out of the parking lot. With nothing to do tonight I guess I'll head back home.

Why is dating so fucking hard? Maybe I should just stick to having a cat and a few plants and call it a day. The idea of never having someone to call my own, someone to come home to at the end of the day, someone to care for, and who will care for me in turn, is seriously depressing, but at least I wouldn't be getting caught up in this kind of garbage.

Not that I needed the reminder, but if I didn't already know it, I do now:

People suck.

Bentley

Well that was humiliating. Finding out my girlfriend of the past three months is cheating on me by meeting her date. I'd decided to surprise her with dinner when she'd texted me to tell me she was having a rough day. We aren't living together, but we had keys to each other's places because we slept over so often it made sense. I'm a massage therapist and own my own business, so I generally don't start work until later in the day. She always leaves first and having a key to her place meant I could lock up after I left.

Today I was off, so I thought I would run home and get some housework done, and then grocery shop before heading back to her place and making her favorite meal. I'd offered to take her out to dinner, but when she'd said she just wanted a quiet evening at home, I thought I would cook for her instead. I was going to have a bouquet of flowers waiting for her as well. Figured it would be a nice surprise for her to come home to. Instead, I'm the one who got the surprise. Who knew a "quiet evening at home" was code for "date with another guy"?

I feel like shit. Fortunately I have my best friend to console me as I lie with my head in her lap, wondering how long I would have gone without knowing about this other guy if I hadn't shown up at her place when I did. She clearly wasn't expecting me to be there or she never would have told whatever his name is to pick her up at her apartment.

Jesus fuck, I feel so fucking stupid. The fact that she wasn't at home when he showed up makes me wonder if she was fucking some third guy while we stood there like a couple of dumbasses trying to figure out what was going on.

All those nights she said she was "out with the girls", or was "exhausted and wasn't up for seeing me", or was "working late". Yeah, I'm an idiot.

"Can you believe she was pissed at me when I called to confront her because I wasn't supposed to be there?" I say as Peyton runs her fingers through my hair. "I'm trying to do something nice for her and she's mad at me. I wasn't even planning on staying because it sounded like she wanted to be alone. I was just going to leave the dinner in the fridge so she'd have it."

I left the key to Stacy's apartment on her counter after gathering all the things that were mine that I'd been keeping there. Then I took the dinner and the flowers with me and got the fuck out of there. I called her in the car on the way to Peyton's and broke up with her. She tried to convince me it was only a one time thing, and I just laughed. That pissed her off, but what the fuck ever. What's his name said they'd been out before, so she clearly didn't have any qualms about what she was doing, or any plans for stopping. I wasn't in love with her, but I did care about her. Knowing she didn't give two fucks about hurting me tells me I was lucky to find out as soon as I did, though.

Fuck. Why do people suck so much?

"Well, now it's in my fridge," Peyton says. "And I am going to enjoy the hell out of it because you are an amazing cook and she doesn't deserve a goddamn thing you make ever again. And the flowers look lovely on my table, too, by the way. She's trying to put the blame for her shitty behavior on you, babe. I never did like her."

I sigh. I did know that. Peyton has never kept her dislike for Stacy a secret. "I should have listened to you," I say.

"I wish I'd been wrong, if it makes you feel any better." She keeps running her fingers through my hair and it feels so good I think I might just fall asleep, until she speaks again.

"Wanna watch *Supernatural* and get drunk? I have wine, beer, and vodka."

"That sounds good," I say, managing a small smile. Peyton and I have been friends since we were kids and she always knows how to make me feel better. We both fell in love with Sam and Dean Winchester when the series first started and we were only twelve years old. It's got fifteen seasons now, and tells the story of two brothers who fight monsters and demons that most of humanity doesn't realize exist, and save lots of lives in the process. There's witches, banshees, ghouls, demons, angels, and so many other creatures, and beings that make the show entertaining, but it's got a lot of heart and depth, too. We grew up with the Winchester brothers, and now at thirty-two we get to watch reruns of our favorite episodes whenever we want.

Peyton, of course, has a massive crush on Jensen Ackles, who plays the older brother, Dean, and she'll just pause the show at random moments and stare at him, letting out a dreamy sigh while I roll my eyes. I can't say I blame her. I'm straight, but I'm not fucking blind, and the guy is handsome. She does the same thing with the character Abaddon, a sexy female demon.

I sit up and she makes her way into the kitchen. We stay up far too late for two people who have to be at work the following day, but we get drunk, make each other laugh, and pass out together on the sofa. And even though I know I'll wake up with a massive headache, I do feel a little bit better already.

Chapter Two

Bentley

"Hey, that was your last appointment," Peyton says, knocking on the door to the massage room I'm currently cleaning and disinfecting after my last client. It's been a week since my breakup and I've been kept pretty busy with work. Peyton is my assistant, and by that I mean she does pretty much everything, from taking calls and scheduling appointments to managing our social media accounts, advertising, and marketing, and she created our website as well. I honestly don't know what I would do without her. It's just the two of us in this little hole in the wall building, but we've done well for ourselves since we started up our business six months ago and are getting more and more clients every day. "What do ya say we hit up a new queer bar I found? I'll buy you a drink." She smiles at me mischievously and I raise an eyebrow.

"Does this new bar happen to have an attractive bartender you are hoping to ogle, or maybe even fuck?"

Her grin widens. "A lady has needs."

I groan and roll my eyes, then make the mistake of

looking back at her as she gives me a pouty lip and big pleading hazel eyes. Fuck. "We haven't been out since your breakup and you know it would be good for you. Maybe you'll find a gorgeous woman with big tits that can take your mind off of Stacy, if I don't snag her first."

I groan louder. "Jesus Christ, I wasn't even thinking about Stacy."

She eyes me.

"Okay, maybe I was thinking about her a little bit," I admit. I honestly don't know that I miss her, per se, but I do miss having someone. I'm not so desperate that I want to get involved with just anyone though. I don't mind casual sex, but I also really like the idea of meeting the right girl and having more. I want commitment and forever, and the knowledge that I'm the best thing in her life, just like she is in mine, not just a passing fancy.

"So, come on," she pleads again, bouncing on the balls of her feet.

"Fine," I acquiesce. "Just let me finish cleaning up and I'll meet you there. I'm not going out in scrubs."

"Clearly, darling," she says, and winks at me. "Wear those jeans that hug your ass okay? Gotta show off the assets. I'll text you the address." She disappears and I finish tidying the space before closing up and making my way to my car; a black 1967 Chevy Impala (the same car Dean drives in *Supernatural*) because yes, I'm that obsessed.

I head home and take a quick shower, then change into my ass hugging jeans and a long sleeved off white button up that I leave untucked and roll the sleeves up on. I tie my hair up in a messy bun again and grab my jacket before heading out the door to meet Peyton.

When I arrive at the address she texted me I park my car and climb out. I often tag along with Peyton to gay bars, more to be her wingman than to find someone for myself. This place is called *Johnny's*.

She said she's here and found a table so I head inside and scan the room for her. It's a nice place. A mixture of high top tables and booths resting on gleaming hardwood floors, and the soft, dim lighting invites a relaxed atmosphere, as a country song about riding something I'm fairly certain isn't a horse, plays overhead.

Peyton spies me and waves and I make my way to where she's sitting at one of the high top tables. She's dressed in an off the shoulder long-sleeved shirt and skinny jeans and she's sipping on a soda when I slide into the seat across from her.

"You look nice," she chirps, and grins at me.

I just shake my head as someone stops at our table. A young man with dark hair and pale skin. The name tag on his shirt says Tommy, and *manager*, underneath.

"Can I get you anything?" he asks, looking at me.

"Just a beer," I say. "Whatever's on tap."

He nods and looks to Peyton. "And you?"

"Gin and tonic please," she says with a smile, and he scurries away.

"Is that the guy?" I ask.

She sighs. "Alas, no. I haven't actually seen him yet. I was here the other night with the book group, though, and oh my goodness." She fans her face and I chuckle. Peyton has lived in Massachusetts longer than I have and she's made friends through a queer book group and her former workplace. She's introduced me to everyone and I enjoy them well enough, but Peyton is my ride or die, and I prefer just spending time with her. Plus, I don't really read.

My best friend is a bit of a slut, and I don't mean that in a bad way. She just enjoys sex a lot, with both men and women, and is on the prowl more often than not. She's gorgeous, with long brunette waves and hazel eyes. Sparsely scattered freckles adorn her pale skin and she has a captivating smile. Most people who see us together assume we're dating, or have at least hooked up, but we've only ever been friends. And we've both promised that if the person we're dating can't handle our friendship and see it for what it is, they aren't right for us because we are not going to lose each other over someone else's insecurity.

Our drinks arrive shortly and we sip on them while we chat, after which she slides off of her chair and grips my hand, pulling me with her onto the dance floor. It's not long after that a woman about our age taps Peyton's shoulder and whispers in her ear. Peyton grins and turns to face her as the other woman's hands grip her hips.

I excuse myself and return to our table, watching my friend and the rest of the couples, taking a few more sips of my drink.

"Hello," I hear, and turn to see a beautiful blonde woman next to me, dressed in a very short dress that showcases her gorgeous legs and is also cut low enough that an ample amount of cleavage is visible. God, normally I would be getting hard just looking at her, but it's not happening tonight. So when she runs her hand along my arm and asks if I want to dance, I politely tell her, no thank you. She frowns but moves on, and I sigh as Peyton returns to our table.

"What was that?" she asks. "You sent her away? She was practically undressing you with her eyes."

"I know. I just don't feel like it tonight," I admit.

"Why not?"

I bite my lip, staring at my drink. "Do you think Stacy cheated on me because I was bad in bed?"

There's silence, and when I look at Peyton she's frowning and her eyes are narrowed, arms crossed over her chest. "I think she cheated on you just because she's a selfish cunt. She never treated you right. She always took advantage of your kind nature. And you deserve so much better than that. If she wasn't satisfied with your sex life there are a million things she could have done other than cheat."

"I know, but it doesn't make me feel any better, wondering. I don't want to get out there again and humiliate myself."

Peyton sighs and gives my arm a squeeze. "I don't think you have anything to worry about, but if you aren't comfortable with it, you aren't comfortable with it. You don't have to rush back out there. I just don't want you sitting here convincing yourself that you're the problem, because you aren't."

I nod. But before I can get another word out Peyton is gripping my arm so tightly I grimace, as she squeals like a fucking school girl. "He's here!"

"What?" I yank my arm away from her vice-like grip and turn towards the bar where she's staring with fucking heart eyes, only for my heart to drop into my stomach as the blood leeches from my face.

"Shit!" I gasp, sliding out of my chair and grabbing Peyton's small frame, hauling her in front of me as the guy's gaze flits around the room and I duck behind my best friend.

"What the fuck are you doing?" Peyton hisses, looking back at me. "Are you drunk already?"

"No, I'm not drunk," I hiss back. "That's him."

She turns towards the bar again, and then back at me. "That's him? The guy who Stacy cheated on you with?"

I nod. "Yes, and I can't let him see me. It was fucking horrible enough the first time."

"Oh, boy," Peyton mutters. "Hon, if your goal is to not

be seen, I think picking your five-foot-two friend to hide behind is a bad choice."

"Shh, we have to go. Just move sideways towards the door so he doesn't see me."

"Oh my God," Peyton sighs. "You can't be serious."

"Very. Now go." Peyton grabs our coats off the back of our chairs and then does as I ask, as I stay crouched with my hands gripping her waist and we make our way slowly across the bar and towards the door. I let out a relieved sigh once we're outside in the chilly night air, and take my jacket from Peyton before sliding it on, just thankful that What's His Name didn't see me, because running into him again, after how fucking awkward it was the first time, would just make all of this shit with Stacy ten times worse.

Chapter Three

Bentley

So, how's it going? Peyton texts a few days later as I sit in the coffee shop and google apartments in my area. On top of having my girlfriend cheat on me, I also need to find a new place to rent since the lease on my place is up in a couple of weeks, and I'm hoping to find something a bit closer to work, and ideally a bit nicer.

Fine, I reply. *I have a couple of places lined up to go look at.*

What does it say about us that we work together and spend almost all of our free time together, and when we're not together we're texting each other? she asks.

I think it says we're codependent best friends who probably need therapy.

We'd probably do that together, too, she replies, and I laugh.

So, from one codependent friend to another, how off the table is the hottie from the bar?

Seriously?

Ugh. He's so cute, though. Lip biting emoji.

I reply with an eye rolling emoji, and she responds with a laughing emoji.

I glance up just as the door to the coffee shop opens only to nearly shit myself when I see him again! What the actual fuck? Is he following me? Why am I running into him everywhere now? He's got a dark peacoat on and his raven hair has snowflakes in it. I watch as he brushes his hand over his hair and stomps his boots on the floor to get rid of the snow.

"Shit," I whisper when his gaze lands on my spot near the back corner, and I duck, trying to hide underneath the table. When I peek back up he's in line and looking at the menu behind the counter, so I quickly close my laptop and shove it in my bag, then stand and shrug my coat on, before grabbing my coffee cup and holding it in front of my face as I make my way to the door.

I'm stopped abruptly when I slam into someone, courtesy of staring at the floor while I walk instead of actually watching where I'm going, and my coffee cup flies out of my hand. I hear a startled "Shit!" as the remaining coffee splatters all over the front of What's His Name.

Fuck! I'm so flustered and absolutely mortified that I don't even stop to help him. I just rush out of the damn coffee shop like my pants are on fire.

"God, if you love me you will never ever let me see that man again," I groan as I sit in my car, banging my head on the steering wheel and wondering if it would be less painful to just drive off a cliff and get it over with, because this slow death by humiliation is just not for me.

Alex

A week later I'm chuckling as I dump a load of laundry into the washing machine, remembering the incident at the coffee shop. I probably deserved what happened, honestly. I definitely wasn't expecting to get lukewarm coffee all over my nice clothes, though. But after seeing Bentley through the huge window I couldn't help going inside just to see what he would do when he saw me. Fuck, I don't even drink coffee. Him ducking under the tiny table and thinking I didn't see him had me holding back a laugh. Just like the other night at the bar when he was crouching behind his petite female friend, or date, maybe? But their dynamic said she was a friend. Either way she is maybe five foot two and him thinking she provided any sort of cover was hilarious. The guy sucks at hiding.

A grin is still on my face as I start the wash. If he knew how much entertainment he's given me over the past couple of weeks he'd probably be mortified. I can't say I blame him for not wanting me to see him though. Finding out your girl-friend is cheating on you has to suck, and running into the guy she was cheating on you with certainly wouldn't help. I really hope he gets back out there and finds someone who will treat him right, because even though it was only a couple of awkward minutes that we exchanged, I could tell he was a nice guy, and those seem to be few and far between these days.

I change into a clean T-shirt and a pair of sweats, then simmer some water on the stove before pouring myself a cup of earl gray tea and settling on the sofa. I pick up my book, the pages worn and the spine creased and cracked from all the love it's received.

I don't work tonight, and while I did do some grocery shopping and still have some things on the to-do list, I'm also going to spend as much time as I can with Josephine March and her sisters. I've read *Little Woman* a dozen times at least but it's a comfort read for me and it never gets old.

I take a sip of my tea as Marble, my Himalayan, jumps

up on the sofa and then proceeds to settle onto my lap over top the blanket I've draped across myself. She purrs as I pet her soft fur. "You know you're spoiled, right?" I tell her. She lifts her head, tilting it to the side as if to say, *Yeah, what about it?* Before making herself comfortable again as I scratch her neck.

I must doze off because I'm awoken by the sound of voices in the hallway, and they don't belong to my neighbors. I'm on the bottom floor in my building, currently with a vacant apartment across the hall, my brother living above me with his husband, and my parents across the hall from them. Yes, my whole family lives right next to each other, and while I know a lot of people would hate it, and no doubt think it's a bit strange, I love it. My parents and brother are everything to me and having them close gives me comfort. My parents own the apartment complex and have always taken great care of it and their tenants. Each building in the complex houses four units and there's a dozen buildings in all.

I grab Marble and move her onto the floor as I stand. She stretches and yawns, then hops back up on the sofa and sprawls out on her back.

I stretch and pick my book up off the floor, setting it down on the coffee table, before I make my way to the door and peek out through the peephole. There's someone moving in next door and there's a few different movers carrying boxes and furniture into the apartment. Call me curious, but I have to know who my new neighbor is, so I open the door and step into the hall. I nod at one of the movers as he steps out of the open apartment door and moves back down the hall towards the door of the building, while another guy heads inside, passing him on the way. This guy isn't wearing the movers' shirt and hat. Instead he's dressed in a thick tan coat and jeans, carrying a very large, very familiar plush penguin. No way. It can't be him.

It's not until he turns towards the door to his apartment that I see the long blond and brown hair pulled into a messy bun at the back of his head and my suspicions are confirmed.

Oh. My. God. He doesn't see me because the penguin is covering the entire right side of his face and blocking me from his view.

"Hey there," I say, and he nearly jumps out of his skin. Okay, I honestly didn't mean to scare him, but that was kind of funny. "Sorry," I add with a chuckle. I can't help biting the inside of my cheek to keep from laughing even more when he turns around with the giant penguin in front of his face and says nothing.

"You uh, you okay?" I ask. No response. "You do know I can see you right? I mean that's a big penguin but it's not that big."

He sighs and lowers the giant plush penguin, his cheeks flushed crimson as he averts his gaze. I decide to go easy on him.

"You want some help bringing your stuff inside?"

His gaze meets mine now and he blinks at me, like he can't believe I offered to help him. His mouth opens but no words come out.

"I can give you a hand if you want," I say. "Just let me get my shoes and coat on." I disappear back into my apartment and return a moment later ready to lend a hand. He comes out of his apartment, cheeks still flushed, but leads me to his car when I tell him to show me the way. It's a pretty cool car, too. I mean, I know shit all about cars but this one looks like it's vintage and in great shape.

He hands me a box and I make my way through the snow and back inside with it, setting it down inside his apartment and wondering just how absurd it is that this man is the one who ended up being my new neighbor. Hopefully he doesn't hate the idea of living across from me.

I go back outside and grab another box, carrying it inside. Once everything is out of his car he shuts the trunk and then proceeds to remove the messy bun from his hair and run his fingers through it. It's honestly the most gorgeous hair I've ever seen, thick and full and falling to just below his broad shoulders. I know lots of women who would be very jealous of that hair. Hell, I might be jealous of that hair. He's also wearing a gorgeous turquoise scarf that looks like it's knitted and incredibly soft. And I don't normally notice things like this, but it's bringing out the color in his eyes.

He catches me staring and flushes again, and I realize I am probably being a bit creepy, so I decide to introduce myself. "I'm Alex," I tell him, holding out my hand. "Alex Florez-Romano." He bites his lip, then turns to face me and takes my hand in his.

"Bentley Emerson," he says, shaking it, that southern twang making me want to get him a cowboy hat and a rope or something.

"I like your scarf," I tell him, and he looks down, then gives a soft smile.

"Thanks, my Gram made it."

I nod. "It's beautiful." There's a bit of an awkward pause so I say, "Listen, I know this is probably weird for you, but I swear I haven't seen Stacy since our last date, and it really was just two dates. We didn't even sleep together. I hope that helps, and I swear I didn't know about you or I never would have gone out with her at all. I'm not like that."

He nods, some of the tension leaving his big body. "Thanks," he says, voice soft. God, the guy looks like a

Viking but I have the impression he's nothing but a sweet teddy bear.

"You must be hungry. Why don't you come to my place for dinner tonight since you've still got all that unpacking to do? I'm not much of a cook but I can do spaghetti and throw a salad together."

He shuffles his feet, hands in his coat pockets. His gaze doesn't meet mine. "Oh, uh, that's okay, you don't have to feed me. I'll manage." Shy much? Or just uncomfortable because it's me?

"Look, it's what, three o'clock ish now? Why don't you take some time and think about it, and if you decide you want to take me up on my offer, just come knock on my door around six. Maybe you can get a nap in beforehand. You've probably had a long day."

He nods and I leave him be, heading back to my apartment. I find myself really hoping he'll come for dinner, because something about him tells me he's worth getting to know a bit better. And while I love my family, Lord knows I could use a friend.

Chapter Four

Bentley

"You hid behind a what?" Peyton says, then descends into laughter.

"A giant penguin," I mutter and hear her snort, she's laughing so hard.

"It's not funny," I grouse.

"It is a little bit funny," she says. "Oh my God, what are the odds?"

I groan, sitting on my sofa surrounded by boxes, convinced that if God does exist he has some twisted sense of humor. This is the exact opposite of never seeing the guy again. Of all the apartments in the entire city, I just happened to find the one that was right next to Alex.

"He wasn't mean or anything was he?" she checks, her voice sharper and her laughter dissipating.

"Worse," I grumble. "He was really nice. Offered to help me move my stuff inside and invited me over for dinner."

"Oh, really? That's great."

I sigh. "I don't know if I want to go."

"Listen, I get that it's kind of uncomfortable, but the guy didn't do anything wrong, right? Didn't you say he didn't know about you when he went out with Stacy?"

"So he says."

"You don't believe him?"

"No, I do. He looked genuinely horrified when he found out I was her boyfriend." I pick at some of the lint on my pants as I grumble.

"And he's extending an olive branch. Plus if he ends up being your friend and then you happen to introduce him to me..."

"No," I growl.

She sighs. "All right, fine. Spoil sport. Seriously, though, go have dinner with the guy. He sounds nice, and maybe it will end up being a good thing. It wouldn't hurt you to have another friend, right?"

Ugh. She's right. I know she's right. I've lived here for over six months and other than Peyton and the sort of friends from her book club, I don't know anyone. Having another friend would be nice, and we can't live next door to each other and avoid each other forever, though if it weren't for Peyton I would certainly be willing to give it a try. The only reason Peyton and I are friends is because she's extroverted and adopted me. Even meeting Stacy was because she was a client of mine first and she asked me out.

"You're going, right? I'm going to ask you how it went tomorrow when I see your beautiful face."

"Fine." I wish she could see my face now because I'm working an epic pout.

"Good boy," she says. "Now, get a nap and don't forget I'm coming over tomorrow to help you unpack. Bye, babe."

"Bye." I end the call and toss my phone on the coffee

table. I grab the blanket and pillow that I brought with me in the car since my bedding is all still in boxes, and curl up on the sofa.

When I wake and check my phone it's two hours later, so I decide to do a small amount of unpacking. Mainly the necessities. I get my toiletries and towels in the bathroom, find the box with my bedding and get it set up on my king sized bed, get my bedside lamps on my matching night-stands and plug them in, unpack some clothes, and get my television set up on my TV stand.

I shower, change into some fresh clothes, and then make my way out of my apartment and across the hall to Alex's. It's literally two steps and I take a breath and let it out before knocking on the door at exactly six pm.

It opens so fast I startle and he grins. "Hey, you came. Come on in." He gestures inside and I step through the doorway, greeted by the smell of garlic and wheat, and the next thing I know a gorgeous cream and chocolate colored cat is winding its way between my legs, purring.

"Oh, this is Marble," Alex says. "She's usually more antisocial than this so she must like you. I've honestly never seen her take to anyone so fast before."

I can't help the smile that splits my face as I bend down to pet her and her purring gets louder. "Hey, pretty girl." She stands on her hind legs and paws at me so I scoop her up, and Alex's eyes go wide.

"Shit, she never lets anyone but me hold her, other than my brother-in-law. Not even my parents and brother. You some kind of cat whisperer or something?"

I shrug as Marble rolls over in my arm, letting me cradle her and giving me her belly. I pet her and her eyes roll back in her head, making Alex laugh. It's a nice sound and I find it filling me with warmth as we make our way into the combined living room/ dining room area. The kitchen is just off to the right and there's a bar with chairs set up. I like how he has the space decorated. Simple and cozy.

Alex reaches over and scratches behind Marble's ears. "She's a slut for belly rubs," he says, and I feel my cheeks heat, but grin at the same time.

"Dinner will be ready soon. I only know how to make like three things, and one of them is pancakes from a box so don't expect too much." He's still grinning as he makes his way into the kitchen. "I even splurged and toasted garlic bread!" he calls out. "Make yourself comfortable!"

I keep Marble in my arm, making my way through the small space. It's nothing fancy but it's nice enough. Alex has a beige sectional with a couple different soft looking blankets draped over it, making it look warm and inviting, along with a matching ottoman. There's a lot of bookshelves packed with different books set up throughout the space. One behind the sofa and against the wall, and a couple more on either side of the electric fireplace, which is roaring. A few small plants rest on the windowsill and bookshelves, and there's a photo of Marble, and another one of whom I'm assuming is his family. A petite Latina woman with dark hair streaked with gray, gorgeous caramel colored skin and rich brown eyes is standing next to a much taller Caucasian man with fair skin, thick gray hair and blue eyes, and on either side of them are two boys. One is Alex, his hair and skin tone matching his mother's, and the other looks familiar but it takes me a second to place him.

The bartender from the bar Peyton and I were at when I saw Alex and skippity-do-daw'd out of there. The one who brought our drinks. His complexion is paler, like his father's, though his hair is as black as Alex's and their mother's, and his eyes are hazel whereas Alex's are blue like his father's. They're a striking family.

"This your family?" I ask, as I continue to stroke Marble's belly, and Alex looks up from where he's setting the table, grinning.

"Sure is. Come on and sit down, cowboy, it's ready."

I blink. "I'm not a cowboy."

He grins. "Yeah, I figured that, but your accent just makes me think of cowboys. I won't call you that, though, if you don't want me to."

I shrug. "It's fine."

His smile gets bigger and he gestures for me to sit again. I'm a little disappointed that I have to put the cat down, but I do and she follows me over to the table, sitting at my feet.

"Jesus Christ, I don't think she's gonna let you go," Alex says with a laugh as he sits and Marble rubs her head against my shin. "If she's bothering you at all just tell her to go lie down and she will."

"I don't mind," I say, then look at the huge plate of spaghetti in front of me, along with the bowl of salad and the bread. It smells amazing, the steam from the spaghetti wafting up and filling my nostrils, making my mouth water.

"Dig in. If you don't like it just pretend you do."

I chuckle and shake my head, picking up my fork. "Is the TV in your bedroom?" I ask as we eat. I noticed there isn't one in the living area.

He shakes his head. "No, I actually don't have a TV."

I nearly choke on my water and he laughs. "What? Why?"

He shrugs. "Don't need it. I spend most of my free time reading anyway, or working out, going for runs."

I blink at him. "But, how?"

He laughs again and takes a sip of his water. "Did I break your brain?"

"I...I think maybe," I reply, and he chuckles. "I can't

imagine not having a tv. Maybe because I don't like to read. Jesus, you're missing out on some great shows, though."

"Yeah? Like what?" His eyes twinkle as he leans back in his chair, and I find myself getting lost in them for a second. Such a pretty shade of blue. And that smile is adorable. Huh, I don't think I've ever thought "adorable" about a guy before. Animals, yes, children even, but a grown man, never.

I clear my throat. "Well, there's *Supernatural,* which is the best show in the history of shows," I proclaim matter-of-factly.

He chuckles. "Is that right?"

I nod. "*Schitt's Creek* is super good. My friend Peyton got me hooked on *Once Upon a Time* and *Heartstopper.*"

"Hmmm, well, maybe I am missing out," he says, "but not much I can do about it without a TV. I guess you'll have to invite me over to watch at your place."

My eyes widen. "Oh, uh..."

"Unless you don't want me to come over? In which case I'll just have to remain ignorant."

I hesitate a little but then say, "You can come. If you bring Marble."

He laughs. "So that's how it is, huh?"

I grin and shrug.

"Alright. Deal. You, me, Marble, and *Supernatural.* Next Thursday night. That way you have time to get settled a bit before we invade your apartment."

I nod, and we eat in silence for a moment before he says, "Peyton, is she the friend you were with at the bar?"

My cheeks heat and I groan, burying my face in my hand. "Shit, you saw me."

He laughs, but it's not unkind. "Yeah, sorry. Valiant attempt buddy, but my detective skills are pretty good, and it's not too hard to spot a six foot two inch guy trying to hide behind a woman a foot shorter than him."

I groan again. "Fuck. Kill me now."

Another laugh, and it actually makes me smile. Especially when he nudges my foot under the table. "Look, I get why you did it. Our first run in was a bit awkward. But the only person who has anything to be ashamed of or embarrassed about is Stacy. You, my friend, didn't do anything wrong."

I clear my throat and look at him. "Thanks for feeding me. It's really nice of you. Especially after I was acting so stupid, and spilled coffee all over you the other day."

"Was that you?" he teases, and I laugh. "No problem. You uh.... you and Stacy still together?"

I shake my head.

"Good," is his reply. "I hope you don't mind me saying so, but she wasn't worth your time. I did notice you kept the penguin though."

God, am I going to stop blushing sometime tonight? "What gave it away?" I ask, and he lets out a guffaw, his eyes lighting up again, and I can't help my grin.

"Oh, he's funny," Alex chides, slapping me on the shoulder. "Seriously, though, I'm glad you kept it. I'm sure it'll be much happier with you."

We finish our meals and then Alex starts taking care of the dishes. I can't stand by and watch so I pitch in and we have the table cleared in no time. I'm about to head out when he offers me a beer, so I decide to stay for a bit longer and we settle on the sofa, Marble between us at first before she saunters over and settles down with her chin on my leg. Her eyes close and she purrs again when I pet her.

"So, where are you from?" Alex asks. "Your accent tells me you're from the south."

"Yeah, I'm from Georgia," I tell him.

"That where your parents are?"

I shake my head as I swallow a sip of beer. "My dad has never been in the picture, and my mom died when I was ten. My grandma raised me. She passed away last year and I came out here to be near Peyton. She's been here for a while and had been begging me to follow her. We started up our own business about six months ago."

"Oh, nice. Sorry about your parents, though, and your grandma."

I give a soft smile. "Thanks. What about you? Are your parents nearby?"

He chuckles. "Yeah, about as nearby as you can get. My parents live above you and my brother and his husband live above me."

"Oh," I say, surprised.

He laughs again. "It's okay, I know it sounds weird."

I shake my head, "No, it sounds amazing, actually. I'd love to have family around me. I just have Peyton."

"Well, if I introduce you to my parents they'll probably adopt you on the spot." He grins and there goes my blush again. "They own the building so us living in it is kinda a no brainer." He winks and I chuckle.

He asks about the business that Peyton and I are in together and I tell him about being a massage therapist.

When I leave an hour later it's with plans for him to come over the following week so I can reciprocate the dinner invitation, and introduce him to the first episode of *Supernatural*.

Before I go to bed that night I look through the box of things I packed and put in my car so I would be sure not to lose or break them, and pull out the photograph I have of me and my grandma at her last birthday. We had gotten dressed up and I had taken her out to dinner. Then we'd come back to her place and I'd dished us each a giant slice of the gooey chocolate cake I'd baked for her.

The photo is a selfie I took of us with the cake. Gram is smiling widely, her blue eyes sparkling, and my chest aches as I look at the photograph of the best woman I've ever known. She never complained once about raising me after my mom died, never acted like I was a burden, never made me feel anything but loved and wanted. She got me the therapy I needed, let me crawl into bed with her on all those nights I couldn't sleep or was having nightmares, sang to me as I clung to her and cried.

Living with her was how I met Peyton. She lived across the street from me and saw me outside in the cul-de-sac kicking a soccer ball around, and invited herself to play with me. We've been best friends ever since. She would come over several times a week to hang out, and once I got to know her better and wasn't as shy, I started going to her place, too, and her parents treated me like I was their own. We painted ornaments together every Christmas, baked cookies with Gram, colored eggs together every Easter, went trick-or-treating together every Halloween, and I even took karate classes for a few years with Peyton and ended up really enjoying it. Gram would buy Christmas presents for Peyton every year and attend her choir concerts with me. She adored Peyton just as much as Peyton's parents adored me.

She was such a lively, vibrant person, and I miss her every day.

After she passed I found out that she'd left everything to me, and I was able to use some of the money to make the move out here and start my business. I wish so much she could be around to see me making my dreams come true, but I know she knows, and that she's proud, and that eases the ache in my chest a little. I chuckle to myself thinking of the words she would have had for Stacy if she were here. There would have been some colorful language, that's for sure. No one messed with her little boy. Even as big as I am, she was my protector. I wonder what she would think of Alex. I think the two of them would get along pretty well.

I kiss my fingers before touching them to the photo and setting it on my nightstand. "Love you, Gram."

I turn the light off and close my eyes, then slowly drift to sleep.

Chapter Five

Bentley

As promised, Peyton spends the following day helping me unpack. Well, she's supposed to be helping me unpack. What she's really doing is looking out the peephole every two seconds hoping to catch a glimpse of Alex. Of course, as short as she is she has to get a step stool to fucking reach it. It's been a few hours already and I swear she's only moved off her perch twice, once because the dinner we ordered had arrived, and the other time because I had to take out the trash that was piling up.

"I thought you were over here to help me unpack, not stalk the neighbor," I tell her.

She looks back at me from where she's standing on said step stool and grins. "Luckily I can multitask."

"You're literally not multitasking," I point out. "That's the whole point of this conversation. Unless standing and creeping through the peephole is multitasking."

She ignores me.

"The guy's not *that* good looking," I mumble.

That gets her attention. She turns to me, hands on her hips. "Hush you."

I roll my eyes and grab the giant bag of trash we've been collecting over the last hour. "You'll have to give up your perch again so I can go throw this out."

She reluctantly steps down and moves the stool out of the way, letting me out the door. On my way back inside I run into Alex coming out of his apartment and he gives me a wide smile.

"Hey, cowboy, how's unpacking going?" he asks.

I don't get a chance to answer because my door opens and Peyton steps out. "It's going fine, handsome," she practically purrs, then thrusts her small hand out. "I'm Peyton. Bentley's friend."

"Ahh, yes, I remember you from the bar," Alex says, shaking her hand. "Nice to meet you. I'm Alex."

"You don't want to come in and lend us a hand do you?" she asks.

"I wish I could but I'm actually headed to work." He turns to me. "I'll see you later, right? *Supernatural?*"

I nod and he gives me another grin. "Great." He turns to Peyton. "See you later, too, gorgeous."

Lord, I think Peyton might pass out when Alex winks at her before he saunters off.

"No," I say when he's out the door and Peyton's gaze is still locked on his retreating figure.

"You're so mean," she chides as I grip her arm and pull her back inside the apartment. She turns to me. "Also, did he call you cowboy?"

Jesus Christ. My cheeks flame. "Maybe," I mumble.

"Uh huh, and what did he mean, *Supernatural?*"

I shrug. "He hasn't seen it so I'm introducing him."

I swear her eyes have hearts in them. "Ahh, you guys are

going to have the cutest little bromance." She punches my arm.

I have no idea why, but I'm actually blushing. "Work, woman," I tell her, shoving her towards the mountain of still full boxes. We've made some progress, but there's still quite a bit left to do.

She sighs but grabs the scissors and starts on a box labeled "kitchen" while grousing, "I don't get paid enough for this."

I just shake my head and keep unpacking.

Alex

It's a few days later that I'm sliding my winter jacket on and shoving my feet into my sneakers, ready to head to work for the night. I'm in a bit of a hurry since I'm running late. I went on a run this morning, and by morning I mean eleven because I was up past two in the morning working. After showering and drinking a smoothie I worked on my taxes until I thought my brain was going to explode, and then curled up on the sofa with Marble and *Pride and Prejudice,* only to proceed to fall asleep an hour later. And now I'm hustling so my brother doesn't give me grief about being late again. He's a stickler for punctuality. He used to drive me to work, but stopped since I was never ready as early as he wanted me to be. To be fair, his idea of on time is ten to fifteen minutes early. Now, though, I'm running about fifteen minutes late and I can just picture the look on my little brother's face when I walk in. Tommy might be seven years younger than me, twenty-two to my twenty-nine, but of the two of us, he's the hard ass. Well, with me anyway, and our other coworkers, which is why our parents made him the manager as soon as he turned twenty-one. With his husband, Pierre, he's a mega softy. Pierre's such a sweet guy, though, I don't think anyone could get mad at him.

I leave my apartment and make my way outside, only to stop in my tracks when I see the mounds of snow on top of my car and encasing it on all sides.

Shit. I tilt my head back and groan. I am going to hear about it from Tommy for sure now. I'm pulling my gloves out of my coat pockets, ready to put them on and get to shoveling when Bentley pulls into the parking lot and glides into the space a couple spots over from mine.

I wave and he waves back, his headlights going out before he climbs out of his car. I'm just thinking about how not fun it's going to be to shovel in the fucking dark when he says, "You need a hand?" And what the fuck? Why is my dick twitching at the sound of his deep southern drawl? I don't know, but a shiver races down my spine that has nothing to do with the cold. I really don't have time to psychoanalyze that right now, however, so I shove whatever that reaction was aside and dig my phone out of my pocket, ready to text my brother and let him know I'll be half an hour late. Fuck.

"Yeah, if you have a minute, and an extra shovel, that would be amazing," I tell Bentley. "I'm late for work and Tommy is gonna bust my balls."

"Tommy, your brother?" he asks, hands shoved into his thick, thigh length coat, shoulders up around his ears. He has his turquoise scarf on, too, and there's snowflakes in his hair and beard, and clinging to his long eyelashes. He shivers visibly.

I realize I'm staring at him when his cheeks flush and I clear my throat. "Yeah, he works with me at the bar and he's a bit anal about being on time."

"You want me to give you a ride?" he asks, looking like he might just turn into a human popsicle if he doesn't get inside soon. It's cold out, for sure, but being in the low twenties is normal, and I've adapted over the years. I mean, don't get me wrong, I don't stand out here for shits and giggles, but I can tolerate it. "Might be faster."

"That would be amazing," I tell him, shoving my phone back in my pocket without texting Tommy, then hurrying over to the passenger side door of Bentley's car and climbing inside. He slides into the driver's seat a second later and starts the car, his teeth chattering as he does, making me laugh.

"Cold?" I ask as he pulls out of the parking spot.

He blushes again. "I'm from Georgia, remember? And this is the first winter I've experienced up north. You all are crazy for living here on purpose."

I laugh. "You'll get used to it. Aren't you here on purpose?"

"Nah, I'm here because I can't say no to Peyton."

That pulls another laugh from me and I feel my chest squeezing when he gives me that soft smile.

"I assume we're heading to *Johnny's*?"

I nod. "Yep. My home away from home."

"You and your brother always work together?"

"Yeah, we've been working at the bar since we were teenagers in some capacity or other. My parents own it, so…"

He raises an eyebrow. "Is there anything in this town that your parents don't own?"

I chuckle. "A few things. My brother is gay, and when he came out they wanted to make sure he was safe and that he and other queer people in town had a place where they belonged, so they opened their own queer bar and had official underage nights where they didn't sell alcohol, but the younger queer crowd could come and hang out and dance. They still do it once a week and it's a big hit. That was after taking him to the pride parade every year and putting rainbow magnets on their cars, and a ginormous flag in their street facing window. They still make a rainbow cake for him every year on his 'coming out aversary.'" I put the words in finger quotes, picturing the look on Tommy's face when our parents "surprise" him with it every year. There's the eye roll, and the groan as Mom and Dad stare at him with wide smiles on their faces, and he reluctantly lets us all inside to celebrate. Sweet Pierre always blushes furiously when they tell him how happy they are that their baby boy found someone so wonderful. And even though my brother acts like he hates it, I'm pretty sure he'd be disappointed if we ever stopped.

"Your parents sound pretty great," Bentley says.

"Yeah, they're characters, but I love them to bits."

There's a moment of silence and I take it to appreciate the car. It really is a beauty. Leather interior, bench seats, a tan dashboard and door panels, a cassette player which I honestly don't know if I've ever seen before in real life, and crank windows.

"Nice car," I tell him, and he grins again.

"Thanks, it's from *Supernatural*."

"Oh, yeah? Wow, you must really like that show."

"I'm mildly obsessed," he admits, his cheeks pinkening again as he bites his bottom lip. "Peyton and I grew up on it."

"Oh, cool. We still on for watching next week? You've got me all hyped up now."

He nods. "But don't forget Marble. You don't bring her, you don't get to eat."

God, he makes me laugh more than anyone I've ever been around, and he's so easy to talk to. How is it that we've only known each other a few days? The best part is it feels like he's already coming out of his shell with me. There's no doubt he's shy and introverted, but I can see more and more of his humor and his kind heart every time we're together.

"Here we are," he says, pulling up to *Johnny's* and putting the car in park.

"Thanks again, man," I tell him, climbing out. "You saved my ass. See you later." I shut the door and wave and he drives off.

I brace myself for my brother's wrath as I enter our family's establishment and make my way towards the bar. Tommy is behind it, and I do a double take when I see him serving drinks with a megawatt smile on his face. I don't think I've seen my brother smile unless it has something to do with Pierre. And when he's at work he's all business. His pretty little twink of a husband is nowhere in sight.

I blink when he turns to me and his smile gets even bigger. What the actual fuck?

"Alex, glad you could make it," he says, slapping me on the shoulder.

"Excuse me?" I say.

"What?" he asks, as he mixes a drink.

"Who are you and what have you done with my brother?"

"What do you mean?"

"Uh, you're supposed to be chewing me out for being almost a half an hour late."

He laughs. Fucking laughs. Okay, what episode of the fucking *Twilight Zone* am I in?

"Are you okay?" I ask, genuinely concerned. "Should I call Pierre? Maybe you're having a stroke?"

Another laugh. "Very funny." He shrugs. "I'm just happy."

"Well cut it out, it's weird," I say, pinning on my name tag. "You and Pierre get it on in the back room right before I came in or something?"

He smirks. "No. Pierre is out with Toby."

Toby is Pierre's foster brother and his best friend. "Okay, so what is it then?"

He glances briefly over his shoulder and I follow his gaze towards a table near the back where an older gentleman is sitting, nursing a beer and scrolling through his phone. He's got to be at least twenty years older than Tommy, with thick salt and pepper hair and a decent amount of stubble. He's wearing a snug fitting dress shirt over his broad chest and shoulders, and has a pair of reading glasses on.

"Mmmm, I see," I tease, and oh my God, my never smiles, never laughs, never shows any emotion ever brother, fucking blushes. I don't think I've ever actually seen that before. It's like a rare animal sighting.

"Knock it off," he grouses as he moves around with me on his tail. "Start working."

I ignore him. My brother and his husband like to invite an occasional third into their bedroom once in a while, but I've never seen him this flustered or smitten before. Usually it's just one and done. "He must have rocked your worlds for you to be looking at him like that."

He shrugs, but I know better. The only other person that has ever made Tommy behave like a love sick fool was Pierre. "It's nothing serious," he tells me. "But it was good, yes."

I grin, because getting even that much out of my brother is a big deal. It took months for him to even admit his interest in Pierre even though our parents and I knew he was taken with the pretty French boy from the moment he saw him.

"Now, get to work," he says again.

"Yes, sir," I tease with a salute.

It doesn't escape my notice that both my brother and

the handsome older man are casting glances in the other's direction all night, until the older man heads out a couple of hours later, and Tommy blushes all over again, biting his lip when the guy winks at him.

I'm fucking exhausted when I finally clock out seven hours later and then wait for Tommy to finish closing up so he can take me home. The snow stopped falling a while ago but there's several more inches accumulated on the ground now and I sigh as I remember that I still have to unbarricade my car.

"Who dropped you off tonight if you didn't drive?" Tommy asks as he stops at a red light on the abandoned street. I can tell he's wiped. He works longer hours than I do and I hope that whatever is going on with him, Pierre, and their mystery man, works out the way they want it to, because he could use someone to take care of him, pamper him, let him let go for a while. Pierre is a sweetheart, an excellent cook, amazing with animals, and super smart, but he's definitely not low maintenance. Tommy loves him to pieces, but I think they would both benefit from having a more permanent third, rather than just a casual fuck once in a while.

"Our new neighbor, Bentley," I tell him.

"Oh, yeah, I should probably meet him. God, I've just been so busy." How am I just now noticing the circles under his eyes?

"He's really cool. Shy, but super sweet."

There's a pause and I say, "You okay?"

"Yeah, of course," he says, so fast I know it's a lie.

"You sure? Cause you can always talk to me if you're not. Pierre okay?"

Tommy sighs and rubs a hand over his face. "He's been having more night terrors lately. It happens sometimes, even with the meds and counseling. We'll be okay, though. I just haven't slept much the past few days."

We pull into the parking lot of the apartment complex and Tommy turns off the car. I blink when I realize that the mounds of snow encasing my car are gone. Not melted, just gone.

"Holy shit," I breathe. It could have been Mom and Dad who cleared off my car but I don't think it was.

Bentley, that golden retriever Viking. God, he's gonna make me all gooey inside or some shit if he doesn't stop being so fucking nice.

Chapter Six

Bentley

The following evening I'm unlocking the door to my apartment, practically dead on my feet after another long day at work, when the door above me opens and Alex's parents come out into the upstairs hall, laughing as they make their way down the stairs.

I try to get my door unlocked before they see me because I don't feel like interacting right now, or ever really, but I hear, "Oh, hi, you must be the new neighbor." I turn just as they hit the bottom floor. They look like they're dressed for a night out, him in dress pants and a button up, and her in a lovely maroon dress and heels, her hair up in a twist and her makeup immaculate. They're both smiling at me.

"I'm Johnny," Alex's dad says, and I blink as I shake his outstretched hand. He's tall and broad and his grip is firm.

"Like the bar?"

They grin wider. "You've been?" the woman asks, then holds her hand out for me to shake as well. "I'm Isabella."

"Bentley," I reply, "and yes, I went with a friend of mine the other night."

"How lovely. Well, I hope you go back often. And it's lovely to meet you. We're Alex and Tommy's parents."

"Alex told me. I'm a friend of his."

Isabella laughs and there's a twinkle in her eye when she says, "He told you we were the crazy family who lives next door to each other, huh?"

I flush. "He didn't put it that way."

She laughs. "I'm just teasing you, Bentley. But I'm very glad you are friends with my Alex. He needs more people in his life."

"It's nice to meet you," Johnny says. "We're on our way out for dinner and dancing but we'll see you around I'm sure."

"Have fun," I say, waving as they walk away.

Okay, so that wasn't so bad.

When Thursday rolls around I find I am actually looking forward to seeing Alex again. We've barely seen each other since I dropped him off at work. Our schedules being off means we run into each other occasionally when I'm coming home and he's leaving, but that's it, and as much as I enjoy spending time alone, I could use some company too. And I like that I am cooking for more than one person.

My apartment is pretty much in order now, everything in its place, pillows and blankets on the sofa, pictures of me with Mom and Gram set up on the mantle and the single bookshelf I own, decorations on the wall, and it's starting to feel more like home each day.

I hear a knock just as the oven beeps, letting me know

dinner is ready. "Just a second!" I call. I shouldn't be nervous, really. Alex is my friend. But even though I'm looking forward to seeing him I can't help but be a little anxious, too. The only people I've ever cooked for are Peyton and Gram. I hope he likes what I made. I also hope I'm not too awkward. I know I'm not the best at conversation. Alex is pretty good at it though so I hope things don't get too weird.

I pull dinner out of the oven and then turn it off before heading to the door. When I open it, Alex is beaming at me and holding up a six pack of beer in one hand, carrying Marble in the other. She doesn't look overly pleased about being manhandled, but as soon as she sees me she scrambles out of Alex's grip and practically leaps into my arms, startling me.

"Jesus, girl, at least pretend to be hard to get," Alex chides her playfully. We ended up exchanging numbers when he came by to thank me for shoveling his car out the other day, and told me I was welcome to come visit Marble while he's at work if I want to, just to use the spare key he keeps under his doormat, so I did go over a few times in the evenings and cuddle her a bit, and now Alex says she's spoiled.

"Ready to get this show on the road?" He laughs at his own joke and it makes me chuckle. "See what I did there? Show? Cause we're watching a show?"

"Yes, very clever," I deadpan, stroking Marble as she gives me her belly, and he laughs.

He sniffs the air. "It smells amazing in here. What did you make?"

I follow him into the kitchen where he sets the beer on the counter. "Baked ziti," I tell him.

He leans over the pan on the stove and inhales, his eyes closing. "Oh, yum. Can we eat now? I'm starving."

I nod, but hesitate putting Marble down. I haven't gotten my kitty fix yet.

"You're clearly busy," he says, his eyes twinkling. "Why don't I dish it? Where are your plates?"

I smile softly and direct him, and in no time at all we've got two steaming plates and Alex is carrying them to the table. "It's looking really good in here, too. You all unpacked?"

"Yeah," I say as I sit down with Marble still in my arms. She purrs and rubs her head against my chest.

We talk about work as we eat, me finally setting Marble down after realizing how challenging it is to eat with one hand and also not wanting to accidentally drop food on her. I don't think she would forgive even me for that. She saunters over to the oversized ottoman that's used as a coffee table and jumps on it, turning around a couple of times before settling in for a nap.

"You should bring her over here from now on instead of coming to my place when you want to visit her," Alex says.

"Really?"

He shrugs. "Why not? I know she's safe with you. Just toss her back in the door when you get sick of her."

I chuckle, and for some reason the fact that he knows his girl would be safe with me warms my chest. "Okay. Thanks."

"Not much for you to do over at my place if you don't read." He gives me a friendly smile. "Speaking of which, I was thinking that if you are introducing me to your shows, I should introduce you to my books, if you're up for it."

I grimace.

"Okay, maybe not," he says with a laugh.

"Sorry, I've just never been a fan of reading. I only do it when I have to."

"Any reason?"

I shrug, my cheeks heating a bit. "I was never very good at it, so it isn't something I can do to relax or unwind. It just stresses me out. I take forever to read anything and I just end up getting frustrated." I hesitate for a second, then say, "I have a language disorder, and it's gotten better with the therapy Gram got me, and I get by okay, but words just don't come easy to me. I struggle with vocabulary and I always hated reading comprehension. When I was in school Peyton and Gram helped me with my reading homework. Heck, Peyton still helps me when I'm struggling with something."

"Helps you how?" He takes a sip of his water, and I finally make eye contact with him. There's no judgment in his tone, only curiosity and it relaxes me a bit.

"Reading it out loud to me. It's easier for me to absorb that way. I'm not great with written words, or even knowing what words to use to communicate what it is I'm trying to say sometimes, but I'm real good at memorizing things people say to me. I can remember an entire recipe if someone tells me what to do step by step, but reading them never works. I just get overwhelmed by all the directions being there at once. Gram realized it was easier to teach me to cook by just talking it out, rather than having me look at a recipe book. I've been cooking from memory for a long time."

"Wow, that's actually really impressive," Alex says. "And I could do that."

I feel my cheeks heating again. "Do what?"

"I mean, if you want me to. I could read the books out loud to you. And if there's any words you're having trouble with you can ask me what they mean and I'll do my best to tell you. I'm not a wizard or anything when it comes to read-ing, but I'm decent enough. There's some great stories out there you shouldn't be missing out on."

Shit. Why is the idea of him reading to me making my chest squeeze? That's really damn sweet. He must really want me to know these stories.

"If you really don't want to, though, I won't be offended, I promise," he tells me. "I don't get offended easily, really, so if I'm ever bothering you just tell me to fuck off."

I chuckle. "I don't think I could do that. That was more Gram's domain."

He laughs. "Yeah, your grandma sounds like she was quite the character."

"Yeah, you could say that. I think you would have liked her."

"I think so too." We eat for a bit longer before he says, "God, this ziti puts my spaghetti and meatballs to shame."

I blush again. "Thanks, it's Gram's recipe."

"You have a picture of her somewhere?" he asks, and I gesture.

"On the bookshelf."

Alex helps me clear the table and then makes his way over to said shelf. He sees the photo of Gram and me dressed up for a Halloween party. She was Cruella and I was a dalmatian. She got decked out, too. Looked like the real deal, and I got a shit ton of candy that year.

"Oh, man this is epic," he says, picking up the framed photo. "And you were adorable."

My cheeks heat even more and I'm grateful he isn't looking my way as I load the dishes into the dishwasher.

He sets the photo down and moves to one of us at the ocean we went to every summer. I'm a bit older in that one, late highschool, and we both have wide smiles on our faces. Her with a big beach hat on her head, her graying hair back in a ponytail. I'm pretty sure that was also the trip where I got a really bad sunburn and Gram nursed me back to health with aloe and ice water. Then we spent the rest of the trip indoors and she kicked my ass at Mario Kart. I chuckle as I remember the ridiculous victory dance she did every time she won.

Fuck, the memories make my chest ache.

Alex's laughter brings me back to the present when he sees the third photo of us at Universal Studios in my early college years, standing near Doctor Doom's Fear Fall. Gram has her tongue sticking out and both hands in the air with just her pinky and pointer finger up. I'm next to her just trying not to laugh.

"Man, she was trouble, wasn't she?"

I laugh. "Yeah, she was. In the best way."

I grab the beers Alex brought and make my way to the sofa, and he joins me, stopping to admire the blanket draped over the back before he sits. "Did your Gram make this, too?" he asks, looking at the large throw in pink, blue and purple yarn. He runs his hand along it like it's fine china.

"No, I did," I tell him, and he gapes.

"Seriously?"

I flush and nod.

"Dude, it's gorgeous, and like, amazingly soft. I can't believe you made it."

"Yeah, Gram taught me to knit and I do it when I can. Usually while watching TV."

"Are you knitting anything now?" he asks, taking a seat on the sofa. Marble hops from her spot on the ottoman to the open space between us.

"Yeah, actually, I'm making a blanket for Peyton for her birthday. She's been asking for one forever."

"You gonna work on it while we watch? I don't mind."

"Nah, not this time, but I probably will if you decide you like it and we want to keep watching."

"Hey, there he is," Alex gestures to the giant plush penguin sitting in the corner of the room. I haven't quite figured out what to do with him yet. He's so damn big. Probably a good three feet tall and very chubby, with a giant bow tie around his neck. It makes me happy, though, to have him, even if he was intended for Stacy. Maybe there's some spite there if I'm being honest, though I guess Stacy doesn't know the difference because she never saw it, but thinking of her having anything from Alex makes my skin crawl, and I also like that I have this constant reminder of how Alex and I met, even if things were a bit awkward at first. Seeing the penguin in my apartment, having Alex in my apartment, makes me happy.

"He have a name?" Alex asks, nudging my arm with his elbow.

"A name?"

"Yeah, all stuffed animals need names."

I look at the penguin. I didn't have a lot of stuffed animals as a kid. Not past the age of nine or so, I don't think, but there are a few that I keep in tubs in storage that I got from Mom or Gram and have sentimental value. One sits on my bed, actually. A worn out teddy bear named Jean-Luc Teddy, because Gram got him for me, and we loved to watch *Star Trek* together. Jean-Luc is my favorite character.

"How about Tux?" I say, looking at the gigantic penguin with the bow tie.

Alex chuckles. "Nice. Tux it is." He hands me a beer and then clinks his beer bottle against mine. "Did you know that some penguins give pebbles to their potential mates as a sign of affection, and that when people send messages now to friends and family throughout the day, little things that remind them of that person or that they know they'll appreciate, like gifs or memes, or just random texts, they call it pebbling? It was originally adopted by the neurodivergent community, I think, as a way for people who are nonverbal or have trouble expressing emotions with words to have a safe way of communicating and showing they care, and then over time it's become more popular in the neurotypical community, too."

"How do you know that? You a penguin expert?" I tease.

He laughs. "No, hardly. But my brother-in-law, Pierre, loves animals, and he knows a lot. And I asked him what the most romantic animals were because I wanted to find something to give to Stacy as a gift, something different, you know, because I thought it would be romantic, and he suggested penguins. A lot of them mate for life, too. And they're really affectionate with each other. Turns out Stacy doesn't deserve Tux, or you, so glad he's here."

I grin. "Me, too."

He slaps my arm. "Okay, show me what this *Supernatural* show is all about, cowboy."

We end up watching the first three episodes before I tell Alex it's getting to be my bedtime. He genuinely seems to like the Winchester brothers and their family business of saving people and hunting things, as they say on the show.

"Same time next week?" he says, standing. I only just realized he didn't even bother wearing shoes over, and I kinda like it.

"Sounds good."

"You let me know about the books. If you do decide you're okay with me reading to you we can figure out a time." He scoops up Marble, who hisses at him before letting him scratch behind her ear.

"I know, princess, I'm gonna miss Bentley, too," he tells her, and my cheeks heat for the millionth time that night. When I close the door behind Alex it's with a smile on my face. Peyton was right. It is nice having another friend.

I groan when my phone buzzes on my nightstand a few days later. It's not my alarm. I don't work today with it being Sunday. And I was planning to sleep in. I reach for it, opening one eye and keeping my face smashed against the pillow. The first thing I notice is the time. I guess I did sleep in because it's after ten. The second thing is that I have a text from Alex.

Alex: Rise and shine, gorgeous! You have plans.
Me: I do?
Alex: Very much so

The next thing I hear is a pounding on my front door and it makes me jolt. Jesus Christ.

Alex: Come let me in
Alex: Hurry
Alex: I have to pee

I groan again and roll my eyes. Also, did he call me gorgeous? I scroll back up just to double check. He sure did. And why do I like it so much? I don't know but it's making my heart flutter and my dick twitch in my pajama pants. It's only then I realize I have a good old case of morning wood. And fuck, no time to do anything about it with Alex outside my door.

I climb out of bed and slide my bathrobe on over my pajama pants so I can hide my hard on, then make my way out of the bedroom and through the living area to the front door, where Alex hasn't stopped knocking. And now he's calling my name.

"Bentley, let me in, I gotta tinkle!"

I fling the door open and give him a menacing glare. Well, I try to, but I've never really been good at that and from the wide smile on his face it's not very effective.

Honestly, I also can't bring myself to actually be frustrated with him because I'm glad he's here. I'm not so great at making plans with people, and if they don't take charge and insert themselves in my life, like Peyton did, and now Alex, I'd just spend all of my time alone. "You do know you can use your own bathroom, right?" I tell him, rubbing my eyes, still trying to wake up.

"Where's the fun in that?" he says, and I open my eyes again to see him grinning wider.

I blink when I see what he's wearing. A red tank top and black athletic shorts with a black baseball cap on, and sneakers, and he's carrying a coat and a duffle bag. Fuck, why am I staring at his biceps? Or the fact that you can see pretty much his entire chest through the armholes of that tank? Or the fact that his nipples are dark and perky. Shit, what the hell is wrong with me? I've never had this kind of reaction to a guy before. Never *noticed* them like this. What is it about Alex that has me so discombobulated? And why is my dick twitching again?

"You okay, cowboy?" he asks, and I flush crimson when I realize I've just been staring at him. Shoot, not just staring at him, checking him out.

"I uh, yeah," I mutter, and step aside so he can come in. "Where are you going dressed like that in this weather?" I ask him as he strides inside and I close the door. My heart rate has picked up and I'm trying really hard not to let my eyes roam over his body.

"*We* are going to the gym," he tells me. "So get ready. I'll wait for you. I really do have to pee though, do you mind?"

I shake my head and he drops his things near the front door and makes his way to the bathroom. When he comes back out he plops himself down on the couch and gives me a shooing motion.

"Uh, help yourself to food and water," I tell him. "I'll

just go take a shower." I have to find a way to get rid of this erection because it is not going away on its own.

As I step into the bathroom and close the door behind me, I let out a sigh and try to calm the pitter patter of my heart. I hang up my robe and turn the water on before I strip. My dick is leaking now and I take it in hand and give it a few slow pulls, biting my lip to keep from moaning too loudly. God, it feels good. Maybe my reaction to Alex has more to do with the fact that I haven't given my dick attention for quite a while and less to do with Alex himself. That has to be it. It would make sense, right? Ever since I broke up with Stacy I haven't really had much desire for sex in general. Maybe because I'm scared? I still worry that she cheated on me because I wasn't satisfying her, which has made it hard to want to hook up with anyone, and I'm too shy to go meeting someone at a bar or something. In the past, the girls I've dated have been ones that Peyton introduced me to, or that I met through my job, like Stacy. And I've honestly been so tired and busy with everything, I have had no desire to get back out into the dating scene. I haven't been with anyone else in weeks, but I haven't been jerking off either, so I'm probably just going through a dry spell or something.

I'm starting to get louder and more desperate as I touch myself, so I step into the shower and let the warm water cascade over me as I start to work myself again. I've always been able to produce a good amount of precum and it means I rarely need lube. Fuck, a whimper leaves me as I circle the head of my cock and then slide down my shaft before gripping tighter and moving back up. I shake as plea-sure envelops me and I close my eyes, planting one hand on the tiled shower wall and shivering. With each stroke I come more and more undone, and when I move my hand to my chest and pinch my nipple a cry leaves my throat that I have no control over. "Oh, God," I murmur. I haven't felt this good in a long time, and when I shoot my release all over the shower wall seconds later, I tell myself that picturing Alex with his mouth on my nipple and his hand wrapped around my cock doesn't mean a goddamn thing.

Alex

I have sweat sliding down the back of my neck and my heart is racing, and if I'm being honest with myself, only part of that is due to my workout. I have never been more distracted in my life than I am right now watching Bentley. I have no fucking clue what is going on with me. And ogling him was not at all a part of my plan when I told him he was coming with me today. I've never stared at another man while he exercised before, but something about the way Bentley moves, the way those powerful thighs bunch and flex underneath his gym shorts as he works his legs, and the corded muscles in his arms bulge when he's working his upper body, has me hypnotized. I've also never been one to get turned on be sweat, but holy fuck, he's covered in it and I find myself wanting to know what it would be like to lick it off his gorgeous, hard body.

And that hair. Jesus Christ, that hair. He had it down again when he opened the door this morning and the way it tumbled around his shoulders, I was clenching my fists at my sides to keep my hands from just flying into it. It looked so damn soft. Even now as I watch him he has a few loose strands of hair falling into his face and it looks so damn sexy.

Fuck, what is wrong with me? I've never wanted to touch another man before. Not that way, anyway. And I've also never looked at another guy and thought "gorgeous" before, or "sexy". I've noticed guys I thought were good looking, I guess, on occasion, but none that made me want to lick them, for fuck's sake. What is it about Bentley that's got me so....sexually frustrated, I guess?

I'm so focused on him I've barely gotten any of my own workout in, and my arms are about to fall off because I've been doing the same reps with the same dumbbells fifty times by now as I stare through the full length mirror on the wall and watch him breathing in and out as he sits at the chest press machine, the sounds of the gym filling the space around me, people grunting and breathing, the belts of the treadmills moving, the "clank clank" of the weights, people's murmured voices, and the music playing overhead.

It really isn't helping that I am pretty sure he was jerking off this morning in the bathroom, and I've got the image of him with his hand on his dick, stroking and moaning, embedded in my brain.

And when have I ever thought about another guy's dick? Never, that's when. So why am I thinking about Bentley's? He's my friend and if he knew I was having these kind of thoughts about him he'd probably be freaked the fuck out, so I need to get it together.

"Hey," he says, after making his way over to me. I'm still standing here with dumbells in my hands, doing I don't fucking know what, other than staring at him in the mirror as a bead of sweat slides down his face. The strands of hair that have fallen out of his messy bun are slick with sweat, and more sweat glistens on his beard.

He has a towel in his hand and is using it to wipe his face and neck, and I almost groan when he lifts the hem of his shirt and uses it to fan himself. Jesus God mother fucking fuck, Christ on a cracker the man is ripped. Part of me is amazed that someone as built as him can be so gentle on his massage patients, and then a shiver goes through me at the thought of him having those big, strong, but gentle hands on me.

Okay, I have to snap out of it. This is ridiculous. Maybe I need to go on a date with a pretty girl so I can get my very straight friend out of my messed up head. I haven't been back on Tinder since Stacy, and I'm probably just in need of some female companionship. Not sex, at least not right away. I'm not a sex for the sake of sex kind of guy. Fucking is a bigger deal to me than just finding a random stranger to stick my dick in. Nothing wrong with that, and I know it works for a lot of people but it's never been me. I realized in high school, when all my friends were talking about the hook ups they were having, that that just didn't appeal to me. I need to get to know someone a bit before I'm going to feel comfortable getting into bed with them. Sex for me is very much tied to my emotions, and the idea of being that vulnerable with someone, getting naked in front of them, letting them touch me, is something I could never do with a stranger.

The problem is I only have two evenings off a week, and I don't really want to spend them with a girl. I want to spend them with Bentley, watching *Supernatural* and drinking beer, and making each other laugh, not worrying about the pressures of dating.

"Alex?" I hear and realize he's been talking while I've been lost in my head again.

I make eye contact with him through the mirror and he grins.

"I'm gonna head to the showers," he tells me. "You coming?"

Fortunately, before I blurt, *No, but I bet you could make me,* my brain catches up with my mouth and I nod. "Yeah," I squeak out, then clear my throat and try again. "Yeah. I'll be there in a minute." What the hell was that? I'm a fucking

mouse now? And why was I having thoughts of us showering together? I know that's not what he meant. God, this is
ridiculous. How do I get my fucking head screwed back on
straight? No pun intended. I haven't watched porn in a
while. Maybe that'll do the trick. A lot of porn doesn't work
for me, because once again, I need that emotional connection, to feel like the couple really care for each other, and
not that they're just having a steamy one night stand, and
there's a few couples that I follow that are pretty good at
getting me off when I don't have a woman to warm my bed
and need some good spank bank material. With a plan of
action in mind for how to stop lusting after my friend, I
breathe a little easier and make my way to the showers.

Chapter Seven

Bentley

Christ, that was intense. After warming up on the treadmill with Alex next to me on his own treadmill, we hung around each other for about a half an hour doing our workout side by side. But when I couldn't stop staring at him and was terrified of popping a boner, I had to move to the other side of the gym and will myself to keep my thoughts and my eyes off of him. Easier said than done when he's doing his absolute best to torment me with that body and the beads of sweat rolling down his neck, catching on his exposed nipples before sliding down his toned abdomen. I can't remember how many times I lost count of the number of reps I'd done and just had to guess. Irritated me like nothing else.

It's driving me insane that I'm so fucking...aware of him. When did this become a thing? I've never been so mesmerized by another man before, and I thought jerking off this morning would have taken care of things, so to speak. Instead I'm finding myself growling while I towel myself off in the men's locker room and change into my jeans and T-shirt, because I've never been more confused in my life than I am when it comes to Alex and the things he's making me feel, the way he's making my body react. And I swear I saw him looking at me more than a couple times, too, but I tell myself it doesn't mean anything.

The most frustrating thing is, I don't want him to realize that I'm...I don't know, attracted to him, because if he did he'd probably never want to see me again. And I hate the thought of losing him. He's quickly becoming someone I'm very much enjoying being with. So I guess, if these feelings persist, I'll just have to figure out a way to work around them and not make myself obvious, or make him uncomfortable. Because not spending time with him isn't an option.

"Hey, you ready to go?" he asks, and I blink, realizing he's standing next to me, fully dressed in dark wash jeans that cling to his slender legs and a black long-sleeved shirt that looks amazing against his caramel colored skin. He runs his fingers through his dark hair and gives me that Alex smile that has my heart tripping a little bit in my chest. Goddamn it.

"Yeah," I tell him, grabbing my bag. "You wanna come back later this week?" I don't really know why I'm asking him this except that I must be a masochist, because putting myself through this again is such a fucking dumb idea, but I never claimed to be smart, and like I said, he's my friend. The best one I have next to Peyton, and I need the companionship. Having a workout buddy is going to be so much better for me than trying to come up with the willpower to do this by myself, and I haven't really been working out nearly as much as I should have been since I moved here.

"Yeah, how does Thursday sound? We can make it a weekly thing if you want."

"Sounds good," I tell him.

"You wanna go out for lunch? There's a really great burger joint down the road."

I grin because there's nothing I like more than a mouth-watering burger. "Lead the way," I tell him. We came together in his car so I follow him out of the building and into the bitter cold winter air. Even my winter coat isn't enough to keep me from shivering as soon as we step outside, and I tell myself I need to maybe get some more long-sleeved shirts or sweaters to wear because this Massachusetts winter is kicking my ass.

Fortunately Alex doesn't mind when I crank the heat to max as we make the short drive to the burger joint. He just chuckles and shakes his head. The rotten little turd is acting like twenty degrees is nothing while I'm blowing on my hands and my teeth are chattering.

"We'll be there by the time the car warms up," he tells me.

"Shush," I reply, waving my hands in front of the vents as if to coax the warm air out faster, and he laughs. "I don't need your negativity."

"So I was thinking, maybe after we're done eating we could go back to your place and you could read to me?" I say as we sit eating our burgers a few minutes later. It's a fun place, not real big, with black and white checkered floors and red topped circular tables. There's lots of chatter around us as the customers enjoy their food, and the smell of grease, smoke, and onions floats through the air. His face lights up and it makes my heart do that pitter patter thing.

"Yeah?" he says.

I nod. I figure I owe it to Alex to at least try listening since he was kind enough to offer to read to me. Especially since he was willing to try something I enjoyed. Besides that, though, I don't want my time with him to end.

"Awesome. Okay, why don't we start with *Little Women?* It's a classic."

"Are those your favorite?" I ask, then take a swig of my drink.

"Probably, but there's not much I won't read. Also, if there's words you don't understand, don't feel bad. I had to look up quite a few of them the first time, too." His blue eyes are shining and his face is slightly flushed, his dark waves falling over his forehead, and I swallow, because he looks... beautiful.

When we arrive back at the apartments I scurry inside the building as quickly as possible, Alex laughing at me as I do. He unlocks his apartment and invites me in. Marble hops down from her spot on top of the sofa and hurries over to me. I crouch down and pet her, and she immediately starts to purr. After removing my coat and hanging it on the hooks near the door I scoop her up. I see her almost every night now, and we cuddle while I watch TV until I'm ready for bed, and then I bring her back to Alex's.

Kicking our shoes off, we head over to the couch and I settle on it with Marble in my arms while Alex grabs his book off one of his many shelves and sets it on the coffee table.

"I'm gonna make tea, you want some? Or something else?" he offers.

"Just water since your brain isn't screwed on right and you don't have a coffee maker," I tease.

He smirks at me. "You have one across the hall, you know. You could go make some and come back, or we could go over there."

"Nah, I'd rather complain."

He chuckles and makes his way into the kitchen. I decide I'd rather lie down while he reads so I grab one of the throw pillows and situate it just right before I slide onto my side, taking Marble with me. She curls up against my stomach and I stroke her back.

Alex returns and sets my water glass down. I expect him to tell me to move my feet since I'm taking up the entirety of one length of the sectional, but he just grabs my feet and picks them up, before settling down and letting my feet rest on his lap.

Why is my heart rate picking up again? If that wasn't bad enough he grabs the blanket off the back of the sofa and drapes it over me, then rests one of his hands on one of my feet as he reaches forward and grabs the book. His hand only leaves for the brief second it takes him to open the book, and then it's back on my foot, rubbing circles into it absentmindedly while he starts to read.

Jesus, he's barely touching me and my body feels like a livewire. I'm flushed and way too turned on for the amount of physical contact we're having. My dick is perking up and I'm starting to be more and more thankful for the blanket over me. I should ask him to stop so I can fucking pay attention because I have no idea what he's reading, but I can't make myself because it feels so good. I give massages to people all day every day, but other than Peyton's hugs, I haven't been touched since I broke up with Stacy. The more he does it the more my body starts to relax, and my brain turns to mush, even as goosebumps break out all over my skin. God, it's like some form of exquisite torture.

"If you decide you want to be done, let me know," he says.

"I'm good, but can you maybe start over? I was spacing there for a bit."

He chuckles a little. "Sure, cowboy." He pauses and asks, "You don't wanna be knitting while we do this? I don't want you losing precious minutes."

I shake my head. "I can't knit unless I'm watching something I've seen before, or don't really need to pay that much attention to. I think I better be paying attention to this."

And I do pay attention this time, though when he tries to do different voices for all of the characters I can't stop laughing because they're awful. A voice actor he is not. He stops and I relax again, the sound of his voice soothing. I find I enjoy hearing about the March sisters, and I think Beth is my favorite. She's just so sweet. I really like Jo too, though, and how she rejects societal standards and is unapologetically herself. Her independence, strength and spirited personality remind me of Gram.

We get a few chapters in before I start to nod off and Alex is yawning, too. I had to stop him just a couple of times to ask him about words and what they meant, like "cabalistic" and "warble", and he told me each time without any frustration or irritation in his voice. Just that kindness that I'm coming to find is so very Alex.

"Okay, time for a break because my throat is getting sore," he says, setting the book down. "You haven't told me to stop so I'm assuming that means you aren't hating it."

"No, I'm really enjoying it, actually," I tell him, and he smiles. "But I am falling asleep."

"Nap time, then," he says, and moves the other pillow on the sofa, resting it on his side and stretching out behind me, his feet near my upper back, before he pulls the other blanket down and drapes it over himself. He grabs his phone and says, "Hey Siri, set an alarm for six pm."

"What's at six pm?" I ask, still trying to register that we're napping together. I could go home, but I don't want to.

"Dinner at my parents' place," he says. "We do it once a month to visit and catch up. You're coming, too."

I hide a grin. "I am?"

He snuggles into the pillow and closes his eyes. A yawn

escapes him, and I know that whatever this attraction or crush or infatuation is, it's not going away any time soon because who the actual fuck sees someone yawn and thinks it's cute? Jesus.

"Yep," he says. "Night, Thor."

I chuckle, and my heart pitter patters again. "Night."

Alex

I wake before the alarm goes off, my body alerting me that I have to pee. God, I don't want to though. This is the best nap I've ever had, even if we both barely fit on this couch the way we are. Having Bentley's body heat around me, sharing the space with him, the scent of ocean and rain that clings to him, the sense of safety I feel with him near, is addictive, and my body is heavy and boneless as I groan. When I open my eyes I come almost face to...foot I guess, with his large sock-covered feet, and even though I'm not typically a foot person, I have an overwhelming urge to press my lips to his, and I nearly gasp when my cock jerks at the thought.

Okay, time to get up before I embarrass myself by doing something incredibly stupid and inappropriate. Inviting him to dinner with me was stupid enough. What I need is a break from him, but it's the last thing I want. And I know he doesn't have family, so I want him to feel welcome with mine. If that means suffering by being in his company for another few hours, I'll survive.

I climb out of my cocoon of warmth and coziness and over Bentley's long legs, making my way to the bathroom.

When I return he's snoring softly with Marble lying on his hip like it's the most comfortable place in the world, and I can't believe I'm jealous of a fucking cat. I mosey over to them and stare down at her. "You're going to have to get off you spoiled feline," I tell her, arms crossed over my chest. "He's coming with me."

She raises her head, blinks at me, and then puts it back down. I sigh. The alarm is going off in a couple of minutes, but since I feel like it might be nicer to wake Bentley gently rather than being shocked awake, and not at all because I want the excuse to touch him, I turn it off. And then, even though what I really want to do is run my fingers through that thick, gorgeous head of hair, and feel how fucking silky it is under my fingertips, maybe grip it and use it to tilt his head back while I suck marks on his thick neck–okay that was oddly specific and I realize that definitely falls into the inappropriate and possibly creepy category–I rest my hand on one of his broad shoulders instead. Fuck, even that has a zing of electricity shooting up my arm.

"Pull it together, Alex," I murmur.

"What?" he mutters, and I almost shriek, stepping back as his eyes blink open slowly.

"Jesus, I thought you were asleep," I say, catching my breath, really thankful that I didn't say any of the other things I was thinking out loud. Lord Almighty.

"Sorry," he chuckles, his eyes opening fully, before he yawns. "I haven't been awake for long. What are you pulling together?"

"Uh..." my cheeks heat and I scramble to think of something. "Never mind, it's not important. Upsy daisy, we have to be there in fifteen minutes."

"Isn't it upstairs?" he asks, reaching over to scoop Marble into his arms and rubbing her belly as she flops over. She looks at me upside down from where she's nestled in Bentley's strong arms and I swear she grins. I take the opportunity to glare at her.

"Yeah, but don't you need to get ready, or something?"

He looks at himself. "I don't think so. Do I need to change?"

I shake my head. "You gotta pee or anything?" What the heck? Why did I ask him that? Is he five?

He chuckles. "I will in a minute."

"Will your brother and his husband be coming?" he asks. Why am I staring at the way his arms fill the sleeves of his T-shirt as he pets my cat? Jesus fuck.

"Uh, yeah, they will be. You haven't met them yet, right?"

"I sort of met Tommy at the bar. He waited on me and Peyton, and I met your folks, but I've never met Tommy's husband."

I blink. "You met my parents? When?"

"A few days after I moved in. They introduced themselves when we ran into each other in the hallway. They were real nice."

I smile. "Yeah, they are really nice. And both of them love to cook, which unfortunately is a talent they only passed on to Tommy."

He laughs. "Well, you got the gorgeous eyes," he says, fucking staring right at me, like he isn't saying the most romantic thing in the world and impregnating me on the spot. Fuck, this man.

He flushes when I just stare at him open mouthed, and then sits up and plants a kiss on Marble's head before shuffling to the bathroom. I groan and slouch in my spot, patting my lap to invite Marble over. She looks at me like, *You aren't Bentley,* and hops onto her cat tower instead. I get up and get my fussy traitor queen her dinner.

When Bentley returns he's in the process of putting his hair back up in a messy bun, and there go those muscles again, flexing like nobody's goddamn business. His shirt rides up and I catch a glimpse of his blond treasure trail, leading from his belly button to the waistband of his jeans.

Goddamn it, every second I spend with him makes it harder for me to convince myself I'm "just going through a dry spell." But there's no way I'm going to stop spending time with him either. Just the thought of that makes me depressed as hell. Not to mention he's got me hooked on that show of his already and ever since he moved in, I haven't felt quite so lonely.

However, I have to make it a couple more hours before I am allowed to have a mini crisis over my sexuality and the fact that I'm starting to think maybe I'm not as straight as I thought I was.

"Ready?" Bentley asks in that southern drawl that makes my stomach fill with butterflies and my cock twitch.

"Yeah," I manage, hands in my pockets.

Bentley scratches behind Marble's ears once more as we make our way to the door. I decide she's been mean to me and doesn't deserve my affection so I stick my tongue out at her and keep walking.

Bentley laughs.

Chapter Eight

Bentley

Alex doesn't bother knocking when we get up the stairs to his parents' apartment.

"Mom, Dad, I'm here and I brought Bentley with me," he calls as he walks inside.

His mom comes out of the kitchen seconds later with an apron on and her arms outstretched to greet her son, and his dad isn't far behind.

Isabella kisses her son on the cheek. "Alejandro, mijo, so good to see you." His dad is next and he gives Alex a warm hug. Then Isabella is turning to me and gripping my cheeks, planting a kiss and making my face flush.

"Bentley, so glad you're joining us," she says, her smile bright, and I know she means it.

"Thank you for having me," I tell her.

"It's a pleasure," Johnny says, holding his hand out for me to shake.

"Are Tommy and Pierre coming?" Alex asks.

"They better be," Isabella says. "Someone has to eat all this food. Make yourselves comfortable and dinner will be ready soon." She makes her way back to the kitchen and Johnny looks at us.

"Can I get either of you a drink?"

"I'm good, Dad, thanks," Alex says.

"Me, too," I say. "I can wait for dinner."

"Suit yourselves." He gives a kind smile and heads back to the kitchen.

Alex sits and I walk around, looking at the different decorations and family photos. Their home definitely has a different style than Alex's but it's just as warm and cozy. There's a big brown leather sofa and matching recliner. A gorgeous woven rug with bright colors in an intricate pattern sits in the middle of the living space with a large wooden chest on top of it that serves as a coffee table. The drapes over the large window are olive green. On one wall is a painting of a sunflower field. Above the large flat screen TV is a painting of an elephant.

I spot a photo of a younger Alex on one of the bookshelves. He's probably in highschool, and it looks like a senior photo. His arms are crossed and he's leaning against a brick wall with one knee bent and his foot planted on the wall. He's dressed in snug fitting dark wash jeans and a black button up, untucked, casual but nice, and he looks mischievous and sexy as hell giving that Alex smile.

Shit. I clear my throat and look away like I'm afraid I'm gonna get struck by lightning just for having those thoughts about him, or that he'll somehow know that's where my mind has gone. And I'm still trying to figure out why my thoughts even went there. I know Alex is a good looking guy. I've known that since we met, but that knowledge never made me look at him or think about him as anything other than a friend until very recently.

I'm saved from the uncomfortable thoughts swirling

around in my head when I hear the front door open and someone shouting, "We're here!"

I turn and see Tommy, and who I am assuming is his husband, holding hands as they walk through the door.

Why that makes my heart flutter I don't know, but maybe it's the fact that they're clearly so gone on each other that they held hands just to cross the hall. Kinda adorable.

Speaking of adorable, Tommy's husband is a little sprite of a man, maybe five foot four, with wavy blond hair that's short on the sides and longer on top, and pale skin, dressed in white skinny jeans with holes in them and a cropped baby blue T-shirt that has Care Bears on it. He's young, but then so is Tommy, and they're looking at each other with so much affection it nearly makes my heart burst.

"Hey, baby brother," Alex says, standing and giving Tommy a hug. Tommy groans, his arms limp at his sides, clearly not one for physical affection, unless it's coming from Pierre, it would seem. Pierre giggles as he watches the two brothers.

Alex turns to Pierre next. "Hey, squirt," he says affectionately, and Pierre presses up on his tip-toes to hug him. "How you doing?"

"I am fine," Pierre says, his French accent thick, his voice almost angelic. "Don't worry about me."

"You guys haven't met Bentley," Alex says, ushering me over. "He's our new neighbor."

"Hi," Tommy says, shaking my hand. "I remember you from the bar, but I'm sorry we haven't gotten around to officially introducing ourselves. We've meant to come and say hi and welcome you to the building."

"It's not a problem at all," I assure him. "It's good to meet you."

"Bonjour, I'm Pierre," Pierre says, voice soft, but a sweet smile on his face as I shake his hand. It's so small it gets swallowed up by mine. He's really a stunning guy. Very delicate features, big blue eyes and full pink lips, three sparkly earrings in each ear and a belly button ring. He grips Tommy's hand again and nuzzles his husband's arm with his nose, and Tommy presses a kiss to his hair.

"Have a seat everyone, dinner's on the way!" Isabella calls from the kitchen.

We take our seats, Alex and I on one side of the table and Tommy and Pierre on the other as Isabella and Johnny carry steaming dishes into the dining area and set them on the table. It smells amazing, and looks even better. There's two different kinds of rice, pork, fried potato pancakes that Alex tells me are called llapingachos, and beans. And my mouth waters.

There's so much joy and laughter at the table that it makes it almost hard to eat the delicious food because I can't wipe the smile from my face. Isabella and Johnny regale me with tales of Alex and Tommy as kids and all the mischief they got up to. Tommy tells me about the time Alex shot him in the ass with a pellet gun and he couldn't sit down for a week, and Alex reminds him that he got him back by making Alex do all of his chores for that week, complaining they were too painful.

They ask about my work and Isabella tells me she'll have to book a massage soon to see how good I am, making me flush.

Johnny tells the story of how he and Isabella met in college, and he knew as soon as he saw her that she was the one, but that it took her a while to catch up.

"I couldn't stand him," Isabella says with a wide smile, and we all laugh, even though I'm sure I'm the only one who hasn't heard the story yet. "Thought he was an arrogant asshole. Which he was." She winks at her husband and there's nothing but love in that gaze. "But he was also kind and caring, smart, funny, and my parents didn't scare him away."

"I knew what I wanted," Johnny says, a twinkle in his blue eyes and that same smile on his face. Pierre nuzzles Tommy's shoulder with his nose, his cheeks pink and a huge smile on his face. I've yet to see Tommy smile, but I know that doesn't mean he isn't as crazy about his husband as his parents are about each other, or as Pierre is about him. I have also noticed that throughout the meal Tommy hasn't stopped touching Pierre once. Not in a way that is inappropriate, but just simple things, like stroking his finger down Pierre's back, or resting his hand on his leg, or even holding his hand while he eats with his other hand, and how content Pierre looks with his husband's ministrations, almost like Marble when I'm petting her.

Isabella tells me that Alex told her about my Gram passing and me moving out here, and I get the most heartfelt condolences from everyone at the table. When I find out Pierre lost his parents when he was a kid I feel an immediate connection to the little guy. He's barely said a word the whole meal but his eyes were so soft when I spoke about losing Mom and moving in with Gram, and I know he understands grief like that. I just wish he didn't. I can tell what a sweetheart of a guy he is and I've only known him for a couple of hours.

When I ask what he does he tells me he's in school and does some cam work on the side, and I feel my cheeks heating, but he seems completely comfortable talking about it, even in front of his in-laws.

"Sorry, I'm making you uncomfortable," he says.

"No, it's fine," I assure him. "I just wasn't expecting it, that's all."

I ask him what he's in school for and he beams and talks about his plans for becoming a veterinarian.

We eat dessert in the living room after the table has been cleared, and Isabella and Johnny offer us wine. I can't help my gaze from straying to Alex every so often as we visit some more and the room is once again filled with smiles and laughter.

It's been a long time since I had this, since I had anyone but Peyton.

When we leave it's almost midnight, and Isabella kisses me on the cheek again. Johnny asks if he can give me a hug and all six feet and two inches of me almost melts when he wraps his strong arms around me, because it's been a long time since I've experienced any sort of fatherly affection, and he's giving it so freely to someone he barely knows.

"You are welcome any time, son," he tells me and fuck, I have to keep the tears from filling my eyes. I don't think I can speak so I just nod.

I exchange numbers with Pierre and Tommy, and Alex and I make the very short trip down the stairs. We stop in front of my door first.

"I'm really glad you came," he tells me, then rests his hand on my arm. "Night, cowboy." He turns to walk away and I say his name, making him face me again.

I clear my throat. "I'm off tomorrow, if you wanted to hang out at all before you go to work."

That smile that I want to capture and keep tucked away in my pocket splits his handsome face. "I would like that very much," he tells me. "I'll text you."

"Sounds good." He winks at me and I head inside, unable to keep the smile from my face.

Alex

I have one goal in mind when I close the door to my apartment and make my way to the bedroom. Porn. Good old fashioned guy on girl porn. Because I have to get these thoughts of Bentley out of my fucked up head and I don't know how else to do it.

I close the door even though I'm alone. I don't know why, it just feels weird to leave it open while I jerk off. Marble moseys over to her cat bed and lies down.

Sitting on my bed I open the laptop and go to Only-Fans. I pull up the account of one of the married couples I follow. They have uploaded a few new videos since I was last on here, and they all look promising.

I undress down to my boxer briefs and then sit at the head of the bed with the laptop on my lap and click the play button. I've been half hard all fucking night so it doesn't take long for me to get fully hard as I watch the couple lying in bed next to each other. They start off partially clothed, in just their underwear, facing each other, sharing gentle caresses and soft kisses. But it's the way they're looking at each other that really gets me going. You can tell they share a connection on a deeper level, that they genuinely care for and love each other.

I'm stroking through my briefs as they start to make out, and I moan when they begin to undress each other, and precum slides down my shaft. My breathing picks up and goosebumps erupt over my skin as the woman tilts her head back and exposes her neck, letting her man kiss and suck, while at the same time unhooking her bra. My cock jerks and I start to stroke myself harder as her gorgeous breasts are bared, her bra being tossed aside. Then the man is sucking on her tits and I reach into my underwear now, a groan leaving me as I come in contact with my bare length.

The gorgeous woman lies on her back and the man works his way down her body, kissing, licking and sucking on her skin, drawing gasps and whimpers out of her and me in turn. When he gets to her pelvis he breathes her in, before grabbing her panties and sliding them off, letting them join her bra on the floor. They're both so turned on, if the way they're breathing and the erection the man is sporting is anything to go by, but they're still looking at each other like they're the most beautiful thing the other has ever seen. Fuck, I want that so bad. When my thoughts go straight to Bentley I shove them aside and focus on the sexy couple in front of me.

They're both naked now, and the man spreads the woman's thighs, before he goes down on her, licking and sucking her pussy, making the most debauched noises as he does, like he's never had his mouth on anything so delicious.

She arches her back and moans like a fucking whore as he devours her, and her body starts to shake.

The man pauses briefly and raises his head. "Touch your tits, baby," he instructs. "I want you to come just like this."

She moans and does as she's told, and I'm yanking my underwear down around my thighs, stroking myself, so damn hard. Yes, fuck, this is what I needed. So good.

The woman cries out not much later, her body shaking with the man's tongue still eating her out, and he growls. Then he's shoving his bare cock inside her and thrusting hard and fast. God, this is so damn hot.

I'm about two seconds from blowing my load when Bentley's face appears in my mind again and my hole spasms. Holy shit. When I come, it's so hard and I shout so loud, I hope he didn't hear me across the hall.

Fuck. It almost worked. I look down at my spent cock and the load of cum on my belly and chest. Then slowly move my fingers to my hole. I've never even played with it with my fingers before, but it was clearly into what I was doing and I've never had any reaction down there when I jerked off with someone's face or body in my mind. But thinking about Bentley made it perk up. I touch the pucker, run my finger over it a couple of times and shiver at the sensation. Jesus, why is the idea of having something inside me so appealing all of a sudden?

I move the laptop aside and rest my head back on my pillow, my arm behind it as I stare up at the ceiling.

Okay, well, that didn't work as well as I'd hoped, because if anything I think I'm just thinking about Bentley more. What it might feel like to have him on top of me, his heavy weight pressing me down, those strong arms around me, and his dick, fuck, his dick buried inside me.

My hole spasms again and I groan in frustration.

Goddamn it.

Goddamn him.

When I wake up the next morning I shower and eat some breakfast, then feed Marble, before texting Bentley and seeing if he's okay with me coming over. I add that Marble will be coming too. When his reply comes in I smile before I even know what it says, and I swear I must have the dopiest grin on my face.

Cowboy: ready when you are

Me: on my way

Cowboy: just come in, no need to knock

Why is my grin getting bigger? *Stop it, Alex. Pull yourself together.*

I groan as I tuck my phone in my pocket. Then I look down at my dick tucked away in my jeans, and give it a stern talking to.

"You behave yourself," I tell it. "I know he's gorgeous, and super sweet, and cooks like a God, and makes me laugh, and his fucking feet smell like heaven which should totally be illegal, but he's just a friend and you need to remember that. Don't embarrass us."

With that settled I grab my cat even as she fights me, letting me know she doesn't like being manhandled. Well, not by anyone but Bentley anyway. He could pick her up when she's in the middle of eating, or napping, and she'd happily oblige. "Look here, you primadonna, I would give my left nut to be you right now and let that Thor look alike get his hands on me, so you hush, okay? You can handle me carrying you for five seconds. I just need five seconds of kitty cuddles before you leave me for him."

She meows but settles in my arms, and we make our way across the hall.

Chapter Nine

Bentley

I lasted about an hour lying in bed last night with a raging hard on before I gave up and touched myself. After turning the picture on the nightstand of Gram around, because it just felt weird with her "watching" me do that. She was always very sex positive, even bought lube and put it in the shower for me when I hit puberty. Embarrassed me to pieces at the time but I'm grateful now. Though I also realized I didn't actually need it because apparently my body produced enough precum it got the job done by itself.

I swear I did everything I could to get Alex off my mind but my dick wasn't having it. I came so hard I almost blacked out, too. He's coming over here any minute and I've made sure I'm wearing jeans today because if I get hard being around him I do not want it being plain as day which is exactly what would happen in my sweats. Not only do I produce more precum than I think is average, I'm also not small, and normally I like the size of my dick, but when I'm hard and don't want to be, it's a problem. And If I'm leaking it could end up soaking through to my pants pretty quickly, and sweats will make it embarrassingly obvious, so jeans it is.

"Hey!" Alex calls, and a fucking shiver runs down my spine where I'm standing in the kitchen getting coffee. My dick twitches and I growl at it.

"Everything okay?"

I fucking yelp and nearly spill my coffee, turning to face him. I wasn't expecting him to be there. Jesus what is he? A vampire? I didn't even hear his footsteps.

"Yeah, of course," I say.

"Really, cause you were growling," he says, and I try and fail to keep my cheeks from heating. Meanwhile, Marble saunters into the kitchen and starts walking in between my legs, purring.

"It's nothing," I lie. "Just, uh, burned my mouth on the coffee." I lift the cup I'm holding as though it's evidence.

"Oh, sorry. Did I scare you? You said to just come in."

I shake my head. "No, you're fine." I set my mug down so I can pick Marble up in one arm and grab my drink again.

"I've got tea, if you want any," I tell him and the smile that splits his face is, well, goddamn it, it's adorable. Especially when those gorgeous blue eyes light up.

"Yeah? You got tea just for me?"

I flush and shrug. "No big deal."

"You're just showing me up. Now I'll have to get coffee for you."

"Nah, it's fine."

He looks over my shoulder at the stove behind me and his grin gets even bigger, before he steps around me. I'm blushing even harder when he grips the tea kettle on the stove. "You got this, too, didn't you? You didn't have this before."

"Maybe," I mumble, before taking a sip of my coffee.

"I'll give it a try later. Right now I want to see what those Winchester brothers are up to. And," he holds up the book he brought with him, "when we're done with that I can read to you some more if you want."

I nod, and we head into the living room.

We watch one episode of *Supernatural*, me knitting this time with Marble lounging against my hip, before Alex says he needs a bathroom break.

"Hey, you have popcorn?" he asks, when he gets back.

"Yeah, sure, but you want popcorn at eleven in the morning?"

He shrugs. "It's the snack of movie watching, I'm just following the rules."

I chuckle and point him towards the pantry.

When he returns he sits a little bit closer to me than he was before, the bowl of popcorn in between us, and his honey and vanilla scent fills my nostrils. It's all I can do not to let out a groan and bury my nose in his thick dark waves.

My dick jerks and I am thankful that my knitting supplies are covering my lap. If Alex saw me getting hard while he was sitting next to me it'd freak him the fuck out. And hell, I'd be humiliated.

He laughs at something Dean says and then reaches for the popcorn at the same time as me, and our fingers brush. Holy fuck, how does that miniscule skin to skin contact have my body lighting up? Jesus Christ, this is so fucking stupid. I feel like a middle schooler with a crush.

I'm torn between trying not to reach for the popcorn at the same time as him, and doing it on purpose, because I want to touch him, but I don't at the same time because I know it's a bad idea, just putting thoughts in my head that have no business being there. He's my friend. That's it.

I decide to take my own break a bit later and head to the bathroom, more to cool off than anything else. Being around him shouldn't feel like such fucking torture. I breathe and will my half hard dick to deflate, then splash some cold water on my face.

When I return Alex grins at me and pats the sofa. "You up for one more, cowboy?" he says.

I smile because I love that he's enjoying my favorite show so much, and watching the episodes all over again with someone who's never seen them before is exciting. Besides that I secretly love that nickname, and hearing it come from his lips. "Sounds good."

We watch three more episodes in all, pausing after the second one to have lunch. I've made a decent amount of progress on the blanket I'm knitting for Peyton, too, which I'm happy about.

When we've had our fill of *Supernatural* for the day Alex breaks out *Little Women* and I lie down with Marble tucked against my stomach and my feet pressed against Alex's thigh. It's not the most comfortable, being as tall as I am, my knees bent quite a bit. But I don't want to just assume he's okay with me having my feet in his lap just because we did it once. But when he opens the book, he looks at me.

His cheeks are slightly flushed and he's biting his lip when he says, "You can put your feet on my lap if you want. I don't mind."

Hell, I can't say no to him. I don't want to say no. So I pick my feet up and place them on his lap, and he gives me the biggest grin, his hand immediately finding my socked foot and rubbing circles on it with his thumb. Fuck, that feels good. Better than it has any right to.

"This okay?" he asks, and I nod.

"Feels nice," I tell him, my voice thick, and raspier than

normal, and I swear his cheeks flush even more. I listen, then, while he reads, that smooth, soft voice lulling me into relaxation and taking me to another time and place, allowing me to escape with him, and these four heart warming sisters.

Jesus Christ. I may not be the smartest person on the planet, but I know two things for certain. One, I'll never get enough of him touching me. And two, I'm not getting over this crush on him any time soon.

Alex

Oh my God, I don't know what's wrong with me. What was with all the fucking flirting I was doing yesterday? Could I have been any more obvious? I pulled the famous, "get up and pretend to need something so I can sit down closer to you instead of just scooting over because that would be too obvious" trick. And then telling him he could put his feet on my lap? Jesus, Alex, get it together! Although, to be fair, he didn't seem to mind either one of those things. And the way it felt when our hands touched when we reached for the popcorn at the same time? God, I felt like a teenager with how goddamn giddy it made me.

And, as long as he's not telling me to back the fuck off, what's one more harmless little flirtation, right?

Fuck, okay, here it goes. I take out my phone and open my texts to Bentley, then search for the gif I want. There's several to choose from and I tap one, then click the little paper airplane and let it do its magic.

I get a text back from him a second later.

Cowboy: Huh?

Me: You've been pebbled. Get it? Dwayne Johnson? The Rock?

Cowboy: haha, so clever

Cowboy: Penguin gif

Goddamn it I fucking swoon. And even though I know better, part of me wonders if he knows what I'm doing and is flirting right back. The goosebumps breaking out all over my body are telling me I'm far more gone on him that I even realized.

Chapter Ten

Alex

So, update on me and my self love sessions. It's been a few more weeks of hanging out with Bentley to watch Supernatural, work out, and read *Little Women* to him, which is slow going because we only have so much time together each week, but we're still going strong with it and he's enjoying the story. And I am falling for him more and more every fucking day. Every time we talk, every time we text and send those ridiculous penguin and The Rock gifs, which we're still doing weeks later, or the Supernatural gifs we send every Thursday as our "reminder." Every time he makes me laugh, every time he fusses over my prickly cat, or has a cup of tea ready for me when Marble and I go over to his place. Every time his feet are on my lap and I get to touch him, the few times I rubbed his foot in a way that made him laugh because I was tickling him, the way he smells, the way he blushes. Everything about him is driving me crazy. And I've decided that it's time for me to man up, and do something I've never done before.

We've developed an open door policy, which basically

means we can enter each other's apartments whenever as long as the door is unlocked, and we don't need to knock every time, so I've made sure my door is locked now, because having him barge in on me while I'm in the middle of exploring would suck ass.

I've jerked off to Bentley more times than I care to admit, and it's making me realize that maybe, just maybe, I'm not as straight as I thought I was. Yes, I know, I'm a little slow on the uptake, but I've been fucking nervous okay?

I've also noticed that I find myself looking at the other men in the gym way more now than I used to, too, and I think it's time for me to do a type of exploration I haven't yet. Because if being into guys is something that's a part of who I am, I want to know. I want to know that part of myself, and embrace it, not keep it buried or hidden.

So, I've got my laptop open to OnlyFans, only this time I'm looking for gay content. Particularly videos where I can tell they have a connection, because that's what I need to get off. Scrolling through videos of two men together is making me equally nervous and excited, honestly, because I know that if this is something I respond to, I'll have answers, or at least a better understanding of myself. And I also know that no matter what I discover, I'll have the best support system in the world and people who I know love and care for me to talk through it with, which is something a lot of people don't have, and I can imagine this being so much scarier without that.

I pray to God I don't come across Pierre's content because I think that would scar me for life, and Tommy would murder me. I find a video that looks promising, two men standing in the kitchen fully clothed, close together, one with his arms around the other. I take a breath and let it out, then click play. It starts out with them talking, and the one being held is telling the other about something that happened at work that's stressing him out while his partner rubs his back and plants a kiss on his forehead, soothing him. It's incredibly sweet, and I can tell by the way they look at each other and how comfortable they are with each other that they're in love. And my dick is not offended by this in the least.

In fact, I'm already half hard and these guys are fully clothed.

"How can I help?" the one guy asks as he takes his partner's face in his hands and kisses him softly, just a quick kiss, before pulling away.

"Hmmm," the other one hums, his hands on his partner's chest and their foreheads pressed together now. He's a bit smaller and a couple inches shorter than the other guy. "Make me feel good. Please." He lifts his head and looks into his partner's eyes, and the heat is unmistakable. "I want you inside me."

Fuck. My dick is fully on board now. I quickly strip out of my shirt and pants and down to my briefs as I watch them start to make out. It's slow and sensual at first before it picks up, and they start to use tongue. My dick jerks when the smaller of the two lets out a whimper and the other one groans, taking his partner's face in his hands and tilting his head, deepening the kiss. Shit, the breathless needy noises of the smaller one are revving my engine really good.

I take my cock in my hand and stroke slowly, watching as the smaller one jumps up and the larger one catches him, setting him on the counter before they're at each other again, their clothes quickly coming off and being discarded on the floor. Wow, I am paying way more attention to their bodies than I ever was when I watched straight porn, and I can't lie–I like what I see. The bigger one is hairier while the smaller one is smooth, and he runs his fingers through the other's chest hair like he can't get enough. They're both hard and leaking and I find I can't look away from their straining erections, both of them oozing precum that has my dick jerking and my mouth salivating.

"Fuck, cowboy," I whine as I grip myself and stroke. God, I've never craved another man's touch like I do Bentley's, and watching these two, it's just cementing that fact in my mind even more. I'm not trying to keep him from popping into my mind during these...sessions anymore. I gave up fighting it days ago. My hole flutters and I move the laptop to the side and spread my legs, lying on my back. God I feel like a fucking whore and I fucking love it.

I watch as the smaller one wraps his legs around the bigger one and ruts against his belly. Holy fuck, why is that so hot? The bigger one is growling and has his massive arms around his smaller partner, holding him to him as if to encourage his needy thrusting.

Damn, my cock is leaking like a faucet as I reach between my cheeks and locate my hole. I let out a cry when my finger comes in contact with the sensitive bud, and it flutters wildly against my fingertip. Holy shit. My cock spasms and I groan as the noises on the screen pick up. The smaller guy shouts and his dick sprays all over the stomach and chest of the bigger one, and I don't think I've ever seen anything hotter than one man's cum embedded in the chest hair of another man.

I grip my dick and stroke harder and faster even as I continue to circle my hole and press my finger tip to it periodically. Each touch makes my dick ooze precum and a shiver race down my spine. My thighs are trembling as the bigger guy picks the smaller one up, moves about a foot to the left, and slams him against the wall before impaling him on his monster cock.

The smaller guy shouts but his cries are muffled by his partner's rough kisses. I reach for the lube and coat my finger, knowing this is going to be over soon and if I want to try this now is the time. I slick up my finger and return to my hole, and just as the bigger guy moves his mouth to the smaller one's nipples and starts to suck, I push the tip of my finger into my tight channel. It burns at first, but after only a short moment it starts to loosen up a bit, and I moan at how good it feels to be filled.

I turn my head and watch as the smaller guy is impaled over and over again on the other's dick, and he's so blissed out he's hard all over again. God, I wish I had three hands so I could play with my nipples too.

I stroke my cock at the same time that I shove my finger a bit deeper inside me, and shout, "Holy shit!" when I find a sweet bundle of nerves that has my eyes rolling back in my head and my balls drawing up. Fuck, I'm close. I move my finger as the grunts and pants of the men in the video continue, but all I'm thinking about is what it would feel like to be impaled on Bentley's cock, and I want it so fucking bad I might cry.

I hit that sweet spot again and my orgasm washes over me as I shout Bentley's name, my back arching and my cum shooting out all over my abdomen as I picture those arms on either side of me, that smile above me, that dick buried so deep.

Fuck.

I am so not straight. And I'm falling so hard and fast for my friend. Shit, I don't know if I've ever had a best friend before, but Bentley and I have gotten close in the last month and a half and I definitely consider him my best friend. Maybe my only friend, really, outside my family. There's my coworkers at the bar, but I'm not close with any of them.

But that's the scariest part of all of this. It's not being bisexual that's making me freak out. It's being bi and having feelings for my friend. Being attracted to a man who's a stranger is so much less terrifying, because I have nothing to lose if it doesn't work out.

With Bentley, I could lose everything.

Bentley

Fuck, I'm in trouble. Trying to convince myself that I don't have feelings for Alex, that I'm not attracted to him, has been increasingly harder over the past few weeks. Every time we're together he does or says something, or multiple things, that make the butterflies in my stomach go crazy. It's very fucking inconvenient, because I can't have feelings for him, and I know this, but it's not stopping my heart from pitter-pattering when he's close, or my dick from twitching, or my body erupting in goosebumps every time he rubs my feet, or tells me the meaning of a word I don't understand when he's reading to me, or makes one of his terrible jokes. He does nothing to quell that ache in my chest when he laughs at something on *Supernatural,* or when he asks me about what it was like growing up with Gram, and then actually listens like he really wants to know about her, because she's important to me.

I've gotten so little sleep lately because I can't stop thinking about him and my right hand is getting a workout. I try not to think of Alex when I'm jerking off but it's no use, and I've even begun exploring gay porn to see if other guys do it for me like he does. I don't know why I'm coming across this realization so late in life, but I'm nutting so hard to watching two men fuck and it's making me wonder what I've been missing out on all this time.

But even though I have watched lots of gay porn now, I still can't bring myself to go out with anyone, male or female. I keep telling myself it's because I'm nervous still about my abilities in bed, but I know I'm fucking lying. The truth is, I don't want to be with anyone who isn't Alex, exploring these things with him. And I hate myself for it because I have no business thinking of him that way when he's straight and hasn't shown me any signs to the contrary. For a bit there I thought maybe the texts we were sending back and forth were his way of flirting, but I realized that that was just wishful thinking on my part. And the foot rubs every time he reads to me? Yeah, I don't think he's trying to flirt there either, I think he's just a tactile person and he's being nice.

Ugh! This is driving me crazy! At least one good thing has come of all this though, and that is the fact that I have become very well acquainted with my prostate. Wow! Holy grits and cornbread, that thing is amazing. What would be even more amazing is if I could experience what it would be like to have Alex inside me, making me feel good, making me come. God, I'd give anything to be underneath him.

I'm sitting on my sofa, making myself miserable with how unattainable my friend and next door neighbor is when my phone pings with an incoming text message.

Peyton: We're going ice skating before it gets too warm. Invite Alex. I'll be there in twenty minutes to get you

Me: But I've never been ice skating before

Peyton: That's the point, babe. We gotta get you acclimated with Massachusetts winters. And don't worry. I'll teach you.

I groan but do as I'm told and text Alex before I start getting ready.

Me: Hey, Peyton says we're going ice skating and I'm supposed to invite you

Alex: You mean you don't want to invite me? Sad face emoji

My cheeks heat. This guy drives me bananas sometimes and makes it hard to think, or form words.

Me: No, of course I do

Alex: I'm just being an ass, gorgeous, I know you can't stand to be away from me for a whole day. Be at your place in fifteen.

Goddamn it, why does he have to do that? It's hard enough trying not to fall for him, but when he talks to me like that it makes me weak in the knees. And if I'm being honest, my dick perks up, too every time he calls me gorgeous. Between that and hearing him call me cowboy, I'm fucking screwed.

Me: you can invite the rest of your family too if you want

Alex: sure thing

Peyton is knocking on my door twenty minutes later and I step out into the hall, closing the door behind me. I'm dressed in jeans, a sweater over a T-shirt, and my coat, along with gloves, and a hat and scarf. She beams at me, and when I tell her Alex's whole family was invited she gets even more excited. I don't understand wanting to meet new people but she thrives on it. Instead of knocking on all of their doors separately she just cups her hands around her mouth and shouts, "Let's get this show on the road, bitches!"

My cheeks flame and my mouth falls open as my eyes widen. "Seriously?" I hiss, horrified.

Her grin gets wider. "What? It gets the job done."

Alex is laughing as he joins us in the hallway and gives Peyton a high five. "I like your style," he tells her.

"Thank you."

Johnny and Isabella show up a second later and I can't believe they're laughing, too.

"I like her," Isabella says, then introduces herself and Johnny to Peyton.

When Tommy and Pierre join us Pierre is smiling and Tommy is scowling. When Pierre stands on his tiptoes and whispers something in his ear, then pecks his cheek,

Tommy's face softens ever so slightly. Pierre seems to be some kind of magic charm for Tommy, and I watch as their hands join.

"Ready," Pierre says in that gorgeous accent. I think Peyton is swooning, and I have to elbow her in the side to keep her from flirting with a very gay and very married man.

We take two cars and make it to the skating rink in about fifteen minutes. It's late morning and definitely a bit nippy, especially with the breeze. Well, for me anyway. No one else seems to be as cold as I am. Tommy isn't even wearing a coat, just a sweater, and it's making me cold just looking at him.

"You coming?" Alex asks once everyone has their skates on and I'm still sitting there, hugging myself.

"Eventually," I mumble. "Maybe in June or July." I'm not crazy about the fact that I can't skate and everyone else can, and I really don't want to make an idiot out of myself in front of Alex by falling on my ass every two seconds.

He smirks. "Best way to warm up is to get out there and start moving, cowboy."

I flush and Peyton chooses that moment to show up next to me. "He's nervous because he's never skated before," she announces, and my cheeks heat.

"Oh, that's no big deal, I'll teach you," Alex says, and I must be the color of a tomato when he holds his hand out to me. I see Peyton's eyebrow raise out of the corner of my eye as I place my hand in his. As cold as I am right now I'm seriously wishing I wasn't wearing gloves so I could feel his hand in mine. "We'll go slow. Peyton can help, too."

"Yeah, you know what, Alex, I think you got this. I'll check on you in a bit." My best friend grins at me and then skates off to meet up with Alex's family. If Tommy and Pierre weren't already married she'd end up being in their wedding party by the end of the day. It takes all of two minutes of them talking and skating for Peyton to have Pierre laughing, and I'm pretty sure Tommy is trying not to smile. I hate how easy it is for her to strike up conversations with complete strangers sometimes.

"Hey, come on, I got you," Alex says, drawing my attention back to him. I slowly stand and I'm already wobbling, my hand clasping his tighter as we move towards the rink. I'm a strange mix of embarrassed, terrified, and turned on as he moves closer and puts his arm around my waist to help me keep my balance.

At least with it being so cold outside there's no way I'm popping a boner. My dick has shriveled up and my balls have gone into hiding. I'm clinging to the railing for dear life and Alex is chuckling at me. "I swear I won't let you fall," he says. "You can let go."

"No thanks," I mutter. "That's how they get you."

He laughs and then does something that has my heart going crazy behind my rib cage. He loosens his arm around me, making me yelp and reach for him, only for him to circle around in front of me and grab my hands, giving me the sweetest smile as he squeezes them. "I'm right here," he says. "You got this. Come on."

God, I'm mortified but I'm also so fucking gone on this man. Damn him for being all sweet and tender and shit. I've also noticed that even with all the other couples and families around, he's not hesitant at all to hold my hands or touch me in a way that could be interpreted as intimate. He just doesn't seem to care. And I love that about him. "I feel like I'm a toddler and you're my dad trying to get me to walk."

He laughs again. "Hey, if it works." His voice changes to that same voice parents use when they're encouraging their toddler. "Come on Bentley, you can do it."

I glare and slowly glide forward. "I would give you the

finger but I can't risk it right now. Just know I thought of you."

He laughs more. "It'll help if you pick up your feet so I'm not dragging you."

"I'm good. This is working just fine."

He shrugs. "If this is how you're comfortable I'll drag you with me the entire time." He would, too, even if it meant he didn't really get to skate much himself.

"Hey, looking good, guys," Peyton says, skating close to us with a wide grin on her face as she glides around effortlessly.

"Shut up," I grouse and she cackles, then winks at me, before skating off.

My eyes catch on Alex's family skating nearby, and I can't help noticing how Tommy and Pierre hold hands while they move across the ice. Tommy even twirls Pierre a couple of times and the little guy spins around on one skate, his skirt billowing out around him. Show off.

Isabella and Johnny are holding hands and spinning in a circle, laughing, before Johnny pulls Isabella to him and they kiss sweetly, and my chest squeezes because I want what all of them have so much.

And I want it with the man in front of me.

Chapter Eleven

Bentley

Two days later, I'm making my way into work with my phone in my hands, texting and paying very little attention to my surroundings. I'm just strolling into the tiny little space I have reserved for an office in the building Peyton and I rent for our business, when I hear, "Who you texting?"

I shriek, and almost throw my phone in the air, but fumble and manage to catch it against my chest as I stare at my best friend, who is sitting on my small desk, laughing so hard she's snorting.

"What the cotton-picking hell?" I ask, after I've taken a second to calm down. "Girl, you almost made me shit myself."

She just laughs harder and I have to chuckle some at her snorting at least. "Okay, it wasn't that funny," I say after it's been a full two minutes and she's laughing so hard she's crying now and can barely breathe.

"I'm sorry," she says, calming down a smidge. She wipes her eyes and tries to compose herself.

Another thirty seconds go by before she finally calms down enough to tell me why on earth she's in my office instead of at her desk out front.

"Listen, I had to talk to you, and I thought if I tried out there you would just escape."

"What are we talking about?" I ask hesitantly. My phone chimes and I look down at the text I just got from Alex. We've been texting back and forth all morning about *Supernatural,* after he texted me with a gif of The Rock again. Sometimes it's gifs of actual rocks. We like to switch it up. And whoever didn't send the gif of the rock sends back a gif of a penguin. I have no idea why we do it, but I'm glad we do. It feels like our thing, and it's nice to have that with someone. Right now he's trying to get me to give him spoilers about *Supernatural* now that we're on the second season and he's as obsessed with it as I am, but also very impatient for us to get to the next episode.

A smile splits my face when I see his ridiculous gif of Dean saying, "Not cool," after me telling him I will reveal nothing.

"That," Peyton says.

"Huh?" I ask, looking up.

She's grinning widely. "We're talking about why you have such a huge smile on your face when you text him, and have had for the past several weeks, and why he was so eager to help you at the ice skating rink the other day, and how you're blushing like crazy right now."

"Am not," I say, my cheeks flaming as I bite the inside of my cheek to keep from smiling even more.

"What is going on with you two?" she asks, kicking her feet.

I shrug. "Nothing. And how do you know it's Alex I'm texting?"

"Because he and I are the only ones you text, period, and I know it's not me."

Okay, fair point. That's what happens when you don't have any friends.

I can't help the grin that escapes me. "It's nothing," I say again. I sigh and decide it wouldn't hurt if Peyton knew a little bit. "We just have this thing we've been doing. Kinda an inside joke between us, but I like it."

She raises an eyebrow. "What thing?"

"We're pebbling each other."

"Pebbling?"

"Yeah, like sending each other gifs and memes and stuff. Penguins do it."

She looks at me like I've lost my mind. "Penguins text each other?"

"No, they give each other pebbles as a sign of affection, and when people send texts or gifs or memes or whatever to each other, it's called pebbling." I show her my phone. Her smile gets so big she looks like the fucking cheshire cat as she scrolls through the texts.

"Oh my God," she says. "You guys are totally flirting."

I yank my phone away as if it's in danger. "Are not."

"Okay," she says, raising her hands. "If you say so."

I bite my lip. "You really think he's flirting?"

"Um, I really think you're both flirting. Honey, no guy texts his friend like that. He's seriously got a hard on for you."

My face flames again. "He's straight."

"Maybe. Maybe not." She pauses as I worry my lip between my teeth. "Do you...want him to be flirting with you?"

I meet her eyes and there's nothing there but care and affection. My voice is hoarse when I say, "Maybe."

She squeals and I almost drop my phone a second time. "Omg, you two would be adorable together!"

"Yeah, well, as far as I know, I'm the only one with feelings and it sucks."

"Have you talked to him?"

"No. I can't."

"How come? You'll never know if he feels the same if you don't say anything. And I'm pretty sure he's got heart eyes for you, too, if those texts and the way he was looking at you at the skating rink are anything to go by."

I shake my head. "That's just Alex. He was just being nice." I don't tell her about the fact that he gives me foot massages every week while he reads to me, because she'd probably try to convince me that was him flirting too, and I can't have her giving me false hope. But also because I kind of want to keep it just between me and Alex. It feels more special that way, even if it isn't romantic. I don't want to share that piece of him, of us, with anyone else.

She sighs and hops off my desk, resting her small hand on my arm. "I think you guys would be amazing together. I see how happy he makes you, and I want that for you. I'm just here to support you. You know that."

I nod. "Yeah, I do. Thanks."

She bites her lip. "So, while we're on the subject. There was a package that arrived right before you got here, and I took it because you weren't in yet. And I'm thinking it was maybe supposed to have discreet packaging, but it didn't so much."

"Oh my God," I groan, sliding down the wall and covering my face with my hands. "I'm a turtle, and you can't see me right now."

She laughs. "It's nothing to be embarrassed about. Lots of people buy sex toys. I do."

"Yeah, but you're you."

"Hey, you know what? I'm pretty sure introverts have sex, too."

I remove my hands from my face, managing a small smile.

"I don't see any problem with you exploring. Especially if you think you might be into a guy. It's a good idea actually. It'll help you know what you like if anything does happen. And look on the bright side, at least it came here instead of to your apartment."

I sigh and rest my head against the wall. "Yay for that."

She chuckles. "Come on, we better get ready. Your first appointment gets here in ten minutes." She holds her hand down to me and I grab it, letting her haul me up. As embarrassed as I am, it kinda feels good for her to know, and to not have to hide either my feelings for Alex anymore, or the fact that I'm wanting to try some new things in the bedroom. Even if nothing ever happens between Alex and I, at least I know now that I'm into men and women, and that makes things a little different when it comes to dating. When I finally do get out there again, I want to know what I like. And if I just happen to picture Alex while I'm using my new toys, there's no harm in that, right?

That night I once again have Alex front and center in my mind while I work my brand new flesh colored dildo into my ass, my eyes closed and mouth parted, hair loose and tumbling across my pillow as I move my hips, chasing my pleasure as the magic toy nudges my prostate again and again. I was a bit nervous about sticking something so big up my ass, but after watching a couple of how to videos and using a ridiculous amount of lube, I was finally able to relax and let it slide inside me, and holy fuck, it's been one hell of an experience. The only thing that would be better is if it were Alex's cock buried inside me, making my body sing with pleasure, making me come so hard I see stars.

I can practically feel him holding me down, those plush lips pressing kisses to my neck and chest, before moving to my nipples and sucking on them. I let out a wail as I pinch my own nipple and the dildo hits that rubbery spot over and over, making my body light up.

"Alex!" I cry out, my body shaking as I shoot my release all over my stomach and chest. I take a second to come down from the high of my orgasm, before I slowly slide the dildo out, thankful that I had the courage to purchase it even if Peyton did find out, because the orgasm I just had was worth every single second of embarrassment.

"You get five gold stars, my friend," I tell it. As I stare at it I wonder what Alex's dick looks like. If it's anything like the one in my hand. Is he thick, or long, cut or uncut, does he manscape or does he have a wild bush of hair down there like I do? God, I've never wanted to know what another man's dick looks like until he came along. Even with all the showering and changing we do at the gym I've never seen it. As wild and carefree as Alex is, I've noticed he's also not the type to strip naked around strangers, or even me, and I kind of...like that about him.

I sigh as I stand and make my way to the bathroom. I hop in the shower for a quick clean up before sliding into clean boxer briefs and my warmest, coziest pajama bottoms, that just happen to be Supernatural themed; a gift from Peyton last Christmas. I slide into a long sleeved sleep shirt as well, before I climb into bed.

I grab the picture of Gram off my nightstand as I lie on my back, and just look at it for a second. I see that smile and I wonder again what she would think of Alex, or what she would think of me having feelings for Alex. I have no doubt that she would support me no matter what because that's who she was, and I have tears filling my eyes knowing she'll never get to know that special person that I marry someday. I miss her so much. Her humor, her kindness, her sass. I miss her chocolate chip cookies and banana bread. Even though I have the recipes for all of her delicious treats and meals, it doesn't seem to taste quite the same when I make them.

I miss her carefree spirit and her courage to stand up for what was right even if it cost her. I miss her optimism and that laugh that always made me feel like everything was going to be okay.

God, I could really use some of her wisdom right now. Because as much as she goofed off and joked around, she was also one of the smartest, most thoughtful people I knew.

"I miss you," I tell her as tears slide down my cheeks. "I'm kinda lost right now. I don't know what to do." I wipe my tears and start to talk, like she's really here and can hear me. Who knows, maybe she can. "I met this guy, Gram, and he's, he's really great, and I think I'm falling for him, but he's straight, and," I chuckle as more tears fall and I wipe them away, too. "And apparently I'm not. Did you know that? God, it's strange to be realizing this in my thirties, but I'm kinda glad cause I would have hated to have gone my whole life never knowing this about myself." I take a breath, pausing before I start again.

"Peyton thinks he likes me, too, but I can't let myself believe it, because what if I'm wrong? What if I say something and he doesn't feel the same? I could ruin everything, and I'd rather have him in my life as a friend than not at all. It's really hard, though, spending so much time with him, feeling like I'm falling harder and harder for him each day and not being able to do anything about it.

Peyton says I should say something, but I'm too damn scared.

"I could really use your advice right now."

Alex

I'm leaving my apartment to head to work later that week, and running a wee bit late as usual, when I open my front door and step into the hall in a hurry, only to be stopped by a box sitting on my doormat that has me tripping and nearly falling over. I'm caught by strong arms and inhale the scent of ocean and rain as Bentley lifts me back on my feet.

"You okay?" he asks, his voice warm and soft and as sexy as ever.

"Yeah," I croak, almost whimpering when his arms leave me. "Thanks."

I bend down to pick up the box, and flush when I realize what's inside. It doesn't have any pictures on it or anything but I recognize the return address. It's the sex toys I bought so I could do more in depth experimenting. And the guy I'm undoubtedly going to be thinking about while I'm using them is right fucking here.

"What's inside?" Bentley asks.

My brain fucking shuts down and I can't think of anything to say, so I spew out the last thing I bought. "Coffee maker."

He blinks and eyes it. "You sure? It's kinda small for a coffee maker and kinda a weird shape."

I panic. "Uh, well, you know, they can do all sorts of things with technology these days." I pat him on the chest. "See you later."

"Bye," he says, and I practically shiver as that southern drawl sends electricity racing through my veins.

I get out to my car and open the door, throwing the

stupid box with the stupid sex toys into the stupid passenger seat and then sitting down in my stupid seat. I turn the key with a vengeance, and it's not nearly satisfying enough, so I climb back out of the car and grab some snow in my hand, before throwing it as hard as I can. Okay, owe, that hurt my shoulder.

I want to fucking scream because I'm so damn sick of feeling the way I do for Bentley, like my chest is going to burst or my mouth is going to open and blurt out something that will ruin everything. I turn around and kick the wheel of my car. Yeah, I'm just full of good ideas tonight, and no I apparently didn't learn from the mistake I just made a second and a half ago, and I wince when my toes start to throb.

"Fuck, fuck, fuck," I growl, then climb back in the car and slam the door shut. I rest my head back on the seat and sigh, before I pull out of the parking lot and head to work.

It's busy all night, and even though I get a couple of texts from Bentley, I don't have time to open them. My feet ache and I'm fucking exhausted when the bar finally closes hours later and I head home. It's not until I'm in bed that I remember Bentley's texts, and by then I'm too close to falling asleep to worry about it.

Marble jumps up on the bed and settles on the pillow next to me, and I can't help wondering what it would be like to fall asleep and wake up to a sexy as fuck Viking with a southern accent, to have his scent on my sheets, his warm, hard body curled around mine, those big, strong but gentle hands on me. It's almost enough to make me break out my new toys, but I'm too damn tired. I think of how Bentley holds Marble, and how he fusses over her, and rubs her belly, and plants kisses on her head.

I have never in my life wanted to trade places with an animal until now.

Chapter Twelve

Alex

The following morning I wake up and feed Marble, before eating my own breakfast and having my morning tea. After that I take a shower and dress. I'm supposed to be going over to Bentley's soon but I have a few minutes to spare. I remember the texts he sent me and open my phone. There's three photos, two of him with Marble, her looking as spoiled and satisfied as ever, lying in his lap, curled in a ball in one, and in the other she's on her back, while he rubs her belly. In the third she's sitting and looking up at him, her blue eyes big, and her fur fluffed up, and it's honestly a really cute picture of her. The caption reads, *Marble says hi.*

I text back, *I don't think she likes you at all.*

I'm unloading the dishwasher and wiping down my counters when my eye catches on the bushel of bananas I bought yesterday when I was grocery shopping. I think of the sex toys I still have in a box in my bedroom and wonder if I should break them out, but decide it's better to wait until later tonight when I have more time. The bananas, though, are giving me an idea, and they're right here. Besides, I can always eat it afterwards.

I've experimented with my fingers in my hole, and I got the toys so I could do more experimenting that way, but I've yet to do any oral experimentation, and I've been wondering what it would feel like to have a cock in my mouth. One very specific cock, that is.

I look at my phone. I have ten minutes before I'm supposed to be over at Bentley's, so I finish wiping down the counters and wash my hands, then snap one of the bananas off the bushel. Do I put my mouth on it as is or do I peel it first? Does it matter? Might be easier if I peel it. Okay, here it goes.

I unpeel the banana from the bottom so I have a better grip on it, holding it from the top with the stem down. Here's hoping it doesn't fall off in my mouth and choke me. That's a great way to end up in the ER.

You would think having been on the receiving end of several blow jobs over the years I wouldn't be so nervous, or would at least have a better idea of what I am doing, but even after reading tips online for how to suck a guy's dick, I'm starting to appreciate the girlfriends I've had that made it look easy. I've gotten my mouth over the banana and I'm trying to keep my teeth out of the picture, which is easier said than done, but it's only about a third of the way in my mouth before I'm gagging on it and my eyes are watering. Fuck.

I pull it out and wipe my eyes. "Okay, sir, you're not winning this one," I tell it, before I'm closing my mouth over it again.

I've gotten it in about a third of the way again, and am gagging on it once more, with tears in my eyes when I hear, "What are you doing?" and nearly jump out of my skin. I choke on the banana as it breaks off in my mouth and then

I'm sputtering, trying to decide if I should just eat it or spit it out as tears slide down my cheeks. I go for spitting it out.

I'm panting, and my face is flaming when I turn and see Bentley there, eyeing me. Oh my God. I dump the banana halves on the counter and wipe my eyes. "What the hell are you doing here?" I ask him, my heart thrashing.

"I thought we could hang out at your place," he says. "The door was unlocked so I came in." He bends down and scoops Marble into his arms. She purrs and nuzzles his cheek.

Shit, that was humiliating.

"Are you okay?" he asks, and that just makes it worse.

"I'm fine. Just, don't sneak up on me like that." My voice is harsher than I intend, and I know he didn't actually do anything wrong. I'm just so embarrassed and I have no way to explain what I was doing. I clearly wasn't eating the banana, moving it up and down like I was.

"Sorry," he says, his voice soft, and I know I've hurt him.

I sigh as I toss the banana pieces in the trash. "No, it's not your fault. I'm sorry. I just didn't get much sleep last night and I'm tired, I guess." Total lie, but what am I supposed to say? I was practicing deep throating a schlong?

"You want some coffee?" I ask, trying to make amends, gesturing to the coffee maker on the counter that has yet to be used. He gives me a smile and I count it as a win. Hopefully we can just forget this whole banana thing ever happened, and note to self, lock the fucking door if you ever do that again.

Bentley looks conflicted as he eyes the coffee maker and Marble, trying to figure out if he can hold her and make coffee at the same time. He keeps her in the crook of his arm while he removes the carafe from the tray, and fills it with water. "Do you actually have coffee?" he asks, "or did you forget that part?"

I smirk at him, then open the cupboard above the coffee maker and pull down coffee and liners, setting them on the counter. He grins again and then hands me the coffee to open so he can hold my cat.

I roll my eyes but I do it. "I have no idea how to make coffee, so if you want me to do it you have to tell me how." He tells me how many scoops to put in the basket at the top of the coffee maker after placing the liner inside, and then fills the top with water, before placing the carafe back on the tray and pressing the button. It starts to gurgle and hiss seconds later, and then the apartment is filled with the smell of brewing coffee.

"Thank you," he says. "I know I could bring coffee but you getting that was really sweet."

And, I'm blushing. I shrug. "You did the same thing for me so I could have tea. It's not a big deal."

He sits on the sofa and I grab the book. We're still working our way through *Little Women* since we only have so much time during the week to do this and we spend a lot of that time watching *Supernatural*. He's got me completely addicted to that show and I am not at all complaining about the fact that it has fifteen seasons. I won't lie and say I don't notice how many attractive men and women are on the show either.

We take our usual positions, Bentley lying down with Marble tucked against him and his feet on my lap. This is the only way I get to have any physical contact with him other than our fingers "accidentally" touching every time we eat popcorn together, and I look forward to it every time, even if it is only his feet, which still manage to smell amazing by the way. It's completely unfair. God I want to bring them to my nose and breathe them in, but that might be a bit much. I do tickle him a little off the bat and he lets out the most adorable giggle as he moves his feet away and then proceeds to poke me in the side with them.

"Not nice," he says, a twinkle in those gorgeous blue eyes. "Be good to me. I'm your only access to Sam and Dean Winchester."

I laugh and he places his feet back on my lap again. This time I'm good, rubbing them gently, and I grin when I hear him sigh in contentment as he pets Marble and I start to read. We're nearing the end, and I know Bentley is going to have a hard time with this chapter considering how attached he is to Beth. Her death scene always guts me no matter how many times I read it, and I can't help thinking about what it would be like to lose one of my parents, or Tommy. Fuck, I'm getting emotional just thinking about it. I just hope I can actually read it to him without turning into a blubbering mess.

He asks what a couple of the words mean as I read and I do my best to explain them within the context of the story. Words like "stalwart" and "superannuated." I can tell he's getting emotional as I read about Jo taking care of her sister in her last days, and the poem Beth reads that Jo wrote about her; about the ways Beth's life has touched her, her patience, her kind heart, and her cheerful and gentle spirit.

I manage to hold it together while I read, but I notice Bentley's hand moving up to his face and see him wiping tears from his eyes as he sniffles and his body shakes slightly. And for some reason that only makes me care for him more. My sweet, teddy bear Viking.

My heart melts when he buries his face in Marble's fur, and I rub his foot. "You okay?" I ask. "I always cry at this part." He sits up and I open my arms to him. Then his big body is against me as he buries his face in my shoulder and cries. I wonder if this is making him think about his grandma and I squeeze him a little tighter. And then, because I'm feeling extra brave, I press a kiss to his hair.

Bentley

I've just finished up with a client and am wiping down the massage table when Peyton steps into the doorway.

"Hey, he seemed satisfied when he left," she tells me. "And he gave me this to give to you." She holds out a piece of paper and I take it, unfolding it to see a number written on it. I flush.

"You gonna do anything with it?" she asks.

I shake my head and toss it in the trash. It's been two weeks since we had our conversation about Alex, and I'm just getting more and more crazy about him every time we're together. I know it's not the healthiest thing to just refuse to get back into the dating scene because I'm pining over my friend, but I can't bring myself to date again just yet, and I can't imagine sleeping with someone who isn't him. It fucking sucks.

"Maybe if you're gonna put your love life on hold until Alex comes around, it would be a good idea to actually tell him how you feel," Peyton says, her voice gentle.

I keep thinking of how he held me and let me cry on his shoulder when Beth died in *Little Women* and I was so upset. Being in his arms was so amazing. It felt right, like that's where I belonged, and I shivered when he pressed that kiss to my hair. God, I want so much more. But we haven't touched again like that since, just the normal foot rubs and occasional pats on the shoulder.

I don't think I'll ever forget walking into his apartment and seeing him with half a banana down his throat, gagging on it. Jesus, it put so many filthy thoughts in my head, and I can't tell you how many times I've jerked off to thoughts of him choking on my cock since. Not that I wasn't doing it before, but now I have a visual.

I've also been wondering why on earth he was fucking his own mouth with a banana in the first place if he's straight. Maybe he's not so straight after all? But I can't ask him that. It might not be something he wants to share, which might explain why he was so upset when I caught him.

I've also been a bit stressed since then because if he isn't straight and he starts dating other guys, fuck that's going to hurt. He clearly isn't interested in me that way, whether he's exploring his sexuality or not, and the thought of him being with someone else? God, it makes me sick.

"I don't know how," I tell her. I'm not telling her about the banana incident because I don't think Alex would want me spreading that around. But it's got me more and more convinced she was wrong about his feelings for me.

Fortunately I'm saved from talking about it anymore when the bell above the door rings, signaling my next client has arrived.

Peyton squeezes my arm and leaves the room while I finish up with changing the linens around and getting everything set up for whoever just came in.

I'm startled when I hear Peyton's voice plain as day from the waiting room. "Oh, hell, no."

Then another voice I am familiar with but haven't heard in a while, and honestly never thought I would hear again. "I just want to talk to him," Stacy says, her voice clipped.

"He has a client arriving any minute, and there's nothing you could possibly need to say that he needs to hear. Get the fuck out."

"Who the fuck do you think you are?" Stacy retorts.

"His best friend, that's who. The person he came to

after you fucking cheated on him and he was smart enough to realize what a miserable piece of trash you are."

I can practically see the scowl on Peyton's face and the way she's standing, arms crossed over her chest and her hip jutting out. But I can't let her handle my battles for me. So I make my way down the hall as they're arguing and step into the waiting room.

"Hi, Stacy," I say, and they both turn to me.

"Bentley, I was just asking her to leave," Peyton says.

"I know," I tell her. "Thank you. I'll handle it from here." Peyton glowers at Stacy but doesn't say anything. She doesn't leave the room either, though, and for that I'm grateful.

"What can I do for you, Stacy?" I ask, turning to my ex. She's gorgeous, as always, her blonde hair in a ponytail, her makeup flawless.

"Do we have to talk here?" Stacy says, her voice much more sultry and flirtatious now. "Can't we have some privacy?"

Peyton opens her mouth to speak but I do it first. "No, we can't."

Stacy blanches. I guess she's not used to hearing me tell her no. Maybe that was the problem in our relationship. Maybe I gave in too much in order to accommodate her and gave her the impression she could walk all over me. Maybe she felt safe cheating because she thought I was too much of a softy to make a deal out of it. Who knows?

"Whatever you want to say to me you can say it here," I tell her.

She hesitates but then says, "I want a second chance."

I can tell it's taking everything in Peyton not to go postal on this girl, and it kinda makes me feel good, knowing how protective she is of me. I also know if Gram were here, she'd be doing the same thing.

"I don't think so."

"But we were so good together, Bentley," she presses, stepping closer. "I miss you."

Peyton makes a retching sound and I have to keep from laughing when Stacy glares at her.

"Look, Stacy, I know I'm not the smartest guy out there, but I know that what you want isn't me. It's not us. You don't miss me. I'm guessing your current fella probably broke up with you, and I'm thinking what you miss is having a man to string along, and I'm done being that man. I'm happier without you than I ever was with you, and you cheating on me was honestly one of the best things you could have done because it taught me some things about myself that I might not have learned otherwise. So, no. We're not getting back together. Not now, not ever. And I'm gonna have to ask you to leave now and not come back."

Stacy's face is red and her lips are thinned. She's clearly pissed, but I think it's because I hit it right on the nose. She's coming back to the guy she thinks is most likely to take her back because her other man, or men, have decided they don't want her either, and she can't stand that. I honestly don't know why I was ever with her in the first place, except that she was so persistent and I had a hard time telling her no, and maybe also, because I was lonely. Well, meeting Alex and his family, and having more time to spend with Peyton because I'm not with Stacy has made me realize that what I really needed this whole time was family, and a sense of belonging, and I think I've found that.

Her fists clench, her lips thinning. "Bentley–"

Peyton steps in now and I let her. "I think he told you to leave."

We both stare at her. Well, Peyton glares, and Stacy huffs, then spins on her heels and walks out the door.

Chapter Thirteen

Alex

"Hey, you ready?" I ask, grinning as I see Bentley closing the door to his apartment just as I'm doing the same with mine. He's carrying a pan of brownies that look absolutely mouthwatering, and I have a bottle of wine.

"Yep," he replies, and we make our way up the stairs before stopping to knock on Tommy and Pierre's door. They've invited us over for a game night, which sounds pretty fun. Despite being neighbors and working with my brother, we haven't had much time to actually hang out the past several weeks and I miss him.

We have had one more monthly meal at Mom and Dad's and that was nice, and Bentley and Pierre are getting better acquainted. I was a little worried about Pierre though. He seemed upset, but when I asked Tommy if everything was okay, he said he'd tell me later. I've noticed that the smile my brother has been wearing for the past couple of months at work is gone, and his usual glower has returned, along with a sadness I don't think I've ever seen reflected in his hazel eyes. I have also noticed that the handsome older man who used to frequent the bar and clearly has eyes for my brother hasn't been coming around lately. I have a feeling that whatever is going on with him and Pierre has to do with that.

"Hi, guys, come on in," Tommy says when he opens the door. Bentley steps inside after me and I pull my brother in for a hug that I don't think he's expecting. I know something is wrong when he returns it. Tommy never lets me hug him. Well, hardly ever. And it's even more rare for him to reciprocate the hug. It's just not his thing, but right now he's holding on tighter and far longer than I thought he would.

"Where's Pierre?" Bentley asks.

"Kitchen," Tommy tells him, pulling away from me. "Getting some snacks together."

"I'll go find him," Bentley says, and saunters off with his brownies.

"Everything okay?" I ask when Bentley is out of ear shot.

"No, not really," Tommy admits. "Maybe you could stay a little bit after Bentley leaves and we can talk out on the balcony?"

I nod. "Yeah, of course." I don't think I've ever seen Tommy look so distraught. He's usually the one who keeps everything inside while I'm the one who typically wears my heart on my sleeve. But the fact that he wants to talk to me tells me it's a big deal.

"Just um, be extra good to Pierre. He's having a hard time."

"Yeah, you know I will be." Fuck, a tear slides down Tommy's cheek and it fucking kills me. I don't think I've seen him cry since he was eight years old. Except on his wedding day and those were happy tears. "Jesus, Tommy, you're making me nervous."

"It's nothing life threatening or anything," he assures

me. "I'm just feeling helpless, is all." Fuck, I pull him to me and hug him again, and he lets out a few sniffles as he sobs gently on my shoulder.

"Should we be here if Pierre is so upset?" I ask. "And you clearly are too?"

He nods. "We need this. We need the normal. I'm hoping it'll help distract him, maybe make him feel a tiny bit better. He's been really down on himself lately, convinced his anxiety and depression is destroying everything. Please stay."

"Anything you need," I tell him, and he pulls away, wiping his tears quickly. He takes the wine bottle from me and offers me a small smile, and I follow him into the living area. I can hear Pierre talking with Bentley and he seems like he's doing okay, but I know that doesn't mean much. People who struggle with mental illness do a great job of hiding how they're really feeling a good portion of the time. I hate that my brother in law can't see what a great guy he is because our whole family adores him and would do anything for him, most of all Tommy. But having a brain that lies to you and does its best to convince you otherwise makes it really hard to see that, I know.

I hear him laughing and Tommy's eyes light up just the tiniest bit, like he's not heard his husband laugh in ages. If anyone can make Pierre feel a little bit better it's Bentley. He's so sweet, and seriously funny, too.

Tommy enters the kitchen and sets the wine down on the counter, then turns to Pierre and slides an arm around his waist, drawing him to his side before pressing a kiss on his cheek. Pierre flushes.

"Bonjour, Alex," he says, his voice soft. "So glad you both could come."

"Me, too, squirt." I ruffle his hair and he bats my hand away.

We each grab a plate and put some snacks on it. There's cheese and crackers, chips and salsa, pigs in a blanket, and Pierre has made macarons and crepes, and set out some jam to go with them. I notice Pierre doesn't eat much, though.

We sit at the table with Bentley and I on one side and Tommy and Pierre on the other. We play a few rounds of Giant Uno, and if you haven't played with those cards, they're not kidding when they say giant. The things are huge and it just makes the game even more fun in my opinion, especially when you add in other rules, like slapping the deck every time someone plays a zero, and the last person to do so having to draw four cards, or being able to play out of turn if your card is the same number as the one on top of the pile. I'm failing epically and have accumulated so many cards I can't hold them all and everyone else is laughing as I mock scowl. Normally I might be more irritated, but since I know Tommy and Pierre could use the laughs I don't mind at all.

After Giant Uno we play Unstable Unicorns. The goal is to get seven unicorn cards and you do so by playing certain cards to upgrade your deck, while also playing cards to try and downgrade your opponents' decks. And the cards are so utterly ridiculous we're laughing all over again.

Tommy and I are merciless with each other, though we do go after Pierre and Bentley some, too. In the end, though, it's Bentley that wins.

Bentley leaves shortly after, and Pierre perches on Tommy's lap before kissing him sweetly. My chest squeezes, because I love seeing them in love, even if Pierre is having a tough time. My brother has been head over heels for his husband from the moment they met, and I know Pierre loves Tommy more than anything.

"I'm tired," Pierre says.

"Go to bed, amor," Tommy tells him, stroking his cheek. "I'll take care of everything."

Pierre gives him a soft smile. "Thank you."

He turns to me and says goodnight.

"Night, squirt," I tell him. "Sleep well."

Tommy kisses him again and Pierre scoots off his lap and saunters off to the bedroom, closing the door behind him.

I help Tommy clean up the game and the snacks, and then we each grab a beer and head out to the balcony. It's early spring, so it's warmer out now, but still a bit chilly. The hoodie I'm wearing should be enough to keep me warm while we talk. Tommy grabs a blanket and brings it out with him and we take seats on the chairs they have set up.

"So, talk to me," I say. "What's going on? Does it have anything to do with the older guy you two were having fun with? I couldn't help noticing he's been scarce around the bar lately."

Tommy sighs. "Yeah. It wasn't meant to be more than a good time. Started out as one night, which turned into two, and then the three of us were hooking up on a regular basis. Pierre and I have never wanted more with a third before, but there was something about Cyrus that was different."

"Was?" I ask.

Tommy sighs again, staring at his lap. "Yeah. We haven't been over to his place in almost two weeks, and I'm managing okay. But Pierre..." he trails off.

"What happened?" I ask.

"Cyrus said he needs time. That he's working through some things and he's not sure what's going to happen, or if he'll want to keep doing what we're doing. It's been almost two months of the three of us, and just as Pierre and I were about to tell him we wanted more than just casual, he hit us with this."

"You guys want him to be a permanent part of the relationship?" I ask, just to clarify.

"We do," Tommy says. He gives a soft smile. "Honestly, Pierre and I were both scared of letting the other know that we were developing feelings for Cyrus, and it took a few days of us acting kinda weird around each other before we finally sat down and talked it out, but yeah, we're both kinda head over heels for him it turns out."

"You love him?"

He nods. "Yeah, I think we both do."

"And he doesn't know if he wants this?"

He nods again. "The thing is, I'm pretty sure he feels the same about us, but he's scared. Something is keeping him from letting himself have us completely, but we don't know what."

"So you think that's what he's working through?"

"Pretty sure. But Pierre thinks the reason Cyrus needs space is because of him. He's convinced he's the problem, that Cyrus doesn't want to be with us because Pierre's too "fucked up" as he puts it, and I don't know what to say or do to make him see otherwise. But it's killing me to see him so upset, not just about losing Cyrus, but thinking he's responsible."

"Fuck, I'm sorry," I say. "That sounds really hard."

There's silence for a bit and then Tommy lets out a humorless chuckle. "Did you know that I had to propose to him three times before he actually said yes?"

My eyes widen. "What?"

"Yeah, he had a really hard time believing that I actually wanted to marry him. He was so sure I'd regret it, that I'd want to leave, and he didn't want me to be stuck with him. Wanted me to have a way out, so he kept saying no."

"Jesus."

"I just want to go back in time and throat punch

everyone who made him feel like he was a problem and not worth caring about or fighting for. Everyone who saw him as a burden because he struggled. I think that's what finally won him over, me being a persistent asshole. I just wore him down, I guess." He chuckles again and takes a sip of his drink.

"He loves you, you know that."

"I do. I just wish I could get him to see that he's not just his struggles. That he's so much more than what he gives himself credit for, and that being married to him is the best thing that ever happened to me. Maybe if he believed that, it would be easier to believe Cyrus cared for him, too, and that Pierre didn't push him away."

"You think he's safe? He wouldn't harm himself would he?"

"I don't think so, but I have been checking up on him more the past few days. It helps that he doesn't like to be alone so he's always out somewhere, either with Toby or over at Mom and Dad's doing school work if he's not making a video for his OnlyFans. He's been so anxious lately, though, that both of those things are suffering. Mom has been helping some, trying to distract him by taking him out to lunch, or shopping, or getting his nails done, and Toby texts a lot to see how he's doing if they're not together."

"He could come down and hang with us at the bar," I suggest. Pierre used to hang out at the bar all the time when he and Tommy met, and whenever Tommy wasn't serving a customer he'd be talking with Pierre. It was kinda adorable watching their love story unfold right in front of me.

"Yeah, I might suggest that. I'm not sure it would help though since that's where Cyrus used to hang out and doesn't anymore. Might make it worse for Pierre, not better, if he's blaming himself."

I sigh. "That's tough, man. You know I'm here for you guys if you need anything at all."

He gives a soft smile. "I know. And just talking about it helps. And Pierre has been talking to his therapist, too."

There's a pause before Tommy speaks again. "So what's going on with you and Bentley?"

I blink. "Nothing."

He snorts. "Right, yeah, okay." He takes a swig of his beer.

"We're just friends," I insist.

"Friends who flirt non-stop, huh? And look at each other with heart eyes?"

I gape. "I don't...I haven't."

He laughs. "You absolutely have and do. Watching the two of you is nauseating."

"Hey, look who's talking, Mr. Can't Keep My Hands Off My Man," I retort, and he laughs.

"Look, it's been clear to everyone that you and Bentley have feelings for each other since that first dinner at Mom and Dad's. So why aren't you doing anything about it? He's a great guy."

I scoff. "He's straight."

He eyes me. "So you admit you have feelings for him?"

I flush and scowl. "I didn't say that."

"You didn't deny it, though."

"Ugh, fine. Yes, I have feelings for him, okay? I guess I'm coming out to you as bi now, or whatever. But it doesn't matter because despite what everyone thinks, he doesn't have feelings for me."

"Wrong."

I scowl at my brother again. "What makes you so sure?"

"Like I said, I have eyes. You should tell him how you feel." He takes another drink, while I'm just holding mine, my grip on it tightening as we talk.

I shake my head. "I can't. He's my friend. My best friend. I can't risk losing him by saying something."

"You won't lose him."

I grit my teeth. "I can't know that for sure, and besides, wouldn't it be cruel to tell him how I feel knowing he can't reciprocate? It's pointless and it would just make him uncomfortable. And I would rather have him as my friend than not have him in my life at all because I can't keep my mouth shut."

"It's not pointless if he feels the same way."

"He doesn't."

Tommy sighs. "So you're bi, huh?"

"Pretty sure, yeah," I say. "Took some time and experimenting to figure it out, but yeah, I'm definitely into men, too. I don't know how I'm just now figuring that out, though."

He shrugs. "It's different for everyone. I've known I was gay since I was twelve. But figuring it out later in life doesn't make it any less valid. And you don't have to put a label on it if you don't want to."

I take a sip of my drink and we sit in comfortable silence for a bit longer. I say goodnight to my brother fifteen minutes later and head back down the stairs to my apartment. As soon as I step in the door I get a text from Bentley.

Cowboy: Peyton's birthday party is next weekend and you're invited. She goes to the same Karaoke bar every year with her friends. You can ride with me. Though I probably won't stay very long, because people

I chuckle.

Me: Lol, sounds good, cowboy

Chapter Fourteen

Bentley

It's Monday evening and Alex has just left for work after spending the majority of the day with me. After going grocery shopping together we did the usual, watching several episodes of *Supernatural* before he read to me some more. I never thought I would enjoy books as much as I do when it's his voice I hear, soft and soothing, warm and sweet.

I'm enjoying *Pride and Prejudice* as much as I enjoyed *Little Women*. Elizabeth Bennett and Jo March would get along pretty well I think. Or maybe they would butt heads like crazy, I can't decide.

I've just finished my dinner when there's a knock on the door. When I open it, a smile splits my face.

"Hey there, small fry," I say, and Pierre gives me a soft smile. "Come in." I step aside so he can enter and then close the door behind him. He seems a little timid. More so than he was when Alex and I were at his place for our game night. Maybe because it's just the two of us now and he doesn't know me quite as well as Alex. He's wearing a black leather skater skirt, black fishnet tights, and a black cropped shirt. He has sparkly pink eyeshadow on and eyeliner around his pale blue eyes. His lips are full and shimmering from the lip gloss he's applied and he has a cat ear headband on his head overtop his blond hair. He really is a pretty little thing.

In his slender arms are mixing bowls and ingredients for baking the macarons we had at their place, because after tasting one I shamelessly begged him to teach me how to make them, and he agreed.

As soon as he steps in the door, Marble is twining her way between his legs and purring up a storm. Pierre smiles and crouches down to pet her. She stands on her hind legs and purrs even louder when he scratches her neck. "Bonjour, pretty lady," he coos, his smile only getting bigger.

"Are you sure you still want to do this?" he asks, looking up at me. He seems more comfortable already thanks to Marble, and it makes me happy. Alex left her here and I told him I'd bring her home before I went to bed.

"Absolutely," I tell him. "Come on, you can put those things down in the kitchen." It's not usually like me to invite someone over to my house, but I've really enjoyed Pierre's company the few times we've been together, and it wouldn't hurt either of us to get to know each other more and be friends. I know he has his OnlyFans he works on, and he's in school right now so I'm sure he keeps plenty busy, but it might be nice for him to take a break from working and studying. He also seemed sad when we were there, though I never did find out why, and I am hoping maybe I can cheer him up, or just be supportive and give him someone to talk to if he needs it.

"I'm glad you came," I say. "And not just because I'm dying to have more of these cookies."

He gives a soft smile as he sets his things down on the

counter, and I get out the things he didn't bring; butter, granulated sugar, a mixer, piping bag, a baking sheet, and my food processor. He grabs the powdered sugar, almond flour, vanilla extract, cream of tartar, and salt and puts them on the counter near my things. He also has a glass with egg whites in it, covered in plastic wrap with holes poked in the top. The yolks are separate, in another covered dish.

"Trust me, it helps," he says with a giggle when I stare at it.

"You're the boss," I say, as he sets the glass down near the other items, then grabs the sifter and starts giving me instructions.

I sift, and blend, and mix, and fold, and sift some more. Once everything is mixed Pierre tells me to pipe one inch dollops onto the baking sheet he's lined with parchment paper. When that's done we let it sit for about 40 minutes while we work on the buttercream filling.

We heat the sugar and water on the stove and beat the egg yolks in the mixer. When the water and sugar mix has reached the desired temperature and consistency, we remove it from the stove and drizzle the syrupy mixture into the bowl with the yolks. We then add butter, vanilla, and salt, and Pierre adds pink food coloring, giving me a smile when he does. "Not necessary but way more fun," he says.

Since we have a few minutes before it's time to put the macarons in the oven, I offer Pierre a drink.

"Nothing alcoholic," he says softly. "It interacts with my meds."

"I have ginger ale, tea, and lemonade," I tell him.

He smiles again. "Lemonade sounds nice."

I pour both of us a glass and hand him his. He takes a sip and his eyes widen. "Oh mon Dieu, that's amazing."

I chuckle. "Thank you. I make it myself. It's my Gram's recipe. We used to spend hours in the kitchen together."

He smiles. "That sounds really nice. I taught myself a good deal of what I know, but my parents were both really good cooks and taught me a lot before they died." He pauses, hesitating a bit, it seems, worrying his bottom lip before he speaks again. "Thank you for inviting me. I'm really sorry if I'm not being the best company. It's been a rough couple weeks and I'm not in the best headspace. I was honestly nervous about coming, not because I don't enjoy your company, because I really do, but I struggle to believe sometimes that people actually want to spend time with me, and that I am not inconveniencing them. I mean, not all the time, but more so when I'm depressed or anxious."

His eyes are on the floor now and my chest aches at the thought that he doesn't think people would enjoy his company. "I'm sorry you're having a hard time," I tell him. "For what it's worth I think you're a really cool guy. You're smart, and fun, and kind, and Alex likes you so I know you must be a good person."

He chuckles.

"But it's okay if you're not feeling great. You don't have to be happy all the time, or put on a brave face. It's okay to not be okay, and to feel how you feel. I dealt with depression some after my mom died, and again when Gram died, so I know a little bit about how hard it can be. And if you deal with chronic depression or anxiety, I think that takes a tremendous amount of courage and strength, battling those negative messages all the time. But you're so much more than your struggles, small fry, and I have really been enjoying getting to know you."

He has tears filling his eyes and sliding down his cheeks now.

"Shit, I didn't mean to make you cry," I tell him.

He shakes his head and wipes at his eyes. "No, it's okay, they're good tears." He sniffles. "I've been enjoying getting to know you, too. My brain is just being nasty lately. I know better than to listen, but it's still really hard sometimes. I never did understand why my brain would want to lie to me, you know? Like shouldn't it be on my side?"

I chuckle a little. "I hear you." More tears spill down his cheeks and I can't just stand here while he cries, so I say, "Is it okay if I give you a hug?"

He nods, and then I'm setting my glass down and doing the same with his, before I wrap my arms around him and he rests his cheek against my chest, sobbing quietly.

"I'm here if you want to talk," I say. "But no pressure."

It takes a few moments, but eventually he says, "There's a guy that Tommy and I were seeing, and after two months he told us he needs space, and I'm having a really hard time with him being gone all of a sudden. And even though Tommy is telling me it's not because of me, I can't stop thinking that it is. That if I didn't have so many issues he would have stayed, he would be making Tommy happy, that I'm ruining everything." He cries harder now and I hold him tighter.

"Oh, small fry," I coo. "Shh. It's okay. You're okay." I rub my hand up and down his back, trying to soothe him. "I know it's hard to remember that your brain is lying to you when you feel that way, but trust me, it is. It doesn't take more than a second of seeing Tommy with you, or hearing him talk about you, to know how crazy he is about you."

Pierre sniffles again.

"I don't know what is happening with this guy, but I do know Tommy would be miserable if you weren't his. And if this guy really did end things with you because he thought you were too much to handle, then I already know Tommy wouldn't want anything to do with him."

He chuckles softly and wipes at his tears. "That's what Tommy said."

"You talking to anyone?" I ask, and he nods.

"I have a therapist, and I'm on meds. They help, but they're not a cure all. I have days where I do pretty well, you know, and then days or weeks where I'm really struggling. Sometimes it's for a reason, at least one I can pinpoint. Sometimes it's for no reason at all."

"Did your guy say why he needed space?"

He shakes his head. "No. And he didn't say how long either. I think that's part of what's stressing me out so much and making my brain assume the worst possible things. He's not communicating with us at all, and we..." he chokes on a sob. "We were..."

It dawns on me why this is hurting Pierre so much. This guy wasn't just a casual fling. "You loved him."

He nods and sobs again, holding me tighter. "We both did, or do. I don't know. We wanted to tell him and then he said he couldn't see us for a while, and, I don't know, everything is just wrong now."

I sigh. "I'm sorry, small fry. I really hope things get better for you all soon. That sounds really hard. Please know I am here for you if you need anything."

He steps back and wipes his tears away again. "Thank you."

"You're always welcome here if you need company. I mean that."

He nods again. "I'm really glad you moved in here, Bentley."

I grin and ruffle his hair. "Me, too."

Alex

The night of Peyton's birthday party arrives, and I stand in front of my full length mirror, admiring my outfit. Dark wash snug fitting jeans, a white T-shirt and a black leather jacket. Perfect. I'm actually really looking forward to having a night out. I haven't gone to a birthday party in a long time and Peyton inviting me was really sweet.

I've been mulling over the conversation with Tommy all week long. I still don't believe him when he says Bentley has feelings for me, too. Having to jerk off before I hang out with Bentley is getting increasingly annoying though. I've certainly put my new toys to good use since I got them, and there hasn't been a single thing I didn't enjoy. I'm not sure if that's because the toys were just so amazing, or if it was who I was fantasizing about while I was getting off that really made it incredible. I just know that I love having things up my ass now. I have even been practicing blow jobs more with bananas and cucumbers, though I fucking lock the door now when I do. I'm getting better, I think, though it's hard to know for sure when I don't have a real person telling me how it feels.

I sigh. I'd really love to have one person in particular telling me how it feels to have me suck his brains out through his dick. Fuck, just picturing Bentley staring down at me with his hand in my hair as he fucks my face, his skin flushed and sweat slick, that gorgeous hair loose and pooling around his shoulders, is making my dick perk up again, even though I just came twenty minutes ago.

Goddamn it. I really have to stop doing this to myself, because despite what my brother says, I know better than to think Bentley could ever want with me what I want with him. I mean what are the odds that he all of the sudden started liking guys too? And not just guys, but me? Yeah, right. And if I'm not careful, I'm going to slip up and he'll find out, and I will be mortified.

My phone dinging brings me back to the present and I pull it out of my pocket.

Cowboy: Just getting out of the shower now, be ready in

I groan. Fuck him. He can't tell me he's in the fucking shower. Now I'm just picturing that incredible body all wet and slick, and goddamn it. No, no, no, he's not for me. It's been two months of pining after him and it's killing me. I sigh, telling my dick to calm the fuck down and be good, before I type out a reply.

Me: will do

"Okay, I'm off," I tell Marble, turning to face her where she's sitting on my bed, licking her paw. "See you later, queen." I pet her quickly and then grab the gift I got for Peyton, before I head out of my apartment and across the hall to Bentley's.

Just as I step inside and close the door, he steps out of the bathroom with nothing but a towel wrapped around his waist. Holy fuck, not good. Look away, Alex, look away! But I can't stop staring. His body is fucking gorgeous. All that luxurious blond and brown hair is loose and falling around his face, water droplets dripping onto his toned pecs and sliding down to bead on his nipples before continuing to his six pack and disappearing underneath the towel.

"Hey, I'll be ready in a few minutes," he says, and I finally move my gaze to his eyes. Jesus, Alex, way to be subtle.

"Yeah," I croak, then clear my throat. "Okay." I take a seat on the sofa while I wait for him, beating myself up for being so fucking stupid. If I don't want him to know that I find him insanely attractive and want to jump his bones, probably not a good idea to stare at him like he's a slab of meat while fucking drooling. He's so damn pretty. But his looks aren't the reason I want him. He's also kind, and tender, and so damn sweet. He's caring, generous, thought-ful, soft, but also funny. He makes me laugh like no one ever has before. He loves my family, he adores Marble. He makes me happy in a way I don't think I've ever been, just by being him.

"Ready," I hear, and turn to see him standing there in tan colored chinos that hug his thighs and ass, a white button down, and a jean jacket. Damn, I still say he'd look amazing in a cowboy hat. He's giving me all the sexy cowboy vibes right now, that silky soft hair up in a messy bun once more, his beard neatly trimmed. I can't help but wonder what it would be like to feel that beard against my skin, under my palms, against my cheek, between my thighs.

In his hand is a rather large gift bag which I am assuming has Peyton's present in it; the blanket he's been knitting for weeks now. It turned out amazing and I know she's going to love it. My gift is a candle because Bentley says she's obsessed with them.

I stand and we make our way to his car. It's about a fifteen minute drive to the karaoke bar we're meeting at and I do my best not to gawk at him the entire time. When we get there and make our way inside we spot Peyton sitting at a table, a handful of people already seated around her. She freaking squeals when she sees us and launches out of her seat, throwing her arms around Bentley like she hasn't seen him in weeks even though they work together. Honestly it's pretty cute how excited she is.

"Hey, handsome," she says to me after letting go of Bentley. "Glad you could make it."

"Me, too," I say, and she beckons us to the table where we join the others. She makes introductions, telling us the three other people there, Sarah, Gabe, and Natalie, are from her book club, and I perk up at that. She squeals again when I start asking questions about it and she finds out how much I love to read.

"Omg, how did I not know this? We're going to be

besties," she tells me. "I'll text you the info so you have it and you can decide if you want to come. It's super chill."

I notice a small smile on Bentley's face. He seems relatively at ease, and seems to know everyone else at least a bit, but he's also sitting between me and Peyton. I honestly don't mind sitting next to a stranger, especially if it will make Bentley feel more relaxed.

Two more people show up in the next five minutes and the table is pretty packed now. There's two women on stage singing a Taylor Swift song together and they aren't bad. Plus they're obviously having fun which is even better. It's a lively place, and I can see why Peyton likes it. I also know that Bentley loves his friend because this is definitely not his type of thing, but he's still here.

We order food and take time eating and chatting as more patrons make their way to the stage. When Peyton turns to Bentley and gives him puppy dog eyes and a pouty lip, saying "Please, best friend," I wonder what on earth she's talking about, and watch as Bentley flushes.

He grumbles and then slides out of his seat, and I turn to Peyton. "What's going on?"

Her eyes go wide. "Oh, you didn't know?"

"Know what?" I ask.

She grins. "Our boy can sing."

I blink. What? How did I not know that?

"He's good, too."

I turn my attention back to Bentley as he makes his way onto the stage and picks up the microphone after saying something to the DJ.

I swallow when I hear the music for *When You Say Nothing at All* by Keith Whitley start to play, and then Bentley opens his mouth and I fucking melt right there on the spot. Goosebumps erupt over my entire body as his voice fills the space. It's smooth and silky, like whiskey and sin as it washes over me, and I can't look away. Holy shit, he sounds amazing. He closes his eyes as he sings, and I notice that the entire room is quiet except for him.

"Good, huh?" Peyton says, leaning closer to me with a huge smile on her face. I can't speak, so I just nod, and then swallow when Bentley opens those big blue eyes and stares right at me.

Shit. If I wasn't already smitten with this man I sure as fuck would be now. Stacy was a fucking moron to let him go.

I don't even realize tears are sliding down my cheeks until Peyton whispers, "Hey, you okay?"

Fuck. "Yeah, of course," I lie, wiping the tears away. I'm so screwed. And I have to do something to get my mind off of Bentley because I can't keep doing this, waiting in the wings for something that will never happen.

Bentley gets a huge round of applause when he's done and he's blushing furiously when he makes his way back to the table, sliding into his seat between Peyton and me. She kisses his cheek.

"Thank you," she says. "Best birthday present ever."

I end up leaving shortly after, telling Peyton and Bentley I don't feel well and I'll catch an uber home. I can tell Bentley doesn't like the idea but he lets me go.

When I get back home I do something I never thought I would do. I get on my phone and download Grindr, because I have to get past this crush I have on my best friend and it's the only way I know how. I'm not planning on hooking up, but I think it's time I tried going on a date again, this time with a guy.

Two days later it's Sunday and I am trying not to tell myself that this is everything I want. Me and Bentley, sitting in his apartment watching *Supernatural*, him back to knitting, Marble curled up on the sofa between us as I sip at my tea.

It's so fucking perfect. Well, almost perfect. If I could scoot a little closer, or reach over and press a kiss to his cheek, or squeeze his thigh... If I could run my fingers through that hair or tell him how breathtakingly beautiful he is.

But I can't. Which is why I'm finally going on a date Thursday night. I've been chatting with a guy on Grindr that seems really nice and we agreed to dinner. I don't even want to go because I'd much rather be spending time with Bentley doing exactly what we're doing now. But I know it's the right thing to do for both our sakes. Maybe if I meet another guy who sweeps me off my feet, I can enjoy my friend time with Bentley without secretly hoping for more.

"Alex?" I hear, and turn to face my friend who has a worried look on his face.

"Hmm?"

His brows furrow. "You okay? You've been quiet."

"Yeah, of course," I reply. "Just tired, I guess, and sore. Been working late a lot." It's true, I do feel all those things and I have been at the bar late over the past week, which I'm sure isn't helping anything, so even though it's not really the issue, it's the only thing I can say.

He frowns. "You want me to give you a massage? It might help."

Oh, holy mother of not good ideas, yes, I want that very very much. But, "No thanks," I say. Because there's no way I can let him put his big beautiful hands all over me without doing or saying something incredibly stupid. I'd get a raging hard on in seconds, and while I know that's normal for guys, it would make me feel so icky.

"I hope you feel better soon," he tells me when I leave a couple of hours later, taking Marble with me despite her protests.

"Thanks," I say.

"See you Thursday morning?"

I nod and he closes the door.

Bentley

I'm worried about Alex. He hasn't been himself ever since Peyton's party and I don't know why. I'm starting to wonder, though, if maybe he's picked up on my feelings for him and is keeping his distance because it makes him uncomfortable? I mean, he's still hanging out with me, but he was so spaced out on Sunday, and this morning he's even more so. Plus, he clearly didn't want me to touch him when I asked if he wanted a massage. And because I didn't want to push anything, I didn't even prop my feet in his lap when he was reading to me.

But instead of insisting I put my feet in his lap, and rubbing them like he always does, nothing. He's been responding to my texts but normally he'd be bombarding me with gifs and memes related to *Supernatural*, hounding me for details, sharing facts about the books we're reading or making plans for the upcoming weekend. None of that.

We're at the gym now and he's barely even talked to me since we got here. My chest is starting to constrict because I'm wondering how I fucked up and if there's anything I can do to make it better. I can't lose him.

"Hey," I say, approaching him on the rowing machine. I do my best not to stare at his bulging biceps and toned thighs. "Are we okay?"

He blinks and stops rowing. Sweat covers his skin and dampens his dark hair. "Yeah, of course."

"Are you sure? I feel like things are off with us and I don't like it."

He flushes and his gaze flits away. He clears his throat and then looks back at me. "I uh, I did need to tell you that I," he clears his throat again. "I have a date tonight, so I can't hang out."

Fuck. Why does that hurt so goddamn much? My chest tightens and my throat constricts. "No problem," I manage, my voice coming out as barely a whisper. Is he going on a date to make sure I know he isn't interested in me and trying to draw that line, without saying it directly so he doesn't hurt me? Message received, I guess. And Peyton was so sure he liked me, too. Even Pierre mentioned that he was pretty sure Alex had feelings for me when we were hanging out the other day. I honestly thought maybe I could try saying something to him if Pierre, and Peyton, and Tommy all thought the same thing, but then he was sick at Peyton's party, and Sunday he was just being weird, and definitely didn't want me touching him, and I thought, maybe not. Now I'm really glad I didn't say anything because apparently I would have been turned down.

I don't know why I'm asking this because I don't want to know, but I find myself saying, "What's her name?"

His flush deepens and he runs a hand through his sweaty hair. "*His* name is Greg."

Fuck, my knees almost give out as his words sink in. *His* name? It's a guy? Fuck, so he is into guys, just not into me. The knowledge hits me like a ton of bricks and I find myself holding back tears.

"So I'll see you on Sunday, though, right?" Alex says.

"Yeah, sure," I reply, forcing a smile. "I'm gonna head to the shower." I walk away as quickly as I can.

As soon as I'm under the warm water, I let the tears fall.

Chapter Fifteen

Bentley

I'm a fucking wreck when I walk into work an hour later. After showering at the gym I dressed and drove here, only to sit in the parking lot for another ten minutes trying to gather myself. I feel so fucking stupid being this upset about Alex going on a date, but I can't help it. I knew he would get back out there at some point, I just never expected it to be with a guy. And the worst part is, I'm already upset at whoever this guy is for taking my Alex time away. If they keep dating and it gets serious he'll have far less time to spend with me than he does now, and as it is we only see each other a few times a week. I know that's fucking selfish, and that he deserves to go on dates and enjoy himself. I just wish I could be the one making him happy, sitting with him at a restaurant, or a movie, or wherever the fuck he wants to go, because I'd do anything with him just to get to spend more time together. But now, it's my job to support him while he dates someone else, and I will, because I care about him, but fuck if it's not going to hurt something awful.

I suppose it's a good thing I won't see him for a few days

because that will give me some time to wrap my brain around all of this and hopefully be a supportive friend when he talks about how his date went.

"Morning, bestie," Peyton chirps when I walk through the door. My gaze doesn't meet hers right away but when it does, the tears start all over again, and she jumps up from her seat behind the receptionist desk.

"Hey, what's wrong?" she asks, and I'm sobbing as her arms come around me. I pull away when I realize I'm getting tears and probably snot on her fancy blouse.

"Sorry," I say, sniffling. "This is so unprofessional."

She snorts and then grabs a tissue off the box on the desk and hands it to me. "Hon, you know I will lock this place down and cancel every single one of your appointments if I have to. You don't have anyone for half an hour anyway, and you know better than to think you have to be professional with me. What happened?"

I wipe my nose with the tissue and then my eyes with my fingers, sucking in a breath. "Alex has a date tonight."

She frowns. "What?"

I nod. "With a guy. Apparently he's into guys, just not me. If he was dating a girl I wouldn't be so upset. I mean it would still suck, but fuck, him dating a guy hurts so much worse."

She sighs. "I am not wrong about this. He's probably doing it because he thinks you don't have feelings for him. You need to say something."

"It's too late now, Pey, I'd just make a fool of myself. He's letting me down easy, I guess. Not telling me to my face that I don't stand a chance. And at least he's keeping me in the friend zone."

She sighs again. "You want me to cancel your appointments and we can play hooky?"

I shake my head. "No, I can't afford to do that. Besides, it'll be a good distraction."

I manage not to sob onto my clients while I'm massaging them, or tell them all about how broken hearted I am.

It only makes things worse when I run into Alex leaving for his date as I'm unlocking the door to my apartment.

"Hey," he says, smiling at me. "How do I look?" He spreads his arms and spins, and it's all I can do not to start crying all over again. He's wearing chinos, and he has a blazer on over a plain white shirt. His hair is perfectly tousled and I ache to run my fingers through it.

"Amazing," I tell him, managing to force a small smile.

His grin turns to a frown. "You okay?" he asks, stepping closer.

"Yeah, of course," I lie, plastering another smile on my face. "Just tired. Long day. Have a good time."

He bites his lip but nods. "See you later."

I turn and stumble into my apartment before he sees me fall apart.

I want to cuddle with Marble but I feel weird about going into Alex's apartment now for some reason. And that makes me realize that if he's got a steady boyfriend I probably won't have the same "walk in whenever you want to" privileges. Things are going to change a lot, I think, and it makes my chest ache and more tears spring to my eyes.

I don't feel very hungry so I just eat a protein bar for dinner. I try to watch some *Supernatural* because it's always been my comfort show, but I can't because it only makes me think of Alex.

I have a sick feeling in my stomach the entire evening, thinking about him being on a date with someone, flirting with them, kissing them, maybe even getting fucked by them.

Shit, I don't know how to accept this, and I know I'm

the worst friend in the world for even thinking for a second that maybe his date will suck, and he'll be mine again, even if it's just for a little while.

Alex

I take a deep breath and let it out. I'm sitting in the parking lot of the restaurant where Greg said he would meet me. And all I can think about is that I'm missing out on time with Bentley. I could be sitting on his couch right now, watching *Supernatural* while he knits something and Marble snoozes between us. I could be in sweats and a T-shirt instead of chinos and a dress shirt. I could be surrounded by his smell, his laugh, his smile.

But I told myself I was going to do this so I could let these feelings for Bentley go, so even though I don't want to, I climb out of the car and head inside. I told Greg on Grindr that I was new to dating guys, so he isn't blindsided by me, and he didn't seem to mind. He was very polite and sweet when we talked, and said he wasn't interested in one night stands either, so there was no pressure for sex. Just getting to know each other.

It's warming up, and there's a pleasant breeze in the air as I make my way inside. I spot who I'm pretty sure is Greg sitting at a table sipping on wine, and inform the hostess that I'm here with him.

He smiles when he sees me approaching and stands. "You must be Alex?" he says, and I nod. He waits for me to sit before he does. "You look nice."

I flush and try for a smile but I'm not sure it's convincing. "Thank you. So do you." He's dressed similar to me, his pants and blazer different colors, and his shirt a button up. His dark hair is styled to perfection. He has glasses over his deep brown eyes and he smiles at me again. It really is a nice smile. Everything about him is nice, really. He's a bit older than me, mid thirties I think, and he said he was an architect, which is pretty cool. He's honestly perfect on paper.

Our waiter comes by and I order some wine for myself. I think I need it.

We order our meals once the waiter returns with my drink. We talk for a bit, about ourselves, the typical get to know you stuff that we haven't already talked about over Grindr. Work, families, hobbies. I tell him about *Johnny's* and that my family owns it, and he smiles.

I find he loves to read as much as I do, though he's more interested in science fiction and fantasy, that he loves animals, and has two cats of his own. He grew up in Massachusetts just like I did. He enjoys being outdoors. He tells me his family isn't the most supportive of him being gay and he's had to cut ties with most of them but has a sister he's close to.

When our food comes we eat, and talk a bit more, and I feel like the world's worst date because all I can think about is how perfect Greg is, the ideal guy, really, but not the guy I want. He doesn't smell right, he doesn't have the sexy southern drawl that makes me weak in the knees. He doesn't blush like crazy when I give him the slightest compliment. He doesn't have a smile that melts my heart and turns my brain to mush.

"You're not enjoying this, are you?" he says, and I stare at him, blinking. He doesn't even look upset, just knowing.

"No, I am," I tell him.

He shakes his head. "Alex, it's okay if you're not. I've been on enough dates to know when someone isn't having a good time. You've barely touched your food. You're clearly distracted."

I sigh. "I'm so sorry. It's not you, I swear."

He gives a small smile. "So who is it, then?"

"Huh?"

"The guy you're pining over?"

I flush. "It doesn't matter. He isn't interested."

"Is this your way of trying to forget about your feelings?"

I blink and he laughs softly.

"It won't work. Trust me."

I groan.

"Tell him how you feel, Alex."

I shake my head. "I can't. He's my best friend and he's straight."

"Are you sure? I thought you said you thought you were straight until a couple of months ago. I'm guessing he's the reason you're even on a date with a guy right now?"

I nod.

"Look, if he's as good of a friend as you say he is, it will be okay. I'm not saying he for sure has feelings for you, too, but he won't hate you for saying something, and you'll know for sure how he feels for you one way or the other. That might make it easier to move on if he doesn't feel the same. And if he does..." he trails off. "You don't want to live the rest of your life wondering what would have happened if you had said something."

I sigh and bite my lip.

"Is he worth taking a chance on?" Greg asks.

Okay, I can do this, I tell myself as I climb out of my car and head into the apartment building. I've been talking myself up since I left the restaurant, feeling horrible for being such a lousy date, but thankful my date was so understanding.

I'm telling Bentley how I feel. Tonight. Right now. I'm sure he's up. It's not that late. But when I stop outside his door I hesitate. I take a deep breath and I'm just about to knock when I remember our rule and reach for the door knob. I hear a moan from the other side of the door, and then a curse as I step inside.

"Fuck!"

I stop dead in my tracks when I see Bentley sprawled out on his couch, naked and fisting himself, obscene amounts of precum coating his hand and cock, his skin flushed and damp with sweat, that beautiful golden hair pooled on top of the pillow his head is resting on. Holy fuck. I've never seen anything this erotic before. Not even the porn I watched compares to this. His eyes are wide when he meets my gaze, and it registers in my brain that I should be looking away, or shutting the door and running away, but I don't. I can't. My name pours from his lips as his dick pulses and load after load of cum shoots out all over his stomach and chest. God, I don't think I'll forget that O face for as long as I live.

My brain is short circuiting, and I don't know what to do. "Shit," I say. "Sorry, I'll go." I step back and shut the door, before hightailing it over to my apartment.

My heart is racing as I shut the door behind me and lean against it. That really just happened, didn't it? I actually heard and saw him jerking off to me. It was my name on his lips while he came so fucking hard.

I pace, shaking my hands out as I do, my body filled with nervous energy. Do I go back over there? Do I wait? Shit, I don't know. Is he going to hate me for walking in on him? Jesus, I hope not.

Marble perches on the top of the sofa and meows at me.

"Quiet, I'm thinking," I tell her. In the end I decide to wait for the morning. I'll go over there before he leaves for work and talk to him. With that sorted out I move to Marble and scratch behind her ears. I'm too riled up to sleep just yet, so I change and go for a run. I think about knocking on Bentley's door when I get back, but decide to stick to my original plan. He might need some time.

I head inside again, shower, and fall into bed.

Chapter Sixteen

Alex

It's no surprise that I don't sleep super great and that I'm buzzing with a mixture of anxiety and excitement the following morning as I dress and then have my tea. I brush my teeth, try to do something with my dark waves, but decide it's pointless, and then grab Marble and make my way over to Bentley's. I figure if he is upset with me, or nervous, or whatever, he'll respond better if Marble's there.

"Yes, I'm using you for my own selfish purposes," I tell her. "But you know what? It's about time you started pulling your weight around here."

But when I get to Bentley's door it's locked. Huh, that's weird. He doesn't leave for another hour and he always has his door unlocked if he's home. I try knocking but he doesn't answer, even after I call his name.

Shit. My excitement has vanished now and I'm feeling something a whole lot closer to dread. Is he avoiding me? Fuck, he can't do this. Not now. Not when I've finally made up my mind to tell him how I feel. I mean, I get seeing your best friend watching you jerk off could be a little awkward, but if he thinks he can ignore me because of it he's got another thing coming.

I check outside and see that his car is gone. Fucker must have left early just so he didn't have to face me.

I return to my apartment and text him our weekly gif of The Rock. I wait and see a couple of minutes later that he's read it, but when several more minutes go by with no response, I can't decide if I'm more frustrated or worried.

I think about calling him, but then decide if he really does need some more time before he talks to me, the last thing I should do is push him. Reluctantly I put my phone down and change clothes so I can go for another run.

I text Bentley again that evening before I head to work just asking if we can please talk, and when he hasn't replied by the time I get home at two fucking am, I decide I'm done being patient with him. It was never my forte anyway. So if he hasn't responded by morning, I'm doing whatever it takes for his stubborn Viking ass to hear me out.

That's how I end up at his workplace, that I have never in fact been to before but got the address for by doing a google search for the name, *Dreamscape Massage,* climbing out of my car and barging in like a man on a mission. Because, I am, I guess, on a mission.

I don't even bother to stop at the desk where Peyton is clicking away at a computer, just waltz past her as she shouts, "Hey, Alex, wait, you're not allowed back there!"

"Like I give a fuck!" I volley back. There's three doors down the hall. Two on the right and one on the left, but only the door on the left is closed. The other two are a bathroom and a small office space with a desk and computer, as well a small counter space with a coffee pot.

I stop outside the closed door for a brief second, hearing soft, calming music coming from the other side and quiet murmurs. There's clearly a client in there with Bentley but I don't care. I open the door and step inside.

Bentley's eyes go wide from where he's standing at the head of the massage table working on the client's neck and shoulders. She's an elderly woman who looks completely blissed out but her eyes snap open, too, when Bentley stops his ministrations.

"We need to talk," I say, my voice brooking no argument.

"Alex, what are you doing?" he hisses as he steps towards me. "You can't be here. I'm working."

"Tough," I say, and he blanches as my finger pokes his chest. "You've been ignoring me and I'm fucking done with it. You think you get to just ghost me because we had a tiny little awkward moment? Just because I saw you wacking the walnut doesn't mean you get to treat me like shit."

He blinks, his face flushed. "Wacking the...what?"

I groan. "Tugging the slug, spanking the monkey, choking the chicken, shaking hands with the milkman." I stare at him. Nothing. "Jerking off! You fucking caught me deep throating a banana, okay, and was that awkward as hell? Yes, but did I act like you didn't exist afterwards? No, because you're my best fucking friend. And best friends talk to each other. Because when they talk they realize that their friend was fucking miserable on his date because he wasn't with the one person he wanted to be with."

Bentley blinks at me again and I have a feeling I'm gonna have to try a more drastic approach. "For fuck's sake," I growl, and then step forward and grip his face in my hands before slotting my lips with his. He freezes, his body stiff as a board, and for a second I think I've royally screwed up. But then he's gripping my face in his hands and kissing me right back.

Holy hell, yes. I back Bentley up against the wall and he moans as I part his lips with my tongue and delve inside. Fuck, that moan goes straight to my cock. His lips are heavenly as they move against mine. He tastes like caramel and vanilla, and his beard is soft under my palms and utterly perfect. Fuck, this is everything I imagined it would be and more. Okay, well, maybe not exactly as I imagined since we have company, but it's still pretty damn good.

"Shit," he gasps, pulling away and breathing heavily. We look at each other and he turns his flushed face to his client, who to my surprise, isn't protesting. "I'm so sorry, Gloria..." he sputters.

She grins widely. "Oh, honey, don't you apologize. This is the most fun I've had in a long time. You should do this for all of your clients."

He flushes even more deeply and I have to hold back a laugh.

"I have to work," he tells me.

"Do that," I say. "But next time I text you, you fucking answer, okay, cowboy?"

He nods.

"And when Sunday rolls around, you better have your fucking door unlocked. Got it?"

He nods again.

"Good," I say. "My work here is done, then." I turn to Gloria. "See you later, gorgeous."

She cackles and waves at me, and I plant one more last minute kiss on Bentley's lips before I open the door and walk out.

Peyton has a huge grin on her face when I walk past her and she calls, "It's about dang time!"

Yeah, I knew she was outside that door the entire time.

We text throughout the rest of the day, and things feel normal again between us, but neither one of us mentions the kiss, and I wonder if he's pretending it didn't happen? God, he better not be. I want so much more with him, and if he tells me we're just friends I will fucking lose it. I have to taste him again, feel those full, chapped lips against mine, be surrounded by his rain and ocean scent, his soft beard against my palms, hear his sexy as fuck moans.

But the second Marble and I enter his apartment Sunday morning, it's like all the courage I had Saturday when I walked into his workplace is gone. I'm feeling more nervous than ever, and I don't know what to do. Should I ask if I can kiss him again? Should I back off and try to let him lead? Should I just not say anything? Do we have a DTR? God, do people even do those any more?

He's smiling when he sees us, so there's that at least, and his cheeks are flushed as he holds his coffee cup in both hands and shuffles his foot around. It's pretty endearing actually, watching this big bulk of a man be so flustered.

"You uh, wanna watch *Supernatural*?" I ask, because I don't know what else to say.

He hesitates, then nods, and we settle on the sofa with Marble. I grin when Bentley picks Marble up and sits down as close to me as humanly possible, our legs and arms touching, and sets Marble on his lap.

"This okay?" he asks, and I grin, reaching for his hand and lacing his fingers with mine. His breath hitches, but then he's gripping my hand in his and squeezing gently.

"Is this?" I ask, and he nods, his blush returning. God, I

want to kiss him. Fuck, I want to climb him like a tree and make out until I can't feel my lips anymore, but maybe he needs to take things a little slower, so I rein myself in and try to enjoy what we're doing, because just having him sitting this close to me, breathing him in, having his big, warm hand in mine, is making goosebumps erupt all over my body, and my dick twitch in my sweats.

Bentley is wearing lounge pants, too, and a plain white T-shirt, and he looks so fucking cuddlable, but like I said, baby steps.

About thirty minutes into the first episode I have to pee, but I don't want to get up. I don't want to lose this closeness with him, so I wait for the episode to end and then reluctantly make my way to the bathroom when I can't possibly hold it in anymore.

When I come back out he's got another episode ready to go and I sink back down next to him. His hand finds mine immediately and I grin. I'm probably gonna have to watch these episodes again because I am way too distracted by his proximity to me to pay a lick of attention, and my skin is fucking electrified. Fuck, if just this amount of contact has my body reacting so strongly I can't imagine what it would feel like to be naked with him. Just the thought has my cock jerking and me suppressing a groan.

He slouches down a few minutes into the show and rests his head on my shoulder, Marble hopping off his lap and lying down again on the ottoman, his hand still in mine, and I fucking melt. To have this big, strong, tender sweetheart of a man snuggling up with me is making my heart go crazy, and I almost whimper at the feel of his hair tickling my jaw and neck.

Shit, I'm so fucking hard already and we're barely touching. I know he can see my dick tenting in my pants, and even though we kissed once already and there's clearly something happening between us, I'm still nervous that him seeing me aroused by his proximity will scare him away. He's not moving though and it's been several minutes, and when I glance over I see him tenting in his pants, too.

Fuck, he's big. My hole spasms and I fucking gasp as I think of that big, beautiful cock being burried inside me. God, I want it so bad. I want everything with him. I'm about to open my mouth and say something when I hear him snoring softly.

Well, shit. I can't wake him up when he's asleep against me, but I'm so desperate for him I can't stand it. I last ten more torturous minutes before I give up and nudge his cheek with my shoulder.

"Mmmm," he grunts.

"Hey, cowboy, you fell asleep," I murmur into his hair, my heart thrashing and my skin prickling. I'm about point two seconds away from mauling him when he tilts his head and those beautiful blue eyes are staring into mine. "You wanna keep watching?" I ask, my voice husky.

He doesn't say anything, just reaches his big hand up and cups my cheek, before he closes the space between us and his lips capture mine.

Oh, God. Just the feel of his lips on mine again is making my body light up. My dick is oozing precum as a zing of pleasure shoots straight to my aching balls. I grip his shoulder and kiss him back hungrily. He turns so his body is facing me and he's on his knees now, tilting my head back and shoving his tongue down my throat.

Fuck. I moan as my dick jerks and our tongues tangle. He pushes forward and I fall onto my back on the sofa, him between my splayed thighs as we make out. Our hands are everywhere, touching, seeking, searching, running along each other's arms and down each other's torsos, and through each other's hair. God, his hair is just as soft and silky as I imagined it would be.

Kissing this man is everything, and I'm so turned on that when he captures my bottom lip between his teeth and bites down, I gasp and pull away, because holy fuck.

"Wait, wait," I say, trying to catch my breath. He stares at me and sits back.

"Did I do something wrong?" he asks, and I can't help loving how he looks right now, his messy bun falling loose and his hair disheveled, his lips swollen and spit slick, his eyes dark and face flushed, chest rising and falling. He's tenting his pants rather prominently and there's a wet spot already forming on the front of his sweats. Holy shit.

Focus, Alex. I shake my head and sit up. As much as I love what we're doing I need to say something before we continue. "No, no, I just...fuck." I blow out a breath. "I need to know that we're on the same page with this. I can't...I can't do this if it doesn't mean to you what it means to me."

He blinks.

"I don't do casual," I tell him. "Ever. It's just not me. If I sleep with someone or even make out with someone it's because I have feelings for them, so if you are looking for casual, that's fine, but I'm not your guy. I like you a whole hell of a lot, and I can't get invested if it's not going somewhere. I don't want to be friends with benefits, or treat this like an experiment. If we're experimenting it needs to be with the goal of us becoming more along the way. I mean, if one or both of us decides that guy on guy action isn't for us, that's one thing, but I don't want to treat this like it's no big deal, because it is a big deal to me."

He flushes and bites his lip. "Me, too," he says, and my breath hitches as my heart flutters against my rib cage.

"Yeah?" I say, and I can't keep the smile from my face.

He nods. "I have feelings for you, too."

My smile widens, but then he's biting his lip again and his gaze lowers to his lap. "You okay?" I ask.

"I'm a little nervous, I guess," he admits, and fucking hell, why is he so stinking adorable? My big teddy bear Viking. "I haven't been with anyone since Stacy, and I'm worried maybe I won't be good enough for you. In bed, I mean."

The idea of him not being able to satisfy me in bed is so utterly ridiculous that I almost laugh, but I don't because I love that he's sharing this concern with me and being vulnerable. And I get where he's coming from. I also hate that Stacy made him doubt himself.

I scoot closer and grip his shirt in my hand, tugging him to me. "Baby," I say, my voice low and sultry as my lips brush against his, "I was about to come hard just from you kissing me, so I promise you don't have a thing to worry about."

I feel a shiver roll through him. "Now fucking kiss me, cowboy," I order as I lie down once again and pull him with me. He moves between my splayed thighs once more, and I gasp when he lowers himself and I feel his hard length brush against mine.

"This okay?" he asks, breaking the kiss, and I whimper as I nod and pull him back down. Then we're kissing even more feverishly as he ruts against me and I thrust up into him.

"Fuck, baby, I'm gonna come. Shit, you feel good." My head is thrown back as he kisses and sucks and nibbles on my throat, drawing a desperate whine out of me as I wrap my legs around him and grip his shoulders. "Bentley," I moan. "Fuck, don't stop, baby." God I can't get enough of that sweet sweet friction and those perfect lips against my skin, his beard brushing my neck and jaw, making my body erupt in goosebumps. He's unraveling me. Being intimate with someone has never felt like this before.

"Alex," he pants. "I'm close." He slots his lips against mine once more and then we're moaning and gasping, crying out each other's names as our cocks pulse, spilling load after load of cum into our underwear.

Shit, that was incredible. And we didn't even take our fucking clothes off. I'm worn out but at the same time can't wait to do more.

He collapses on top of me, breathing heavily and burying his face in my neck. My arms come around him and I hold him close, breathing in the scent of rain and ocean, now mixed with sweat and sex. It's fucking perfection. And having him on top of me, my arms around him, is even better than I ever imagined.

"Was it good for you, too?" I ask, and he chuckles, his big body moving against mine and making me grin even wider than I already was.

"It was amazing," he says, and I take a second to remove the ponytail holder from his tousled hair, then start to comb my fingers through it. He hums and nuzzles into me closer. And even though my spunk is already starting to dry and stick to my sensitive skin, and I desperately need to get out of these underwear, I can't make myself move, especially when he lets out a hum that sounds more like a purr and rubs his cheek against my chest.

"You like cuddling, huh?"

"Maybe," he admits and even though I can't see his blush I know it's there.

"That okay?" he asks.

"Always." I sigh contentedly. "Give me ten minutes and I can go again."

He chuckles again and then lifts his head and starts to nibble on my ear. I moan and my dick jerks. "Okay, maybe I don't need ten minutes. Mmmm, why does that feel so good?"

He lets go of my ear and brushes his nose along my neck, before peppering soft kisses there, and then nibbling on my jaw.

"Fuck, cowboy," I groan, already arching my hips again.

"I'll be right back," he says, and then climbs off of me and moves to the bathroom. He comes back later with a package of wipes and no shirt. My mouth waters as I watch him slide out of his pants and cum soaked underwear. Holy fuck, he's naked in front of me and I can't stop staring. He's so damn beautiful it hurts. Those broad shoulders, defined pecs, toned abdomen and thick thighs are a vision, and I can't believe I get to see him this way. Being intimate with someone isn't something I take lightly, and the fact that he's sharing this with me, giving me the privilege of gazing at his beautiful body, means everything. His dick is long and thick, and uncut, like mine, and there's a happy trail leading from his belly button to the wild thatch of pubic hair between his legs.

"Wow," I breathe, as my heart rate picks up and my dick jerks again. I'm getting kinda emotional staring at him, because I honestly never thought we'd be here. That he could care for me the way I care for him. It's like a dream come true.

He grins and blushes fiercely as he wipes the jizz off his dick.

"I was thinking we could do the next part naked," he says, and I nod before peeling out of my own clothes. I've never felt more safe and comfortable being naked in front of anyone before, and when Bentley looks at me like he's staring at a priceless work of art, I can't help it; my cheeks heat and I grin like an idiot.

"You're awfully good looking," he rumbles as he steps

closer and takes my face in his hands, and fuck I just melt on the spot. I have to grip his arms to keep my knees from giving out on me. His fucking accent is going to be the death of me.

He presses a soft kiss to my lips. God, I could kiss him forever. "You wanna be my boyfriend, Alex Florez-Romano?"

I nod. "Yeah. Yeah, I do. You wanna be mine, cowboy?"

He grins. "I reckon," he says, and I'm smiling from ear to ear.

We pull apart and he hands me some wipes. I clean off and then he takes my hand and pulls me towards the bedroom.

He lies down when he gets there and pulls me to him. I stare for a second, once again at his beautiful body, all that golden skin on display, his thick cock half hard, his nipples pert, and all that luxurious hair fanning across the pillow, his blue eyes locked on me.

He tugs on me gently and I climb on the bed and straddle him, the feel of his naked skin against mine making my cock thicken and my body come alive. Holy hell. A shiver races through me as I stare down at him, and he grips my thighs.

"Do you have any idea how goddamn beautiful you are?" I ask him, and my eyes widen when his breath hitches and his dick jumps. "Oh, you liked that, didn't you, cowboy?"

He lets out the tiniest whimper as his hands tighten on my thighs and his pupils darken, his cock almost fully hard now. "You like when I tell you how fucking pretty you are."

He moans and his hips thrust up into me. "Alex."

"Do you know how hard you made me the other night when you were up on that stage singing? I almost came in my pants at the sound of your voice, baby. And when I walked in on you touching yourself." A low rumble leaves my chest and I watch as his dick lengthens and precum starts to ooze out. "God, that was so damn hot. You gripping your beautiful cock and stroking it, watching as you sprayed your perfect spunk all over yourself, shouting my name."

He lets out another whimper and then grabs my face in his hands and pulls me down to him, kissing me hard. My dick is hard now, too, and it brushes against his as we kiss, both of us moaning and gasping and panting at the feel of skin on skin, our bodies melded, every glorious inch of us in contact, our dicks brushing against each other's, sending bolts of pleasure down my spine and making me kiss him harder, sliding my tongue inside his warm, wet mouth and devouring him, getting drunk off the noises he's making as my balls ache to come.

"God, I want to do so many wicked things to you," I tell him, pulling back for air.

"Stop talking," he almost growls, and pulls me back, kissing me harder. I fucking tremble, gasping as his hands move from my face to my ass and he squeezes. Fuck, that feels so damn good. I keep kissing him as I thrust forward, my cock sliding against his over and over and then pushing back into his hands, begging for more of his touch.

"Can I touch you?" he asks, and I nod. When I look down at our cocks nestled against each other's, my eyes widen at the amount of precum leaking from his gorgeous mushroom head. Holy shit. No wonder it feels so damn good. He leaks like a fucking sieve. I mean, I don't have a lot to go on I guess, but I don't have nearly that amount of precum.

"Fuck, that's hot." He bites his lip and his cheeks turn crimson. "Touch me," I say. "Use your precum as lube and fucking touch me, baby."

He eyes darken and he coats his fingers with his own

fluid before he grips both of our cocks and starts to stroke us in tandem, and oh my fucking God. This feels so incredible I can't even bring myself to miss his hands on my ass. Fuck, I'm whining and whimpering and thrusting shamelessly into his hand as he strokes us together, both of us panting and our skin slick with sweat. His cock against mine, his big, strong hand wrapped around us, my dick soaked in his fluid, is turning my brain to goo and my body to fire. I've never felt pleasure like this.

"Fuck, Bentley, I can't," I whine. "You feel too damn good, baby."

His cock is pulsing against mine seconds later as he grunts and then throws his head back, his release shooting out, covering his hand and both of our cocks. Seeing him come undone, spraying so hard his body is trembling, his neck muscles strained and his dick spasming against mine is all it takes for me to shoot my load, too, unloading on his hand, my cum mixing with his.

"Shit!" I cry out, my chest heaving, as aftershocks roll through me and I collapse on top of him. He grabs several tissues from the nightstand and uses them to wipe off his hand.

"I like it when you come," he murmurs against my hair as his arms come around me. Our spunk is sticky and pooled between us, and I have a very strong desire to take a shower right about now.

"I like when I come, too," I say, and he laughs. I lift my head and kiss him. "But I like it better when you come."

He grins. "Shower with me?"

"You read my mind, beautiful."

He narrows his eyes as his dick twitches against my stomach. God, I love that. I love that he gets so turned on by being told how fucking pretty he is.

"You're gonna be trouble with that, aren't you?"

I grin. "Maybe. Can't help it. My boyfriend is the prettiest man there is and he likes when I tell him."

He bites his lip and blushes beautifully even as his cock tries to rally back to life. I kiss him again, because I can, and then sit up. "Also, the amount of precum you produce is seriously sexy. Has it always been that way?"

He covers his face with his hands and I laugh. "Hey, I'm being serious. It's hot. Don't be embarrassed. I'd love to leak that much, not have to worry about lube."

He moves his hands. "Yes, it's always been like that. I didn't realize it was more than average until I started dating and the girls I was with commented on it."

"Like, good comments or bad?"

He shrugs. "I mean, nobody minded. It is a problem if I get hard, though, and don't want to be. My underwear gets wet really quickly and it's uncomfortable, and it can be embarrassing, too, if I leak enough it soaks through to my pants."

My eyes widen. "Oh. Does that happen often?"

"No, but it's happened a few times. I have to be careful about what I wear when I'm around someone I like."

I grin and wiggle my ass. "Like me?"

He narrows his eyes. "Yes, like you. I mean I can do it now because we're together, but there's a reason I haven't been wearing pajama pants and sweats around you much, and was sticking to jeans."

My grin widens. I love that he got so turned on around me his dick was leaking so much. "Well, I love it. It's sexy as fuck."

"Thank you. I think."

I laugh and kiss him. We shower, trading lazy kisses and soft touches, before we climb naked back into bed. Bentley takes me in his arms and I snuggle close, sighing in contentment.

"You said there were a lot of things you wanted to do to me," he murmurs, running his fingers through my damp hair. "Wanna tell me what those things are, darling?"

God, why do I love it so much when he calls me that? It sounds so damn sexy in his accent.

I hum. "Later. Nap first."

He presses a kiss to my hair. "As you wish."

I chuckle. "Did you just *Princess Bride* me?"

"I thought you didn't watch movies?"

"Not much, no, but I watched them as a kid and I've still seen that one a dozen times. It's one of my mom's favorites. The book is better though."

He chuckles. "I like your mom. She has good taste."

Before I can respond, Marble hops up on the bed and tries to plop herself on top of Bentley's stomach, making him laugh.

"Oh, no you don't," I tell her. "He's mine." I grab her and set her down on the foot of the bed and she meows at me, so I narrow my eyes at her. She stretches and yawns, and then lies down against my leg.

We drift off, then, and in Bentley's arms, I'm happier than I've ever been.

Chapter Seventeen

Alex

I wake to Bentley's fingers gently carding through my hair, and I can barely believe I'm tucked against him, and buck ass naked, no less. Jesus, is this real? Is he really mine? That rain and ocean scent surrounds me as I hum, reveling in the feeling of his warmth, his touch, his closeness. I got off with a man twice, and I loved every second of it.

My eyes slowly open as Bentley rumbles, "Morning darling," and I fucking melt. I smirk when I see that Marble has completely disregarded my instructions to leave Bentley alone, and has been comfortably napping on his stomach for who knows how long.

I reach over and pet her even as I scold, "Bad kitty," and Bentley chuckles.

Looking out the window, I note it's dusk outside and realize we must have been dozing for a while. Honestly I could stay in this spot for the rest of the night and be content. I have no desire to move away from my man when his arms around me feel so perfect.

I tilt my head and look up at Bentley, still just trying to

wrap my head around the fact that he's my boyfriend now. That I can touch him, and kiss him, and cuddle with him. That I don't have to try not to be aroused by him, or be terrified that he'll find out about my feelings. That I can ogle him all I want without beating myself up for it the entire time and worrying that I'll scare him off if he catches me.

Shit, just thinking about openly admiring him while he works out has blood pooling south and my dick lengthening against his hip. "How's my beautiful boyfriend?" I ask him, and have the immense pleasure of hearing his intake of breath and watching his dick jerk under the bed sheet. I brush my nose along his neck and plant a kiss there.

"You wanted to know what it was I wanted to do to you?" I say, and he smiles and flushes, burying his face in my hair, and making me grin. I press a kiss to his chest, overcome with the desire to get my mouth on those pert nipples and make him squirm and beg for me. Not yet, though. I press more kisses to his neck and jaw. "I have to use the bathroom. And when I get back, we're going to talk about all the ways I want to explore your beautiful body."

He groans and nods, cheeks still rosy. "Hurry."

I grin and climb out of bed, immediately missing that warm body and those strong arms, and head to the bathroom. I relieve myself and then return to the bedroom to find Bentley petting Marble.

"I gotta pee, too," he says, and gently picks up Marble, placing her on the bed, before he hurries off, but not before I get a view of his gorgeous tight ass and those sinful thighs. Fuck, his body is a work of art, and I want to get my hands and my mouth on it so fucking bad.

When Bentley returns, I'm sitting up in bed stroking my now rock hard cock, and his eyes are smoldering when he looks at me.

"Like what you see, cowboy?" I ask, my voice sultry. He

nods and climbs on the bed in front of me on his hands and knees, leaning in to kiss me. I eagerly reciprocate, carding my fingers through his silky locks and moaning when his big hand grips my throat and he tilts my head back, sucking on my tongue. Holy fuck. My body electrifies and my cock jumps. A whimper escapes me and I'm leaking like crazy when his hand tightens on my throat, not enough to cut off my air supply, but enough to make me feel owned and possessed, and I fucking love it. When we pull back for air we're both panting and our dicks are rock hard, oozing precum. His gaze falls to my groin, his hand still on my throat.

"I love seeing you hard," he breathes, leaning in to plant kisses on my neck and shoulder. "Your cock is so fucking pretty."

It's my turn to suck in a breath. "Shit, cowboy, you can't say stuff like that," I reply as my body trembles. His eyes darken and I groan. Jesus fuck, I want everything with this man. And before I can stop myself I blurt, "I want your feet in my mouth."

His eyes widen as he sits back on his haunches, his hand no longer on my throat, and I fucking whimper at the loss of contact. "What?" he says.

I blink. Okay maybe that was a little out of left field. "I uh," I flush and clear my throat. "I mean, if you're okay with it, that is."

"You want my feet in your mouth?"

"Maybe? I mean, not the whole fucking foot," I clarify. "But I like rubbing your feet, and they smell way better than they should, and I've been wondering what it would be like to kiss them? And maybe more?"

His eyes widen and he makes an "O" shape with his mouth.

"If you're okay with it," I repeat. "That's one of the

things I wanted to try, but if it grosses you out, we don't have to."

He bites his lip. "I don't think it grosses me out, maybe just surprises me. And I guess it wasn't what I thought you would say."

I raise an eyebrow. "What did you think I would say?"

His cheeks turn rosy again. "I don't know, maybe that you wanted to blow me or something?"

I grin. "Oh, don't get me wrong, cowboy, I want to do that, too. Otherwise all those bananas suffered for nothing."

He laughs and leans forward, kissing me again. "I like you."

My chest squeezes. "I like you, too."

"And I'm okay with you doing whatever it is you want to do to my feet. I can't promise I'll like it, but we can try."

I nod.

"How do you want me?" he asks.

"Maybe lay down with your feet in my lap?"

He moves up the bed and rolls onto his back, laying horizontal and placing his feet in my lap. Marble jumps off the bed and scampers into the living room, and I remind myself that after this sexcapade I should get her some dinner.

I grip the foot that is closest to me, and start to massage it. I can tell he likes that when I hear his groaning, but I'm not surprised since he's always liked having his feet rubbed. When I get a bit braver I bring my face down to it and press a kiss to his toes. His feet are soft, and smell amazing, and his breath hitches when my lips come in contact with his bare skin. I look at him and his eyes are lidded, his dick half hard, having softened during our conversation. I press a few more kisses to his toes and then nuzzle my nose against them, and even though I feel a little weird about it, I dart my tongue out and swipe it over his toes, only to grimace at the sensation, and apparently I must make an epic face because Bentley starts laughing so hard he sounds like he's wheezing, clutching his stomach and rolling onto his side, his entire body shaking.

"Hey," I pout. "Not nice. It was a lot sexier in my head." That only makes him laugh harder, and I sit there with my arms crossed over my chest and a mock scowl on my face, waiting for him to stop, though as much as I try not to, I do end up cracking a smile. "Asshole."

He rolls back onto his back, wiping tears from his eyes, and I shift to my knees, crawling over to hover above him. Fuck, he's beautiful, especially with the laugh lines around his eyes and that smile as bright as I've ever seen it. "You're mean," I tell him, my voice not at all serious. Those gorgeous blue eyes sparkle.

"I'm sorry, darling," he says, and my dick twitches. Fuck, I'll forgive him anything if he looks at me the way he is now and uses that sexy as fuck voice to call me his darling.

"Okay, so having your feet in my mouth is a no," I say. "But what do you say we try out one of my other ideas?"

"Which is?"

I don't speak, just lean down and swipe my tongue over his nipple. He sucks in a breath and moans, his hips thrusting upwards as his hands shoot out to grip my arms. "Mmmm," I purr as his eyes darken and he stares up at me. "More, baby?"

He nods eagerly and I lean down and do the same thing to the other nipple, swirling my tongue around the hardened nub and hearing his breath hitch, before I suck it into my mouth and moan as his hips buck up into me, a needy whine escaping his lips. I revel in the noises he's making as I suck and nibble and lick the sensitive flesh, moving my fingers to the other nipple and rolling the bud between my thumb and finger as I tug on the one in my mouth. He fucking wails as he humps the air, and my dick throbs, every noise he makes making me harder.

"Alex," he gasps. "Fuck, that's good." His grip on my arms is fierce now, his skin flushed and damp with sweat. He tosses his head back, my name on his lips again as his eyes close, his neck muscles straining, that gorgeous cock oozing copious amounts of precum, slicking his dick and pooling on his stomach. I pop off of his nipple and suck on his neck, still playing with the other bud between my fingers, and he whimpers.

"Fuck, no, please?" he begs, so much desperation in his sexy voice that I have to give him what he wants. I return to his nipples, taking the opposite one in my mouth again and using the fingers on my other hand to play with the one that's still wet with my saliva. His body shakes and he's babbling incoherently now as he squirms underneath me, still humping the air, desperately seeking friction for his aching cock, rivulets of precum dripping onto his belly now.

God, I don't think I've ever been so aroused in my life. Tasting him, listening to him, watching him. He's so fucking sexy. I bite down gently on his nipple before sucking it into my mouth again and tugging as I pinch the other one, and he cries out my name again as his body shudders and his dick pulses, his release shooting onto his abdomen and chest, some even hitting his chin.

Holy fucking hell. He just came untouched from me just playing with his nipples. I stroke my own cock fast and hard, my release barreling up on me as I stare at him. "Fuck, I'm gonna come," I rasp, and then I'm shooting all over him, my spunk mixing with his just as his eyes open. The way he looks at me makes another spurt of cum shoot out to join the first, pooling on his abs. He groans and his eyes close again as I kiss and suck gently on his torso, his breaths heavy. He's a vision to look at and I can't believe that of all the people in the world, he's giving himself to me. That I get to call him mine.

"Fuck, I could watch you come forever, cowboy," I tell him, then press more kisses to his neck and jaw. His eyes finally open again and he looks dazed and sated, and I can't help smiling because I'm the reason he looks and feels so content and utterly blissed out.

"God, you have a wicked mouth," he says, his voice soft, before he pulls me down for a slow, languid kiss.

I trail my eyes down his body and can't help the touch of possessiveness that courses through me. "You look so damn good covered in our cum, baby." I kiss him again. "You wanna taste us?"

He blinks. "Huh?"

"Our cum? Do you want to?"

"Do you?"

"Yeah, but you don't have to. I'm curious, though, if I'll like it or not. I've never tasted cum before."

He nods. "Me either."

I swipe my finger through the mess on his abs and bring it to his lips. He hesitates, but then his tongue darts out and he swipes it into his mouth. I laugh when his face screws up and he shivers. "That bad, huh?"

"I think it's a texture thing," he says. "But no, not for me. I do love your cum, just not in my mouth."

I laugh. "I'm not offended, but I'm still gonna try it." I'm about to gather more of the essence but he beats me to it, swiping some onto his finger just as I did and bringing it to my lips. I lean forward a smidge before darting my tongue out. The moment the salty taste hits my tastebuds I'm moaning and gripping his hand, sucking his entire finger into my mouth and licking every last bit of our combined spunk off his digit while he stares at me, his eyes wide and his gaze heated.

"Shit, darling, you make it look so much sexier. I'll watch you swallow our jizz down any time."

I release his finger, my dick half hard again as I stare at him and he feeds me more of our spunk. I don't know why I like it so much but fuck, I do. And when I pop off of his finger for the second time I bend over and lap the rest of our spunk into my mouth before swallowing it down and collapsing on top of him.

We lie there for a bit before I say, "I have a feeling there's a bunch of stuff we might want to try together. We probably don't even know what all of it is yet."

"Mmm," he hums in ascent, his finger trailing down my spine. "Good thing we have all the time in the world to figure it out."

"I've been watching porn, so I know some things I might want to try with you, but I'm sure there's other things I haven't seen or don't know about. We might have to do some research."

"Anything off the top of your head?"

"Blowjobs, for starters."

"I want to do those too, but I don't think I can swallow your cum," he tells me.

I pick my head up and look at him. "I think I'll be happy enough just having this gorgeous mouth wrapped around my dick, beautiful," I say, brushing my fingers over his lips.

His big body shivers at the endearment, and holy hell I'm going to have way too much fun telling him how fucking breathtaking he is and watching his body react. Even now I feel his dick twitch against me. He kisses my fingertips and I press a kiss to his chin.

"I really liked when you grabbed my throat," I tell him, flushing slightly, and he smiles.

"I really liked that, too."

"Maybe we should make a list of things we want to try

and show them to each other? We can say what we're willing to try, and what we really don't want to try."

He nods. "I like that."

I sit up, and press a kiss to his lips this time. "Now, I need to get a certain feline her dinner, or there will be hell to pay."

He chuckles and we roll out of bed. Bentley loans me some of his clothes since mine are covered in spunk. They're a bit big on me but they work, and I'm way too excited about the idea of wearing his things. They're soft, and comfortable, and they smell like him, which makes my cock twitch.

Everything is so relaxed as we mosey around the kitchen, him making us dinner and me going across the hall to grab a can of food for Marble and using one of Bentley's bowls to dump it in. She trots over right away and scarfs it down, then licks her chops and meows at me.

We settle on the sofa, eating the meal Bentley made, and turn on *Supernatural* again, sitting as close as humanly possible to each other. When our dishes are empty and our stomachs are full, we hold hands and snuggle up together, draping the blanket Bentley made over us.

When the episode ends and I go to start another one, Bentley squeezes my hand, and I look at him. "Stay," he says, and my heart pitter patters in my chest, because I'd love nothing more.

"Okay," I say with a huge grin on my face. "As long as you don't mind Marble staying, too, and probably sleeping on your bed again."

"If she doesn't stay, you don't either," he says, and I chuckle.

Bentley

Waking up with Alex's warm, naked body tucked against me feels like a dream. Especially in light of everything that's happened in the past few days. I was heartsick when he told me about his date, and jerking off to thoughts of him was the only thing I could do to cope, it seemed. I never dreamed he'd come home early from his date and barge in to find me fisting my cock with his name on my lips, and I was so damn mortified I'd have ignored him for an eternity if he hadn't shown up at my work and barged in on my session with Gloria. Thank God she was the one in there, because I doubt any other client would have responded so positively.

Fuck, having him here, now, I'm so glad he did what he did, because I could have missed out on all of this by being too fucking scared to face him.

My gaze falls to the corner of my bedroom where I moved Tux–the giant penguin Alex left on Stacy's doorstep the day we met–and I can't help smiling to myself, thinking of how we got where we are. I won't lie and say Stacy cheating on me didn't hurt, because it did. But the hurt is drowned out by how grateful I feel to have discovered things I might not have otherwise. If she hadn't done it, if Alex hadn't come to pick her up that day and found me instead, we wouldn't be here now. And if discovering my attraction to men, and having Alex both as my friend, and then my lover, are the only good things that come from my relationship with her, well then I think I did pretty well.

I look over at the picture of Gram on my nightstand and can practically hear her telling me, "It's about damn time." I wasn't really thinking about turning her picture around when I fell into bed and Alex climbed on top of me, but somehow I don't think she minds. I know how happy she'd be to know I've found someone like Alex. I sure do wish she could meet him, though the idea of the two of them in the same room is as frightening as it is heartwarming. I think they would be really good friends, and probably get up to some rather questionable activities, encouraging each other and egging each other on. I can picture her taunting him and him trying to get back at her and it not working out in his favor. The thought has me laughing, and I comb my fingers through his dark hair, making him stir.

"I like waking up with you next to me," he murmurs, and presses a kiss to my pec.

"I like waking up next to you, too," I tell him. He grins and his cheeks flush as I scoop up Marble from her place on top of me once again, and set her down on the floor, before I roll us over so that I'm on top of Alex.

He gasps, and then groans, thrusting up into me and making my already hard cock jerk. I'm already leaking obscenely, and I'm pretty sure the sheets will need to be changed because of it. I press kisses to his naked skin, his neck, and jaw, before making my way down his chest and abs. His dick is leaking and he groans when I pass it by and suck marks onto his obliques, before moving down to his thighs.

"Fuck," he breathes, when I suck and lick on that spot between his pelvis and his thigh. He bucks up and I move closer to his ass, pressing kisses, biting, and nibbling, and making him squirm.

"Fuck, you're being mean," he whines, and I grin at him, then move to his cock and press kisses to it, inhaling his honey and vanilla scent and feeling his dick twitch against me as he whimpers. I nuzzle it with my nose, then brush my nose against it gently, starting at his balls and moving up his shaft. "Holy fuck," he moans, his hands fisted in the sheets.

"I would very much like to try blowing you, if you're okay with that," I tell him, and he nods.

"God, yes. Please. I want that incredible mouth around me so bad."

I flush and grin, then lower my head once more and slide my tongue along his balls, before I suck one of them into my mouth. I've never tasted any man's balls before, but I find myself moaning around his as I suck. He mewls and thrusts upward again, and I move to his other ball, repeating the motion, before I trail my tongue along his shaft ever so slowly. When I reach the tip I lick his precum into my mouth. I'm not crazy about the taste but my desire to please him and to have his gorgeous cock in my mouth overrides my dislike of the salty essence, and honestly it's much more tolerable than swallowing a mouthful of spunk.

When he looks at me the way he does, his cheeks flushed and his eyes dark, nipples hard, his body trembling underneath me, I know there's no turning away.

"You don't have to if–" he starts, his words labored, but cuts himself off with the world's sexiest noise that's somewhere between a gasp and a wail when I take him in my mouth and moan around his head. I suckle on the head for a bit, and then swirl my tongue around it, the taste of him exploding on my tongue and making me ache for more as my dick jerks, and he lets out more desperate, needy noises.

Fuck, I've never gotten so turned on and felt so much satisfaction from going down on someone before. He grips my hair as I bob up and down on his shaft, taking him a bit deeper.

"Oh fuck, baby." I take him a bit deeper still, but my gag reflex kicks in so I move back up, gripping his shaft in my hand and stroking him while I suck on his dick, coming almost all the way off and sliding my tongue inside his slit as I move my hand along the base of his shaft. He undulates his hips, whimpering and writhing, shoving his dick further in and moaning. My eyes start to water as I gag on his length again, and I'm getting even harder at the knowledge that he can't help himself, thrusting into my mouth and making me choke on him. For whatever reason, gagging myself on his dick isn't nearly as erotic as him shoving himself down my throat as he grips my hair hard enough that a bolt of exquisite pleasure races to my balls. "Shit, baby, I'm gonna come," he warns me, releasing his grip on me. I pop all the way off and continue to stroke him hard and fast with my hand, staring into those gorgeous blue eyes even as tears slide down my face.

"Come, darling," I tell him. "I wanna wear your spunk so bad."

His eyes flare and he lets out a wail as he throws his head back and his dick pulses in my grip, his release coating my neck and chest. I reach down and jack myself as he lies, sated and looking so fucking beautiful. All it takes is a few strokes before my release shoots out to cover his cock and balls. I watch, a groan leaving me as it slides down his balls and onto his ass and thighs, some even getting in his crack. I pant, thoughts of getting my mouth on that ass making my dick twitch despite having just come.

Alex doesn't waste any time slicking his fingers up with my release and sucking them into his mouth. And as much as I don't want to swallow cum, watching him feast on my spunk like it's the best thing he's ever tasted is incredibly hot.

He gathers every last drop and swallows it down before he looks at me and fucking whimpers, beckoning me to him. I lean forward and he licks his own spunk from my body, swallowing it down and making me shiver with the noises he's making and the feel of his warm, wet tongue on my sensitive skin.

"Fuck, darling, you're doing things to me," I rasp. He

stares up at me, his chest rising and falling, running his fingers through my hair.

"You're so damn pretty, baby," he says, so much sincerity in his voice that another shiver races through me, and then he pulls me down for a kiss.

"Fuck, that was incredible," he pants, pulling away. "Your mouth is a fucking hoover, cowboy. Where'd you learn to suck cock like that?"

I grin and blush. "I've been practicing, too. You're not the only one who has been traumatizing bananas."

He laughs and pulls me down to him, wrapping his arms around me as we lie tangled in the sheets, the smells of sex and sweat and our combined body wash permeating the air and making me sigh in contentment.

Marble hops back on the bed and makes her way onto the pillow we're not using, and plops herself down.

Alex laughs. "You might never have your bed to yourself again, cowboy."

I tilt my head to look at him. "I'm okay with that," I say, and he flushes again, before I press a kiss to his jaw.

"I was thinking, since I'm off today, and you don't work until later, maybe I could take you out?"

He grins and bites his lip, his cheeks pinkening beautifully. "Yeah?" he says. "Like a date?"

I smile widely. "Exactly like a date, darling." I press more kisses to his jaw and neck and chest. "A late breakfast somewhere and then maybe find a place where we can walk around so I can hold your hand?"

"You don't need to go on a walk with me to hold my hand," he says. "You can do that any time you want."

I press another kiss to his pec. "Not where other people can see and know you're mine."

"Oh." His eyes heat. "You wanna show me off, cowboy?"

"Always," I say, and then press a kiss to his lips. He moans when my tongue slides into his mouth, and opens wider for me. Fuck, I could kiss him forever and never get tired of it. I love the way he melts into me, his mouth soft and pliant against mine, the little whimpers and moans he lets out when I nibble on his lower lip or the gasps I hear when my tongue tangles with his.

"Fuck," he breathes when I finally pull away. His eyes are lidded and his dick is hard again. I grin.

"We need to get up or we'll be in bed all day," he says. "And while that sounds kinda amazing, I am also starving."

I chuckle and kiss his lips once more before we climb out of bed and make our way to the bathroom to shower. We make out while jerking each other off, and then take the time to clean each other.

"I think," Alex says, as we dry off, "you should let me take you out instead because you haven't lived here long, and I can show you the town, as it were."

"All right, but I'm taking you out next time."

"Sounds fair."

Alex borrows my clothes so he can go across the hall and change. When he returns I'm already dressed in jeans and a T-shirt. He's grinning as he looks at me, his eyes bright, and my chest squeezes because I know I'm the one making him so fucking happy, and I hope I can keep doing it for a very long time.

We hold hands in the car, and are both grinning like love struck idiots the entire way to the restaurant. Alex takes us to a little mom and pop place, and when we arrive and get out of the car, he doesn't hesitate to grab my hand again, twining our fingers together as we walk inside. It smells incredible, like cooked eggs, bacon, and coffee, and my mouth waters.

The hostess leads us to a table and we sit. When I open

the menu I notice it's filled with southern dishes, and when I look at Alex he beams at me.

"Thought you might like a taste of Georgia, cowboy."

God, I'm so fucking crazy about this man. I order grits, home fries, and biscuits and gravy, and Alex gets waffles and a side of eggs. He also orders tea while I get coffee.

I'm realizing as we eat that there's no first date jitters, no worrying about making a good impression or trying to impress my date, no nerves at all, because it's him. And we already know each other, and are comfortable together. I've never been so at ease with someone before, or so utterly fucking happy.

After breakfast, Alex takes us to the Boston Public Garden where we take a swan boat ride, and then walk around the different paths, admiring the gorgeous greenery and the incredible monuments and fountains, all while keeping our hands clasped and our fingers twined. The weather is gorgeous, a slight breeze in the air, and the smell of flowers tickles my nose.

"It's really lovely here," I say, and Alex smiles.

"It is. This is where my parents got engaged, and married."

"Yeah? It would be beautiful." I squeeze his hand in mine, then bring it up to my lips and press a kiss to it, and he blushes crimson while biting his lip, then squeezes my hand back.

"I really enjoyed our first date," I tell him when we get back in the car. "Thank you."

"I really enjoyed our first date, too," he says, then leans over to kiss me, and I meet him halfway.

"Mmmm," we both moan as the kiss quickly becomes more heated.

"Home," Alex says, pulling away, his pupils blown and

his voice husky. I can see his dick straining against the zipper of his jeans, and mine is doing the same.

"Agreed," I rasp.

We've barely made it out of the car before we're kissing each other feverishly. We somehow manage to get the door to the building open and then keep kissing as we make our way to my apartment. We break apart long enough for me to unlock the door, and then we're stumbling inside and Alex is pinning me up against the door, both of us breathing heavily, reaching for each other, groping, gasping, and moaning as our tongues tangle and we desperately try to undress each other.

I manage to get Alex's shirt off and he does the same with mine, before we're on each other again. He grips my dick through my pants and squeezes, and I jolt, before thrusting into his hand. God, that feels good. I reach out and do the same to him, my moans getting louder at the feel of his hard cock in my hand and him rutting against me furiously.

Alex's eagerness and exuberance is making me that much harder, and he's unzipping my pants and sliding his hand inside, gripping my dick through my underwear, toying with the copious wet spot that's formed and rubbing the head of my dick with his thumb.

"Mmmnn," I whimper into his mouth as even more precum leaks out and he strokes me through my underwear, the friction from my briefs driving me insane, sending bolts of pleasure straight to my dick and making it twitch on each upstroke.

"Fuck, baby, I love the sounds you make," he purrs as he grips me a bit harder and presses kisses to my neck, making me tilt my head back to grant him better access, practically begging him not to stop. "Don't stop touching me, baby," he tells me as he thrusts into my hand again and again while sucking his marks onto my skin and making me tremble with pleasure. "This feels so damn good. We're gonna come like this, okay? Wanna feel this gorgeous cock pulsing in my hand when you soak yourself. Got it?"

Fuck, who am I to tell him no when everything about this is making me so damn hard? Who knew he has such a fucking dirty mouth?

"Shit, Alex," I moan, my grip on his dick tightening, my movements getting faster and harder as I thrust into his hand and he thrusts into mine.

When he reaches up and starts playing with my nipple I know it's game over. And when he sucks on my neck again at the same time that he pinches my hard nipple, I fucking shout as my orgasm barrels up on me and I shoot load after load of cum into his waiting, eager hand. When I feel his dick pulsing in my grip only a second later, another shot of cum joins the first, and I'm a boneless fucking mess against the door when he, without missing a beat, scrambles out of his clothes and then pulls my pants and underwear down as he sinks to his knees, his cock and balls covered in his release.

"Pick your feet up," he tells me, and I do. He slides my pants away, but picks up my cum-soaked underwear and proceeds to lick them clean while I stare at him, dumb-struck. Holy shit.

He swallows and licks his lips, then leans forward and proceeds to clean me off with his tongue, swallowing every last bit he can get and moaning like a whore when he does.

"Jesus, you have no idea how dirty you sound when you do that," I rasp, my breath hitching slightly as he swipes his tongue over my sensitive skin and I grip his hair.

His gaze meets mine and he smirks at me. "You have no idea how fucking incredible you taste." He presses kiss after kiss to my flagging erection, making me squirm, but unable to get enough at the same time. It's blissfully painful for him to be touching my oversensitive dick, and I want to pull away at the same time that I want to push forward and beg for more.

"Shit, darling," I groan as my dick twitches against his lips. He turns his face and brushes his cheek against it over and over, then runs the tip of his nose along the shaft before going back to kissing it, and I'm fucking trembling as I gasp and whimper.

"I can't get enough of your cock, baby. So fucking perfect."

When I glance down I notice his own dick is half hard again, and it makes mine perk up a little more just at the sight.

"Alex," I gasp, as he licks a stripe up my cock, and I nearly wail at the pleasure pain that spikes through my body.

"I wanna make you come again, cowboy," he tells me, those beautiful blue eyes staring up at me, gaze darkened, his hand on my half hard dick as he rubs it against his cheek once again, practically purring as he does. "I want you to come in my mouth this time." He kisses my cock, then looks at me again. "Can I blow you, baby?" Another kiss and my body trembles. The idea of him sucking me off right now sounds equally erotic and utterly torturous, and I find myself nodding.

His eyes darken even further and he reaches down to scoop some of his own cum from his cock and balls, before gripping my dick and stroking me, using his cum as lube. Holy hell.

The sight of his cum coating my cock and the feel of his hand around me has my dick thickening in his grip even as I whimper at the overstimulation.

"Fuck, such a pretty cock," he murmurs, and I groan as

my dick jerks. Oh, fuck, that was painful, and the sensation sends a shiver down my spine. He licks a stripe up my shaft again, before he slides the tip of his tongue in the slit and I nearly scream even as my dick spasms. I bite down on my fist to keep from crying out so loud his entire family can hear me. God, that's so good. So fucking painful and so damn amazing.

"Look at me, beautiful," he says, then swirls his tongue around the head of my cock. My chest is rising and falling and my skin is slick with sweat as I look down at him, panting. I know exactly what he's doing. The way he's talking to me, telling me how pretty I am while he plays with my dick, and I fucking love every second of it. "I want your eyes on me while I suck your pretty cock."

I nod, and he takes me in his mouth, making me hiss and moan. One of his hands grips my hip and the other grips my shaft, stroking me as he takes me deeper still. Fuck, whatever he's been doing to those bananas has definitely paid off because this feels incredible.

He moans around my cock and I can't get over how utterly blissed out he is at having my dick in his mouth, like this is giving him just as much pleasure as it's giving me. He sucks, and licks, and strokes, making my thighs quake as I stare at him, my hand fisted in his dark waves. Then he's crouching a bit lower and the hand on my hip is moving down to his discarded briefs. He gathers more of his cum on his finger, before pushing up on his knees again, my dick sliding a little deeper still into his warm wet mouth, while his finger moves around to my backside. I gasp and jolt, my hand flying away from my mouth and my dick pushing even further inside him when he slides his finger along my ass crack.

He gags and pulls back slightly, looking up at me, his cum slick finger settled just above my asshole. Fuck, it'll be the first time any part of him is inside me, and God, I want it so bad. I nod and he hums around my cock, sucking as he moves his finger just a smidge, and rests it against my hole. I'm fucking shaking at the sensation of his mouth around me and his finger pressed gently against my entrance. Holy hell. How does it feel this good?

"Alex," I gasp. "Please?" I don't even realize I've started thrusting, my hand still gripping his hair as I support myself on the door, until he gags again. "Shit, sorry," I say, stopping myself. But he just hums and circles his finger before pressing it more firmly against my hole.

I almost fucking whimper when he pops off my cock. "Fuck, you're making me so damn hard," he rumbles, and it's all I can do not to hump the air in front of his face, shamelessly begging him to take me in his mouth again. "You're sexy as sin, baby." He swirls his finger around my hole again and then slowly, gently presses inside. Oh, fuck, that's good, and he's barely inside me at all. I need more and I can't wait.

I thrust my hips forward. "Please?" I beg again.

"In a second," he tells me, and I want to fucking snarl at him. "I want my finger inside you more first, so I can just hold it in you and you can fuck it while I suck you off. I wanna choke on you, baby. Don't hold back, okay?"

Fuck. I nod and grip his hair tighter as his finger slips in a bit more, and he stares up at me. "God, you're so damn beautiful," he murmurs, and I whimper as my cock jerks and my hole spasms around his finger. His eyes flare.

"Alex." I grip my dick to keep myself from coming. Holy fuck. "Please?" I'm going to fucking cry if he doesn't suck my dick right fucking now.

He pushes his finger all the way inside me, and I let out a wail as he crooks it and hits my prostate, crying out his name again.

"Fuck, yes," he breathes. "That's it, fuck my finger, pretty baby." I move back on his finger, moaning at the incredible pleasure, my dick and balls bouncing as I do. Another wail leaves me when he takes me into his mouth once again, and I remember what he told me, fucking his mouth with my cock and chasing his finger with my ass, pleasure overtaking me in only seconds, making me howl his name again as I shoot my release down his throat, my ass clenching hard around his finger. It's not until I've fallen back against the door and my dick has slipped free of his mouth, his finger no longer inside me, that I open my eyes and realize I still have a death grip on his hair. He looks up at me with heavy lidded eyes, tears streaking his cheeks, snot on his face, and my cum sliding down his chin.

"Fuck, are you okay?" I pant. "Did I hurt you?"

He grabs his discarded shirt and uses it to wipe his face, and I see that his dick is once again covered in his spunk and that there's jizz on my floor.

"You came again, too?"

He nods, flushing. "Yeah. Sorry about the mess."

I sink to my knees and grip his face in my hands before kissing him deeply. His hands reach up to grip my face in turn as he grunts and kisses me back. Fuck, he tastes like me, but also like strawberries and maple syrup from the waffles he had earlier today and my dick is trying very hard to spring back to life, but there's no way I have a third orgasm in me right now.

"That was incredible," I tell him, pulling away. "I've never had a blow job like that. You can stick your finger up my ass any time."

He laughs. "I'll put anything up your ass you want me to, baby."

Chapter Eighteen

Alex

Three days later I'm still on cloud nine from everything that's happened recently with Bentley. I've been sleeping over at his place and only returning to my apartment when I wake up and he's left for work. I told him I didn't want to wake him by coming in late after my shifts at the bar were over, but he insisted he wanted me to, and told me he'd leave the door unlocked for me.

Every single night I enter his room to see Marble lying at his feet, or curled up on his back as he hugs the pillow underneath him, or lying on his stomach, since Bentley seems to be a rotisserie chicken when he sleeps. I climb into bed and snuggle up next to him, breathing him in, and letting his warmth envelope me. Everything about it feels so right, and I can't wipe the smile from my face, though I'm not really trying that hard.

We've made love as much as possible over the past few days with our schedules being off, though we still haven't had penetrative sex, and I'm getting more and more eager to try it with him. Getting off with him is incredible no matter how we do it, but I'm craving that closeness. I'm also worried about doing it right and making it good for him, which is probably why I haven't brought it up yet. I feel like there's probably things I don't know and should, regardless of whether I am topping or bottoming. And I don't know if Bentley would want to top or bottom, which, wow, that's not something I ever thought I would be wondering when it came to my bed partners, or myself, but I kinda love it.

I decide I've been putting this off for too long, and if I ever want to make anal sex a thing with us, I better get a bit braver, so I take out my phone as I sit with Marble on my lap, petting her, after having gone for a run and showered.

I chuckle when I see I have a text from Peyton.

Peyton: Bentley hasn't stopped smiling for two days. Glad you guys finally got your heads out of your asses

Me: Lol, same

Peyton: I guess I should give you the best friend speech, so here it is. I don't like saying "don't hurt him" because that's not realistic. You're human beings. You will hurt each other at some point, but I've never seen him happier, so be good to him, or I'll have to burn every single copy of Little Women you own (Bentley says it's your favorite), and that's coming from someone who loves books, which tells you how much he means to me

Me: Got it, and I'll do my very best, I promise

Peyton: thank you, kissy face emoji

I grin when I think of our work out yesterday morning, and how amazing it was to be able to ogle him without worrying about him finding out, just openly staring at him in his shorts and tank top, watching the sweat slide down his neck and making him blush like crazy, then winking at him and seeing his cheeks darken even further as he tried to keep the huge smile from taking over his face. I grin even more when I think about the shower we shared at the gym afterwards, and the handjobs we exchanged. It felt kinda dirty touching each other like that in a public space, forcing ourselves to be as quiet as possible, and we both seemed to really like that. I'm hella curious to find out what else makes my cowboy sing as we get to spend more time with each other and explore things in the bedroom.

Me: Hey you have a minute?

Little bro: I'm meeting Pierre for lunch, but I have a few minutes until he gets here, what's up?

I told Tommy Monday night that Bentley and I are together and I even got a smile out of him. It meant a lot, especially since I know he and Pierre are still struggling. He says they still haven't heard anything from Cyrus. Though Tommy did say Pierre seems to be doing a bit better the last week or so, and he thinks it's in part to how much time he's been spending with Bentley in the evenings when Tommy is at work. I love that Bentley and Pierre are friends now, too. Bentley is so damn sweet, and I don't think he knows it, but he's really easy to talk to.

Me: I need some help

Little bro: with?

*Me: um, so we haven't done *insert peach emoji* stuff yet even though I'm pretty sure we both really want to*

Little bro: okay, tmi, dude

Me: ugh, come on, please help me? I've watched porn but it's not exactly quality learning material so I can't go off of it, and I've read some stuff online too and used some toys, but I just want to make sure I don't fuck it up. I want it to be good for him, for both of us. Please? I don't have anyone else to talk to about this stuff

Little bro: okay, fine, what do you want to know?

Me: I don't know, what do I need to know?

Little bro: if you have used toys you probably have a pretty good handle on it already, just make sure you use lots of lube, go slow, stretch as much as you can first, and talk to each other. And don't freak out if it hurts, that's normal, as long as it doesn't hurt the whole time. Also remember that if you don't like it, that's okay, too

I breathe out and type, my body relaxing a bit.

Me: Okay, thanks. While we're on the subject, is there anything we should know about, like things we may not know or things that we should try?

Little bro: Lord have mercy. Look, I'm not gonna go into detail about stuff, but I'll give you some terms to look up. A lot of stuff, like if you guys are into the kinky shit, isn't specific to dudes and some of it that is you are probably already doing without realizing there's a name for it

Me: okay, thanks

Little bro: I can't believe I'm typing these out while I wait to meet my husband

Me: I love you

Little bro: shut up, you just made it weirder

Me: lol, sorry

Little bro: okay, look up frotting, rimming, snowballing, and docking

Me: got it thank you, seriously

Little bro: I would say any time but that would be a lie

Little bro: you're gonna be fine, just remember to communicate, gotta go, Pierre is here

When I get off the phone with Tommy I text Bentley. He's at work so it might be a while before he responds, but I can't go a whole day without hearing from him. I miss him like crazy when we're not together.

Me: Miss you, my beautiful cowboy

I grin, knowing he'll react so beautifully to my words. I fucking love that telling him he's pretty arouses him, and I don't think I'll ever get tired of it. Jesus, I know I've turned into a fucking sap when it comes to him, but I am one hundred percent okay with it. We still text each other gifs and memes and our silly The Rock and penguin messages, but our texts in general lately have been a bit more mushy in nature, and a bit more sexual, too.

I don't get his reply until half an hour later when I assume he's either on lunch break or in between clients.

My Cowboy: miss you, too, we watching Supernatural tonight?

Me: i hope so, but maybe after other activities?

My Cowboy: hmmm, what did you have in mind?

Me: It involves you and me, and very little clothing

My Cowboy: very little?

Me: Okay, no clothing

My Cowboy: I like the sound of that

Me: You been working on your list?

My Cowboy: yeah, I think it's done for now, we gonna share?

Me: I'd like to, and I thought maybe we could try something we haven't yet?

My Cowboy: such as?

My cheeks heat, but I manage to type out: *Penetration? If that's something you want*

My Cowboy: yes

I chuckle, a wide grin on my face at how quickly that answer came: *Okay, good, me, too. I'll see you when you get home. Meet at your place? I'll have dinner ready.*

My Cowboy: sounds good

I take some time to look up the different terms Tommy gave me, and my cock is hard just reading about them. Rimming sounds hot, but I wonder if Bentley will go for it. I'd love tasting that sweet ass if he'd let me. God, I can picture it now and it's making me salivate. Docking also sounds amazing. When I find out what snowballing is, though, I know that's not going to work. Bentley seems to enjoy blowing me quite a bit, but he does not want to swallow either of our spunk, and that's fine with me because it means I get more of it. Frotting is the last one I look up and realize we've already been doing it, I just didn't know there was a name for it.

I take some time to look over my list of things to maybe try with him and make sure I'm not forgetting anything. I add rimming and docking to the list. I'm so damn hard just thinking about doing these things with Bentley that I find myself sliding my pants and underwear down and gripping my shaft. Marble looks at me from her perch on the windowsill. *Meow.*

I start to stroke myself but pause. "Don't look." Marble has seen me jerk off more times than I can count, but she hops down, stretches, and then moves to her cat tower while I grip my dick, moaning and picturing Bentley's incredible body, remembering the way it feels when his naked skin is against mine. I'm coming with a shout moments later and then snapping a picture of my cum soaked hand and dick and sending it to my boyfriend.

Me: I couldn't wait. Got so hard just thinking about you, baby. There's no reply right away, but my phone buzzes an hour later. His text has me grinning like an idiot.

My Cowboy: Damn, darling. Love that cock. Can't wait to get home to my man

Several hours later Bentley is underneath me, our dinner abandoned on the stove. Fuck, I knew I missed him, knew I wanted him with every fiber of my being, but when he came home and I felt his arms around me, his lips against my neck and his beard brushing against my naked skin, his ocean and rain scent washing over me and making my cock jerk, it was all I could do to get us to the bedroom before I started climbing him like a tree. Don't get me wrong, I'm one hundred percent on board with kitchen sex, too, but not for our first time.

I'm so damn hard right now as I grip his hair and kiss him, straddling his lap, our cocks lined up and brushing against each other as I move, desperate and needy, his naked skin setting my body on fire and making me moan with each glorious brush of our hard cocks. His precum mixing with mine is making us glide so perfectly together, the wetness just adding to the incredible sensation. God, I love how fucking wet he gets.

"Fuck, I want you," he breathes between kisses.

I break away reluctantly, knowing that soon we'll be joined even more than we are now, and my body trembles at the thought, and the desire raging inside me.

"Now?" I say, and he nods. I move off of him for the brief second it takes me to grab the lube and condom from the bedside table. "You wanna stretch me, or should I do it?"

He blinks. "What?"

I blink back. "Stretching. We have to stretch before we can do anal."

He flushes. "Yeah, I know, darling, but the bottom is the one who needs to be stretched and that's me."

I blink again. "That's me, baby. I'm bottoming."

"No, I'm bottoming."

I narrow my eyes. "Why do you get to bottom?"

"Because I want to. Why do you?"

"I want to."

"I've been pretending with dildos for months, and I want the real thing."

"Me, too."

He huffs, and it's kinda adorable, but I'm not telling him that, or letting those pouty lips and those big blue eyes get to me. So what if he's sexy as sin, I am standing my ground on this. I want that cock buried in my ass, goddamn it.

"Okay, there's only one way to settle this," I say. "The Winchester way."

He blinks again and I hold one hand out, palm up, with the other hand over it in a fist.

"Really?" he says, his lips quirking in a grin that is not at all sexy.

"Absolutely. Let's go, big boy. We're gonna rock, paper, scissors our way to pound town."

He laughs now and holds out his hands like mine.

We hit our fists against the palm of our hands three times and then hold them out. I groan when Bentley is scissors and I'm paper.

"Damn it," I sulk.

He grins.

"Shut up," I mumble and he laughs again, then grabs my arm and pulls me to him before gripping my face and bringing me down for a toe-curling kiss.

"You can bottom," he says, and I smile.

"Yeah?"

"Yeah. But I get to bottom next time."

"Deal."

He chuckles and grabs me in his arms before rolling us so he's on top of me. Fuck, I love it when he does that. Love being pinned underneath him, his warm weight on top of me, his firm body against mine. He kisses me several more times before he pulls back and grabs a pillow, sliding it under my hips and then grabbing the lube. He stares at me as I spread my legs. "Goddamn, darling," he rumbles, his voice thick and filled with arousal. "You look mighty fine like that."

I can't help my grin because I don't think his accent has ever been more pronounced than it is now, and I fucking love it. I love that being with me, looking at me, touching me, does this to him. "Come and get me, cowboy," I murmur, my hole fluttering in anticipation.

His eyes flare, but before he pops the lid on the lube bottle I stop him. "Wait. What if you use your precum?" He looks at me. "To stretch me," I say.

His eyes darken. "Are you sure?"

I nod. "I got tested after my last girlfriend, and I'm negative. You?"

"I got tested after Stacy." He licks his lips and his cheeks flush. "What about condoms?"

A shiver races down my spine at the idea of Bentley being inside me without any barriers. I've never done that before, had that kind of intimacy with someone. Never really wanted to, even if it had been an option. "God, I'd love nothing more than to have your bare cock inside me, baby. Your spunk filling me up. But I don't think I'm ready for that quite yet. I'm sorry."

He shakes his head. "Don't apologize. You never have to explain yourself to me. I want you to be comfortable, always."

Fuck, my heart swells with fondness and affection for this incredible man, and my hole flutters as he drops the lube bottle, coating his fingers in his ample precum instead, before leaning over me, pressing kisses to my neck and jaw as his finger circles my pucker and I let out a string of whimpers, gasping when he sucks on the sensitive spot between my neck and shoulder while tapping his finger against my hole. "Relax for me, baby," he says. "Let me in. I'm gonna make you feel so good."

Fuck. I spread my legs wider and whimper even more as his finger slips inside. He continues to make his way down my body, sucking, kissing, nipping, leaving his marks on my skin as he moves inside me, going deeper and then moving out and back in, driving me wild as my nerve endings light up and my body sings. God, even his finger is so much better than the sex toys I used, and the contrast of his beard brushing against my naked skin as his lips ravish me is sending little bolts of pleasure straight to my balls.

I've had Bentley's marks all over me for days now, and I can't get enough of them. My neck, torso, belly, thighs, all covered in his love bites. The only place I haven't had them yet is my ass and I'm determined to fix that soon.

I moan and grip his hair as he reaches my cock and presses kiss after kiss to my shaft, driving me wild and making my cock ache, twitching against his lips as he tortures me in the most delicious way, his finger crooking inside me and making me shout. I don't have time to recover before he's taking my cock in his mouth and sucking at the same time that he adds a second finger to my hole and starts scissoring them. My hole is wet and covered in his precum and I fucking love it.

Shit. He's moaning around my shaft as he moves inside me and I gasp and pant and clutch his shoulders, writhing underneath him.

"Fuck, baby, don't stop."

He growls and takes me deeper into his mouth, bobbing up and down on my cock while his fingers stretch me, pegging my sweet spot intermittently. Not enough to get me to come but enough to keep me on the edge, begging and whimpering.

God, I can't get enough of his fingers inside me and his warm, wet mouth encasing my cock, but I want something else, too. "Kiss me," I beg. "Fuck, baby, please kiss me."

He pops off my cock, saliva sliding down his chin, his pupils blown, and my breath catches at how incredible he looks. Then he's capturing my lips with his again and adding a third finger inside me, nudging my prostate again and again as he readies me for his gorgeous cock.

I'm whimpering and moaning like a fucking whore as he kisses me, and the feel of his hard, wet dick sliding against mine is almost enough to send me over the edge, especially when he deepens the kiss on a growl, sucking on my tongue, his precum coating my cock and making the slide that much more delicious.

"Fuck," I pant, pulling away. "I'm gonna come if you don't stop, baby. And I want that pretty cock of yours inside me when that happens. I want to come so hard on your dick, cowboy."

He growls again and then kisses me once more before he slides his fingers out of me and tears the condom open. Fuck, I can barely breathe as I watch him him sliding it over his cock. Bentley is not small, and I can't help feeling a twinge of nervousness as he slicks up his shaft with lube and positions himself at my entrance. Fuck, this is real. This is happening. I'm going to have another guy's dick in me. And not just any guy, my best friend. And while his size is a bit intimidating, I feel nothing but rightness at the knowledge that it's him about to fuck me. I don't want anyone else but him. His cock inside me, his lips on mine, his hands caressing my bare skin. Sex isn't something I've ever taken lightly, and being here with him, knowing I can trust him to take care of me, body and soul, is everything.

"I'm ready," I tell him, my throat constricting. "I need you."

He gazes at me like I'm the most amazing thing he's ever seen, so much warmth and tenderness in those beautiful blue eyes. He leans down with his hands braced on either side of me, and kisses me deeply once more, as he pushes inside me. "Breathe, darling," he says softly as my body tenses when he's barely breached me. Fuck, he's huge. "You can do it," he coos, pressing kisses to my face and neck, then reaching down to grip my shaft and stroke it gently. My body trembles, and he pushes in a bit further, making me hiss. He pauses and strokes me some more. "You're okay," he says, nuzzling my neck. "Do you want me to stop? We don't have to do this if it's too painful."

I shake my head. "No, don't stop, just keep going slow. I want this. I want you," I assure him. My body is covered in sweat and my skin is flushed, my hole feels like a battering ram is being shoved inside it, and I know I'm trembling slightly, but I want this man inside me more than I have ever wanted anything in my life.

He nods. "Tell me if you change your mind." He kisses my neck and jaw again and again as he strokes me and pushes in a little further still. I take deep breaths and let them out a couple of times as I cling to him, my body relaxing, accepting the intrusion little by little. He pulls out slightly and I grip his arms, shaking my head, and whimpering.

"What's wrong?" he asks.

"Don't go," I plead. He smiles and kisses me.

"I'm not going anywhere, just thought I'd get more lube. I thought it might help."

I flush and nod, and he dribbles more lube over his cock before pushing slowly back in. I sigh as he pushes in a bit more, the sting having lessened.

"Better?" he asks, and I nod. "More?" I nod again.

He keeps stroking my shaft and pressing kisses to my skin the entire time he pushes inside me. "Fuck, you're really big," I tell him, taking another deep breath.

"You're doing so good, though, darling," he coos, pressing kisses to my forehead now, and my nose. "You got this, just a bit farther."

I nod, soaking in his sweet words and the press of his lips and his warm hand still gripping my cock.

"For what it's worth, you feel fucking amazing," he

rumbles, his breaths panting over my face and his big body trembling. "And I swear I'll make you feel so damn good, too, baby."

I shiver and let out another breath as he bottoms out inside me. The burn is almost non-existent now as I grip him and breathe, soaking up the knowledge that he's inside me, feeling so completely full. Holy fuck. My eyes close as he rests his forehead to mine.

"You okay?" he asks, and I nod as my body quivers. Even as we still for a brief moment, soaking up the feeling of being joined in this incredibly intimate way, I feel the need for him to move, to fuck me, to claim me.

"Fuck me," I breathe, opening my eyes and staring into his. "Please fuck me, baby?"

He presses a few more kisses to my cheeks and nose and jaw as he rotates his hips a little, then slowly moves back and presses forward again, and fuck, just that small amount of movement, my body relaxed and ready for him, his dick owning me, has me gasping in pleasure and clinging to him.

His eyes darken, and he groans. "Did that feel good?"

I nod. "Yes. Do it again."

He pulls back and shoves forward again, this time with a bit more force, and my body shakes as I toss my head back on a loud moan. "God, don't stop, Bentley," I tell him, and he doesn't, his hips moving slowly back and forth, brushing along my nerve endings and hitting my sweet spot over and over in torturously slow and painfully exquisite thrusts. I grip his arms as he moves and my whimpers and cries of pleasure fill the room. He picks up his pace slowly and I grip him harder as he thrusts deeper and faster, pleasure overwhelming me as his cock spears inside me and his firm body moves against mine, his stomach the perfect friction against my aching cock.

"Goddamn, baby, you feel amazing," he rasps, his balls

slapping against my ass. I open my eyes to see him gazing at me, his skin flushed and his hair falling loose from his messy bun, his eyes dark.

"You're so fucking beautiful," I murmur, and his body shudders, his cock spasming inside me and making me gasp. His hand flies up to grip my throat and my cock jerks between us.

"Shit, you're gonna make me come, talking to me like that," he says, tightening his grip just a bit more. My dick jerks again and a rumble leaves him as his thrusting changes, from fast and hard, to deep and slow, and oh fuck, that's good. Every press of his dick against my prostate is making me see stars, his grip on my throat only heightening my pleasure. My eyes roll back in my head as his hand tightens even further and I buck up into him.

"Please?" I gasp, not even sure what I'm asking for. He grips my throat a little higher and slots his mouth over mine as he picks up his thrusts again, and I moan into his mouth as his tongue fucks my mouth and his dick fucks my hole. I grip his hair and wrap my legs around his waist, shoving my heels into his ass and making him shorten his thrusts. God, that's incredible.

My whimpers and whines pick up as he sucks on my tongue and pistons inside me. Pleasure rolls over me in waves, and I'm whimpering and tightening my grip on him as I come hard, my cock spilling my release between us as my ass clenches around him. He growls and a second later I feel his warmth filling the condom deep inside me, before he collapses on top of me, both of us breathing heavily.

"Wow," I manage after a second of holding him to me. He chuckles.

"Yeah, wow." He lifts his head and looks at me. "Are you okay? Did I hurt you?"

I brush a strand of golden hair away from his face and

tuck it behind his ear, smiling like a lunatic at him. "I'm fine, cowboy. You were amazing. God, I get so hard when you grab my throat."

He grins and presses a kiss to my chest. "Clean up, dinner, and then lists, or lists first, then dinner?"

"Dinner first, and *Supernatural*. I'm starving."

He kisses my chest again and then slowly pulls out of me. Fuck, after having him inside me and feeling so full it's hard to let him go, and I know it won't be long before I'm begging him to fuck me again.

We clean off, dress and head to the kitchen and our abandoned meal.

After eating and watching *Supernatural* with Marble curled up on Bentley's lap, we get our phones out and I snuggle up against him on the couch as we share what we want to try in bed. I tell Bentley about my conversation with Tommy and he blushes, burying his face in my hair. God, I love it when he does that.

When I explain what docking and rimming are, he blushes even deeper but nods, biting his lip, when I ask if he wants to try them. I tell him I definitely want him to keep grabbing my throat and marking me and he grins, pressing a kiss to the side of my head.

"Anything you wanted to try that I didn't mention?" I ask, nuzzling his jaw with my nose. God, just a couple of hours after we fucked and I'm already so desperate for him again. I can't remember ever being so horny for anyone else in my entire life, but this kind, tender, beautiful man just does it for me.

"I uh..." he starts, but then pauses, and I can tell he's a little tense, a little nervous, maybe?

"What is it?" I ask, looking at him. "No matter what it is, I promise I won't make fun of you or be grossed out. I want to know what you want. You have some kinky shit in mind, hit me with it, baby."

He chuckles and the tension in his body subsides quite a bit, but his cheeks are still rosy. "Ikindofwanttotrywearingpantiesandhavingyouspankme," he mumbles incoherently into my hair.

I chuckle and move away a little so he's forced not to hide against me. "What was that?" I ask.

He sighs, his gaze on his lap, and I grip his hand, giving it a squeeze.

He meets my eyes and swallows. His words are barely a whisper but they're clear. "I want to try wearing panties and having you spank me. Not necessarily together."

I can't help it. My eyes widen. But if he thinks I'm horrified or repulsed he couldn't be further from the truth. "Really?" I ask, and he nods, biting his lip again.

"I have kind of wanted to try it for a while, but I never had the courage to say anything in any of my previous relationships. I didn't feel safe enough."

My chest squeezes. "But you feel safe enough with me?"

He nods.

"That really means a lot to me," I say, squeezing his hand again. "Thank you for trusting me with that. I would love to see my sexy cowboy in some pretty lace panties. I think they would look sexy as fuck on that tight ass of yours. And I am more than willing to try spanking you. Maybe we can mix it with the rimming."

He nods and smiles, burying his face in my neck this time and making me chuckle. He starts to kiss and suck on my exposed flesh and I moan, tilting my head back. My dick is already rock hard and leaking precum when he grips it in his hand and squeezes, making me almost shriek as I jolt.

I try to talk through him stroking my dick through my

pants as he marks me again and again. "Is...nnnnn....is there anything else... you wanted to try?"

"No," he rumbles, his previous shyness gone as he nuzzles my jaw and presses kisses there, before sliding his hand down my pants and gripping me through my briefs. "But I would very much like to try that rimming thing you were mentioning."

"Now?" I ask as I fall onto my back and he hovers over me. Having abandoned my aching cock, he uses his hand to lift my shirt ever so slightly before he kisses and sucks on the bare skin right above the waistband of my sweats.

"Mmmm," is his reply as he raises the shirt a bit more and continues to suck his marks on my belly and torso, making me gasp and squirm, my dick twitching over and over as he works his way up my body, darting his tongue out to swipe along one hardened nipple before taking it between his teeth and tugging.

"Shit!" I cry out as precum oozes out of my cock and gathers on my underwear, my back arching. Bentley releases my nipple from between his teeth, then licks it, before sucking it into his mouth, and the sight is so fucking erotic that when he moans around my nipple like it's his fucking air and he can't get enough, I have to grab my dick and squeeze it to keep from coming. "Fuck, baby, I need to get naked. I need you so bad."

He hums, pressing a few more kisses to my skin before he sits back and lets me strip. As soon as I'm naked I bring him down for another kiss. He's fully clothed and his dick is tenting his pants so beautifully.

He grins, then presses more kisses to my heated skin in between words. "You gonna give me your ass, darling? Or do I have to beg for it? You gonna let me taste that pretty pussy? I had my cock inside it earlier. That wasn't enough for you? You want my tongue inside it, too?"

Oh, fuck. What did he just call my hole? How is my sweet, tender Viking of a man so fucking dirty? Add that to the list because my body lit up at that, and my hole is spasming, making me spread my legs and whine as I grip my dick and stroke it. I can't get over how he can make me melt with his care and affection one minute and have me ready to come from that filthy mouth the next.

"You liked that, didn't you, baby?" he purrs, nuzzling my neck with his nose and making me shake as his finger skates down my dick, along my balls, and over my taint, before stopping at my hole. I whimper, then gasp as he taps his finger against my entrance. He looks down at me as he circles my pucker. Another whimper leaves me when he moves his finger and starts to pull his pants and underwear down.

"Wait," I say. "Use lube this time and leave your pants on. I wanna see how wet you are when we're done." He blushes and nods, then scurries to the bedroom for the lube.

"What about your couch?" I say when he returns seconds later, slicking up his fingers, even though I'm already spreading wider for him, desperate for any part of him to touch me, to be inside me, to make me feel good.

"I have a shampooer," he says, his voice husky, and I can't help but laugh at how serious he is. "I've had to use it a few times," he admits with a flush. His fingers find my entrance again and he circles it a few more times, driving me wild with need, before he pushes inside me, making me moan and spread even wider for him. "God, you like being filled don't you, darling?" he rasps. "Like having your cunt played with."

My breath leaves me on a shudder, my hole spasming, and I grip my dick to keep from coming at his words. Why the hell does that make me respond so strongly? "Bentley," I whine. "Please? I need you to eat me. Suck on my pussy, baby. Tell me how good I taste."

His eyes darken and his nostrils flare. But instead of sliding out of me, he inserts another finger and plays with me some more, scissoring his fingers, pegging my prostate, moving in and out slowly. It's fucking torture, and it's fucking incredible. My dick is oozing precum onto my belly and his sweats are straining with his erection. I only wish I could see how fucking wet he is. How fucking wet I make him.

"You want my mouth on you, darling?" he asks, that accent of his stronger than ever, turning me on even more.

I can't speak so I just nod repeatedly and whimper again and again. When he slides his fingers out of me I can't decide if I'm relieved or not, but when he growls, "Get on your hands and knees," my hole flutters wildly and I gasp, gripping my cock again. I yelp when he slaps my thigh. "Don't keep me waiting, baby."

I stare at him for a brief second before I roll over and present my ass to him, my top half bent over. I hear a deep rumble leave his chest and then his hands are gripping and kneading my ass cheeks. Fuck, it feels so good. I love it when he grabs my ass and we haven't done a lot of it yet. I push my ass back, chasing the feeling and he chuckles and grips my ass cheeks harder, making me moan. "God, that's so good, baby."

"Love this ass, darling," he purrs, then leans over and buries his face in my crack, inhaling deeply. Holy fuck, that's hot. "Mmmm, I don't much care for spunk, but this, baby, this is heaven."

I shiver as he presses kisses to my ass cheeks, right next to my pucker, then moves outward, kissing all over both cheeks before he starts to lick, suck and nibble. God, yes.

"Mark me," I beg. "Please, baby, I want your marks all over my ass."

He growls and bites down hard on my cheek, making me cry out, before he licks over the stinging flesh, then kisses it. He does it again and again and again until I'm fucking sobbing from how incredible it feels and desperate for him to play with my pucker. My cock is throbbing and the couch has a rather large wet spot from where my precum is leaking onto it.

"I need your mouth on my cunt," I gasp through my tears. Shit I've never cried during sex before but this is so much more intense than anything I've ever experienced. It's overwhelming. And I'm not embarrassed or ashamed to cry in front of him.

Bentley hums and presses a few soft kisses to my aching backside before he spreads my cheeks wider and swipes his tongue along my hole. I wail as tears slide down my cheeks, my body shaking with how incredible it feels. "More," I sob. "Please."

"Jesus, you're making me so fucking hard, sweetheart," he growls. "This cunt is so fucking delicious." My cock jerks and my hole spasms as my mouth opens on a gasp. He makes another pass, this time starting at my taint and working his way up to my pucker, moaning as it flutters against his tongue. My arms are shaking so badly I can barely stay upright as he repeats the gesture two more times, before flicking the tip of his tongue over my hole repeatedly and making me shout.

"How wet are you?" I ask through my sobs. I have to know. I need to know. I need to know that he's as wrecked for me as I am for him.

"I'm fucking soaked, baby," he says, his voice husky. "You're so damn sexy you got me leaking through my pants like crazy."

God, yes. He goes back to playing with my pucker, flicking that wicked tongue against it again and again.

"Shit! Fuck, Bentley, please? Please fuck my pussy with your tongue. I need to come so bad, baby. Please?" He tortures me for a handful of seconds more, abandoning my hole completely and sucking more marks onto my ass cheeks, before he spreads my cheeks again, and I let out a wail when he slides his tongue inside. Fuck, I'm not gonna last long at all. This is incredible, and the noises he's making while he feasts on me are just making it harder not to come.

"Shit, I can't," I gasp, tears streaking my cheeks. I'm past the point of no return, and when he grips my balls and tugs, it's over. I see stars as my cock sprays my release untouched, my hole clenching around Bentley's tongue still buried inside me, and it feels so damn good I'm shooting a second time before I collapse on the sofa. It's only after my body has stopped spasming with the aftershocks of my release that I realize Bentley is lying between my legs with his head on my ass.

"Did you come?" I ask, still trying to catch my breath as I wipe the tear tracks off my cheeks.

"Yeah," he says. "Right after you did."

I sigh in contentment. "Untouched?"

He chuckles and kisses my ass cheek. "Yeah, untouched. You were so incredible, darling. I've never had sex like this before."

"Me either," I admit. "Five stars for rimming. Holy fuck."

He laughs and kisses my ass again before squeezing it in his giant hand. "Love this ass."

"Love having your marks on it," I say and he hums.

"They do look nice."

"What about your couch? Can it be saved, or has it met its untimely demise?"

He laughs and kisses my ass cheek again several times, making me grin. "We'll resuscitate it."

I chuckle and then groan at the thought of moving. I'm so fucking blissed out, but I'm also lying in a pool of my own jizz, and I want to see how wet Bentley is, and get my mouth on his spunk before it dries up.

"Can I see you?" I ask. "I wanna see how wet you are."

He lifts his head and I scramble up and turn around. Holy fuck. His pants are soaked in the front like he wet himself. Granted there's a lot of cum in there, too, not just precum, but fuck, that's sexy. And I did that to him.

I grin and bend down to press a kiss to the giant wet spot, making his breath hitch, then I lift my head and look at him. "Gimme," I say, using grabby hands. He blinks, before realization dawns on his face and he stands, stripping out of his pants and underwear. He passes his briefs to me and watches as I lick up every last drop of his spunk, swallowing it down and licking my lips. When I look at him again, his eyes are wide and his dick is half hard again. I'm so fucking boneless and blissed out I feel like I can barely move.

"I don't think I'll ever get tired of watching you do that," he says. He holds his hand out to me. I grab it and he pulls me to my feet. I hobble on shaky legs to the bathroom, where I see my body in the mirror, covered in my spunk and his marks littering me both front and back. I turn so I can see the dozens of marks decorating my ass cheeks and can't help the huge grin that spreads across my face as I look at them.

Bentley grins. "Might be kinda sore for a bit when you're sitting."

"God, I hope so," I say, and he pulls me into the shower.

Chapter Nineteen

Alex

Saturday night at *Johnny's* is a zoo, and even though I'm far from the only employee here, I'm taking orders and making drinks and schmoozing customers until I'm ready to collapse. And even though I saw Bentley just this morning, I miss him like crazy and am aching to get back to him. We haven't had much time for each other the past couple of days with our work schedules differing, so we've barely talked, and the only thing we've done sexually is exchange hurried blow jobs each morning before he leaves for work and I fall back asleep for a couple more hours. I'm still eager to have my turn fucking him and seeing if I can make him come as undone as he made me. And we still need to try docking, which I'm really hoping will happen soon as well.

I'm returning to the bar after taking a couples' order when I see Tommy through the crowd, and even though there's people moving around him and the man he's talking to, I recognize him immediately as Cyrus. And my brother is livid, if the color on his face and his body language are anything to go by. He's poking a finger at the older man while the other hand is clenched in a fist at his side, and though I can't hear what he's saying I know it's not, "It's good to see you."

Fuck, Tommy is tearing into the guy in front of everyone, though fortunately most people aren't paying them any attention. And Cyrus looks absolutely miserable. But Tommy seems like he couldn't care less. I've known my brother for a long time and he's not one to forgive easily, so if that's what Cyrus wants he's going to have to do a lot of groveling, or have one hell of an explanation for why he left my brother and Pierre in the dark as long as he did. And poor Pierre was just starting to come around and accept that he might not see the older man again, from what I understand. I know that the anger and hurt I'm seeing in my brother's eyes isn't because of how Cyrus treated him. It's about how he made Pierre feel. Tommy is ferociously protective of his husband and with good reason, and making Pierre hurt will get you in trouble with him faster than anything.

I'm still staring at them when Cyrus nods dejectedly and then moves away from Tommy, who makes his way back to the bar where I'm still making drinks. I can tell he's trying to hold himself together, but I can't imagine he's okay after not seeing the man for months and then having him show up here again.

"You okay?" I ask, and he nods. I know he's not okay at all, but I can't grab him and pull in for a hug like I want to right now. Fuck, he looks so upset. "Why don't you take a break?" I suggest. "We can handle it out here for a while without you."

I'm expecting him to ignore me, because that's who he is, always toughing it out and putting other people before himself. But to my relief, he nods.

"I'll be in my office if anyone needs me," he says.

Ten minutes later when I go back there to see how he's doing, I hear him sobbing quietly through the door, and my heart shatters.

Fuck.

Biting my lip, and preparing to get my head bitten off, I slowly twist the handle on the door and let myself in. The second Tommy hears the sound of the door clicking open he's wiping his tears and sitting up straight.

"Fuck, Alex, what are you doing back here?" he asks, his eyes red and tear tracks streaking down his cheeks.

"Checking on you. Do you wanna talk about it?"

He shakes his head. "No, not right now."

"Okay, well can I give you a hug?"

He scowls. "Do you have to?"

"I think so," I say. "I hate seeing you cry. You're my baby brother. It'll be fast."

He chuckles softly and wipes away more tears. "Fine."

He complains, but I think he secretly loves my hugs. I move behind the desk where he's sitting and pull him to his feet before wrapping my arms around him and squeezing him tightly, not letting go for several seconds.

"You said fast," he grouses, even as he cries some more.

"This is fast, for me," I tease, and that gets a laugh out of him.

"Let go of me."

I release him and press a kiss to his forehead, which he wipes away as I grin. "Hey, it's gonna be okay, baby brother," I say.

He sighs but he seems a bit better. "Yeah, I hope so."

When I get home that night I'm so exhausted I barely manage to get my clothes off before I fall into bed in my underwear and scoot close to Bentley, taking him in my arms.

I know how happy my brother and Pierre are for me and Bentley, but I hope that whatever is going on with them and Cyrus gets worked out, and that they can be as happy as the two of us are. If there are any two people in the world who deserve good things, it's my brother and his husband.

Bentley

I smell Alex's scent before my eyes are even open the next morning, his honey and vanilla body wash clinging to the sheets and making me crave him. I'm hard and ready to pounce on him when I open my eyes and see him staring at the ceiling with his hands behind his head.

"Morning," I say, and he looks at me. A small smile creases his lips.

"Morning, cowboy."

"Everything okay?"

He looks back to the ceiling and sighs and I scoot closer, tucking myself against him. My erection is pressed against his hip but it's not my priority right now. He folds his arm around me and kisses the top of my head.

Marble, who had been snoozing at the foot of the bed, stands and stretches, then climbs across my legs and plops down on Alex's stomach. He smiles and scratches her neck, making her purr loudly.

"Just worried about Tommy and Pierre," he says finally. "Cyrus was at the bar last night and he and Tommy had words, and I just hate seeing him unhappy."

"That's one of the things I like about you," I tell him, tilting my head to look up at him as I trail my finger over his torso. "You care so much for the people around you and hate to see them hurting."

"But?" he says, raising an eyebrow.

"No but. I just think this is something you'll have to let

them work through on their own, and just be there to support them, like you have been. I think though, that they will be okay."

He places his hand on my cheek and strokes it, then brings his lips to mine. I move up a bit so I can kiss him back, and he shifts his hips, making Marble scramble off of him as he scoots down and rolls on top of me, never breaking the kiss. I moan into his mouth, feeling his hard dick against mine and shove my hips up, seeking friction. God, this man drives me wild. Just being near him, smelling him, thinking about him, hearing his voice, his laugh, seeing that smile; every fucking thing about him makes me hard.

He moves against me, deepening the kiss and letting out a moan. He kisses me slow and languid, the pleasure building with each glide of his cock, each brush of his lips and swipe of his tongue until I'm in danger of coming in my underwear yet again.

I whimper when he sucks on my tongue and then bites down on my bottom lip and tugs, making my cock jerk and ooze precum.

"I believe," Alex rasps, "it's my gorgeous cowboy's turn to bottom." He nibbles on my bottom lip again. "What do you think, baby? Want my cock inside that pretty hole?"

I tremble at his words. "Yes." My precum is leaking through my underwear by now and wetting his briefs as well. "Fuck me, darling."

Alex kisses me deeply a few more times, making my dick jerk again. He moans into my mouth before pulling away. "Love this perfect cock," he says, brushing against me a few times before he slides down my legs and removes my briefs. There's a rather large wet spot on the front, and Alex brings the underwear to his face and breathes them in as if smelling the sweetest flower, his eyes closed and his dick hard as steel, tenting his own underwear. Fuck, that's hot, him practically getting drunk off my scent.

"God, I love how much you leak, cowboy," he says, "and how fucking amazing you smell. I'm gonna make you come so hard your body is covered in your spunk, and then I'm going to swallow every last drop." He drops the underwear on the bed and proceeds to remove his own. Then he's looking at me with so much desire in his eyes that it makes me shiver, before he says, "Spread those legs for me, baby. Show me what's mine."

My hole spasms and I gasp as I do as he says, spreading wide for him, giving him everything he's asking for. "Alex," I breathe as he leans down and buries his face in my ass, inhaling deeply and moaning as he does. He presses kisses to my taint that have me trembling, and even more precum dripping from my cock. Then he's licking a stripe from my taint to my hole and moaning so loudly that between that and the incredible pleasure I feel when his tongue slides over my hole, I have to grab my dick to keep from coming.

"Alex," I say again, breathless as he repeats the gesture. "Fuck, baby, wait."

He lifts his head, spit dripping down his chin, his pupils blown wide and cock straining.

My chest is heaving as I stare at him. His gaze heats even more, and I see his dick twitch when he looks at the thick pool of precum on my stomach and sliding down my cock. He really does love that I leak so fucking much. "Fuck, look at you," he purrs. "Look how fucking wet you are for me. You're ready to come for me already, aren't you baby?" He leans forward and licks a stripe up my dick that has me whimpering, and then he's pressing kisses to it, making it twitch repeatedly, before he sucks the head into his mouth and suckles.

"Fuck!" I shout, and he pops off of me, grinning. Shit, this man is a menace.

"I'm not going to complain if you come before I get inside you," he says.

I shake my head. "No, I don't want to. Please. I need to feel you."

He nods. "We'll resume the rimming later then." I nod and he swipes his finger through the pool of precum on my belly, using it to coat his fingers. "I'm gonna prep you with your own juice, baby."

He moves his fingers down to my hole and spreads the precum around it, using his fingers to circle my pucker. It flutters in anticipation, begging for him. Then he's pressing against it and I gasp. "Does that feel good?" he asks, and I nod, unable to speak. He presses a bit more, and his finger slides inside, making me moan as it fills me. I'm leaking obscene amounts of precum now, just from one of his fingers inside me and I'm instantly aching for more. More of him, always, more of him.

"Please?" I breathe, and he hums before a second slicked up finger slides inside me. God, yes, that's good. I arch my hips up, chasing his fingers as they move, stretching me, spreading me, filling me, my head thrown back and my eyes closed as I moan loudly. "Fuck, yes."

"Jesus, baby, you're so fucking sexy," Alex rumbles, before I feel myself stretching even wider and a burn that makes me gasp in pain as much as pleasure.

"Fuck me," I practically growl. "I want your cock inside me right fucking now."

"Yes, sir," he says, and slides his fingers out. I nearly whimper at the loss, thrusting my hips and spreading wider even as he slides the condom on and gathers more of my precum, using it as lube to slick up his cock. "I'm coming, beautiful," he says, and it only makes me whimper again and more precum ooze out of my cock.

He slathers more of my precum around my hole, and then positions himself at my entrance, before taking a breath and pushing inside. It burns, but it also feels so damn good I feel tears filling my eyes. Fuck, having a dildo shoved up my ass and imagining it being Alex is nothing compared to the real thing, and I'm fucking overwhelmed that he's mine.

"Shit, should I stop?" he says, starting to pull back, but I grab his arms and shake my head.

"No, don't. I'm fine. I just...." I breathe in and let it out. "You feel really good and I can't believe you're finally where I want you. Finally where you belong."

He grins and leans down to kiss me. "I'm all yours, baby. And you're all mine."

I nod. "Keep going."

He pushes in a bit farther. Alex isn't as thick or as long as me, but he's stretching me so wide I feel like he's splitting me in two. I have even more respect for him taking my dick as well as he did, now that I know what it feels like. I take another breath and let it out as he pushes in a little more.

"You still okay?" he asks, and I nod.

"Don't stop."

He doesn't, and a moment later he's fully sheathed inside me, both of us breathing heavily, our skin slick with sweat, our bodies flush and entwined as close as they can possibly be. He rests his forehead to mine even as his body trembles.

"You feel really good," he rasps, hands planted on either side of me. "Fuck, you're so damn tight. Love being inside you."

I look up at him and pull him down for a kiss, soft and slow, before I move my hips, encouraging him to do the same. He pulls back a bit before pushing forward again, then pulls back even farther, before pushing forward a second time, starting a slow and easy rhythm, my body welcoming the intrusion.

"Fuck, that's good," I groan, our foreheads still pressed together, eyes closed as he nudges my prostate with each slow thrust, our breath mingling between us. "Love your cock, darling."

Alex groans in response. "God, I don't want it to end. You're choking my cock so good, baby."

"Faster," I beg. "Wanna feel you so deep."

"Put your legs over my shoulders," he instructs, and I do, groaning at how deep the new position lets him go.

"Fuck, yeah, that's it, beautiful. God, you look so good like this." He thrusts deeper, harder, watching as his dick slides into me again and again before his gaze meets mine. "Kiss me, cowboy."

I bring his face down to mine and slot our lips together, kissing him and letting him do the rest of the work. I'm whimpering as he fucks me so good I can't stop the noises flying from me mouth, my whines and whimpers fueling him and making him move even faster, harder until I feel my balls drawing up and I'm clamping down on his cock as my dick pulses load after load of my release onto my chest and abdomen, my moans of pleasure stifled by his mouth on mine. Seconds later he's crying out my name as his dick unloads inside me, and my body spasms at the sensation.

"Holy fuck," he pants, collapsing on top of me. "That was fucking incredible, cowboy."

My body is still coming down from the high of my orgasm as I wrap my arms around him, holding him close, my spunk sticky between us.

He lifts himself a moment later and lowers his mouth to

my dick, lapping up my release hungrily, his dick twitching inside me as he does. Shit. He's practically salivating over it,

He swallows down a load before going back for the spunk all over my chest and stomach. He swallows it down before licking his lips, and looking at me with a dopey grin on his face like he's drunk off the taste. "Shower time," he says, before slowly pulling out of me.

"In a second," I say, my body heavy. "I need to regain function of my legs first."

He grins. "Was bottoming everything you dreamed?"

"Even better." I take him in my arms again and I'm about to doze off when he runs a finger down my chest, making me jerk. "That tickles."

He chuckles. "Come on, handsome, shower time, then breakfast. We can go back to sleep after that if you want."

I groan and slowly climb out of bed, following him to the bathroom.

We step into the shower and let the warm water cascade over us as we kiss lazily. I groan when I feel Alex's half hard cock against mine.

"You up for trying docking?" he asks, gripping my hips. God, I didn't think I could possibly go another round after the way he wrung me out only minutes ago, but my dick is perking up again already.

I nod and kiss him, making me a little harder still. "Who goes first?" I ask, pulling away and looking down at our nearly hard cocks nestled together. God, even that is enough to make my dick twitch.

"I can," he says. "We'll see if we can do this right. Might be harder than it sounds."

He grips his foreskin, and then tells me to pull mine back. I do, and then we line up our cocks, and he stretches his foreskin open and outward, encasing my head and shaft as much as he can. We both gasp at the sensation of being encased together, our dicks joining so perfectly. "Now you," he says, breathlessly.

"Fuck." I copy his motions, releasing my foreskin and pulling the opening down and over his as much as possible. Holy fuck this is incredible. The combination of our precum leaking out all over our cocks, and being wrapped up so damn tight causes a suctioning effect that makes me weak in the knees. I stumble forward, pushing Alex back, but manage to keep our dicks together, moaning as he starts to stroke us. Holy shit, I'm not gonna last long at all.

"God, that's good," Alex moans, echoing my thoughts. "I'm gonna come pretty damn fast, baby."

"Me, too," I rasp, my hands up on either side of his head as he jacks us, our bodies trembling.

"Shit, baby, you're so fucking wet, all that precum is making this even better."

I groan as pleasure mounts, so intense I have no hope of staving it off. "Alex," I gasp. "Fuck, I'm coming, baby."

We howl our releases together, crying out each other's names, our encased cocks spasming and pulsing, our cum building up inside our makeshift cage until it's overflowing, leaking out, and our foreskin is slowly sliding back and away from each other.

Fuck, that was intense.

"God I definitely need a nap now," Alex says, and I nod. "And some breakfast."

"Me, too."

"Docking gets five gold, very huge stars," he says, and I chuckle, before kissing his cheek and then running my fingers through the spunk on both our bodies and bringing it to his lips.

"Open up, darling, I've got your breakfast right here."

He grins and I slide my fingers in his mouth, letting him lick them clean, before we wash ourselves and then slide into clean underwear. Alex now has a fair amount of his things at my place since he spends most of his nights here.

Marble meows at us as we dress and then prances into the kitchen where she hops up on the counter.

"Nuh uh," I say, grabbing her and putting her back on the floor. She meows again, clearly not happy with me. "You eat on the floor, missy," I tell her.

We make bacon and eggs for breakfast, and once our tummies are satisfied, and Marble has had her breakfast, we crawl back under the sheets and snuggle up together.

Alex is shifting around a lot and groaning in the non sexy way that tells me he's uncomfortable.

"What's wrong?" I ask.

"My back is hurting. I think between the long ass shifts at the bar and worrying about my brother, I'm just more tense than usual."

"I could give you a massage," I say, trying not to sound too excited about the idea. I've wanted Alex to be the recipient of one of my massages for a while now, and the last time I offered he turned me down. At the time I thought it was because he didn't want me touching him that way, but now I'm realizing it was for the opposite reason. He wanted me touching him too much.

"Yeah?" he says, his eyes lighting up. "That would be amazing."

I sit up. "Roll onto your stomach."

He does as he's told and I reach into the nightstand and grab the bottle of massage oil I keep there, then straddle his hips. "Where does it hurt?"

"Everywhere," he says, and I laugh.

"Okay, everywhere it is." I get a small amount of the massage oil on my hands and slather it over his upper back and shoulders, hearing him moan as I do. Then I start working on his shoulders, sliding my hands down his back and back up to his shoulders several times, stopping at the swell of his ass when I reach the bottom, before focusing on just the left side, using a medium amount of pressure and allowing him to relax into it, before I switch to using my forearms along with my hands, and applying a bit more pressure. He moans and it makes me smile.

"Fuck I should have let you do this to me a long time ago," he mumbles, his eyes closed.

"I tried," I remind him.

"I know. I was so fucking horny for you I couldn't let you touch me without getting a hard on."

I grin wider as I keep working. I move down to his low back, and he instantly jerks and lets out a hiss when I hit a tender spot. "Mmmm, you've got a trigger point here," I tell him. "Breathe in and try to relax while I loosen it."

He does, though he's still a bit tense, and I decide to ease up on the pressure, which seems to help.

"Ooh, that's good," he murmurs. "You can go a little harder again."

I do, and the knot in his back loosens gradually, making him sigh. I can't describe how happy it makes me to take care of him this way.

By the time I'm finished and moving his underwear down just enough to press a soft kiss to his ass, he's boneless, and I swear he's asleep until I hear, "You kiss all your clients on the ass?"

I chuckle. "Just the cute ones."

He huffs. "I better be the only cute one."

"You are," I promise, pressing another kiss to his shoulder. "Sleep. I'll be right back."

I move into the bathroom to wash myself off, and then climb back under the covers, scooting close to share Alex's pillow since Marble has managed to confiscate mine.

"Bentley?" Alex says, startling me.

"I thought you fell asleep."

"Sing to me," he says. "I haven't heard you sing since Peyton's party and you're so sexy when you sing, so sing me to sleep."

I chuckle and pull him close, his head resting on my chest and my finger sliding up and down his back. "As you wish, darling," I say. I start singing one of Gram's favorite songs, "Hallelujah" by Leonard Cohen, and Alex is snoring softly moments later.

Chapter Twenty

Alex

Several hours later we're sitting around my parents' dinner table with Tommy and Pierre, eating the arroz con pollo that Mom and Dad made, talking and laughing.

"Alejandro, your brother tells us you and Bentley are dating," Mom says, and then gives me a withering look. "Why did I have to find this out from him and not you?"

I grimace. "Sorry, Mom, it's fairly new and I just hadn't gotten around to it, yet."

"Hadn't gotten around to it," she repeats, and Dad shakes his head, grinning. "I gave you life and this is how you treat me." Her words are stern but her gaze is playful, and I know she's not really upset. "Well, if you decide to get married I hope I find out before the wedding day."

"Mom," I say, flushing, and glancing at Bentley who's doing the same. "We're nowhere near thinking about marriage."

"The two of you would look so handsome wearing tuxes and standing under a beautiful archway," she croons.

"She'll have names for your children by the time dinner is over," Dad says, and she smacks his arm.

"Oh, you are all horrid," she says. She thankfully changes the subject then and I let out a sigh of relief. I'm crazy about Bentley, but we haven't even been dating for a month, and while I want to get married someday, I'm sure not ready to walk down the aisle just yet. Though I have to admit, when I picture my future—one, three or even five years from now, there's no one I'd rather have in it than him. Building a life with him, a home, sounds amazing.

Pierre tells us how his college courses are going, and how busy he is with final exams coming up, and I notice he seems happier, despite the conversation Tommy and Cyrus had at the bar last night.

When the meal is over and the table has been cleared I take a moment to ask how he's doing, and he smiles at me, gripping Tommy's hand. "Still figuring things out, but I'm hopeful," he says.

"We're hopeful," Tommy says, giving Pierre's hand a squeeze. I still can't get over the effect Pierre has on my brother. No one can melt Tommy's heart like his husband can.

When Mom and Dad emerge from the kitchen once more they're carrying pina coladas for everyone, and a virgin one for Pierre. We move into the living room and visit some more while we drink, Mom and Dad regaling Bentley with stories from my childhood and embarrassing me to pieces by breaking out one of our old photo albums. Mom is so excited about it she practically shoves me aside to sit next to Bentley and opens the book on both of their laps.

"He was such a beautiful baby," Mom gushes as she flips through photos of me from when I was an infant, making me groan. Bentley has the biggest smile on his face though, and I can't complain when he's so fucking happy.

He laughs when he sees a picture of me at age eight, in a dress and shirt from the 1860s, holding a book in my hand and smiling widely.

"He wanted to be Jo March for Halloween," Mom tells Bentley. "I watched the movie with him and he fell in love with it. I think he had a crush on Jo."

"Oh my God," I groan, burying my face in my hands.

"It wasn't until he was ten that he read the book and it's been his favorite ever since."

Bentley nudges me and grins. "You look pretty stinking cute."

"Shut up," I say, shoving his face away, and making everyone laugh.

"Oh, look at this, his senior portraits. Such a handsome young man, my Alejandro." She reaches over Bentley's lap to squeeze my hand, and I'm pretty sure if Bentley wasn't there she'd be pinching my cheek instead.

"Beautiful baby and handsome young man," Tommy quips, "wonder what happened."

Mom stands up to reach across the coffee table and slap his leg and we're all laughing again. "You be nice to your brother," she says.

"Yeah, be nice to your brother," I say, and Tommy sticks his tongue out at me, so of course I do the same right back.

"Oh mon Dieu," Pierre groans, with a grin on his face. "You two are ridiculous."

"He started it," I say, and that just makes everyone laugh more.

When we leave a couple of hours later, after a round of Pictionary and a cutthroat game of musical chairs, which Pierre "wins" by sitting on Tommy's lap when my brother gets the last chair seconds before Pierre does, and claiming Tommy's lap counts as a seat, then making them go again and getting the actual chair first, it's late, but I'm not quite ready for bed just yet.

Seeing Bentley with my family, how seamlessly he fit in with everyone, how he belonged there, and how happy everyone was that we are together, just made me want him all over again. I know he's been with them before as my friend, but having him as my boyfriend and everything feeling so perfect, it makes me realize how lucky I am, and how much I want him to always belong among the people I care for most.

"Wanna watch *Supernatural?*" Bentley asks when we close the door to his apartment after stepping inside, and I realize how completely natural it was for me to come in here with him, to assume he wanted me here, that this is where I belong. How natural it was for me to leave Marble here while we were gone and how natural it is now to see Bentley scooping her up and letting her cling to him, nudging his jaw with her head.

"We could," I say. "Or..."

He eyes me. "Or?"

"Or we could finish what we started in the bedroom earlier today, and I could rim that delicious ass of yours until your pretty cock is leaking all over your bedsheets and you're begging me to fuck you again."

Bentley shivers and I grin wickedly when I see the bulge in his jeans.

"As far as options go, that's not a bad one."

I chuckle and step closer to him, gripping his junk and squeezing it, drawing a yelp out of him that I fucking love. He jolts and Marble scrambles out of his arms and hops down, then glares at me.

"Bed, beautiful," I tell Bentley. "Ass in the air." I squeeze his cock and balls once more and he nods, scurrying into the bedroom. I'm grinning widely as I follow him, stripping out of my own clothes as I go. I shut the door and Marble meows at me from the other side. My cock twitches when I see Bentley on his hands and knees, waiting for me, that tight ass just begging for attention.

"Fuck, you look good like that, baby," I tell him, slipping my briefs off. I can't help wondering what his ass would look like in a pair of lacy pink panties, how pretty his cock and balls would be, nestled in the feminine material, or even better, his gorgeous dick hard and straining, leaking all over. Fuck. The thought has precum leaking out of my rock hard cock. "Look at you," I say, kneeling on the bed behind him. "You're soaking the sheets with how fucking wet you are already."

A tremor rolls through him and more precum oozes out of his cock and onto the sheets. I grip his ass cheeks in my hands and squeeze them, making him moan. I press several soft kisses to his cheeks, and he squirms and juts his ass out more.

I chuckle. "You want something, baby?"

"I want your tongue on my hole," he whines. "And I want you to spank me."

"I'll get there," I say, and he groans. I swipe my tongue over his ass cheeks several times, nice and slow, before moving my tongue slowly up his spine, and back down, then press more kisses to the taut globes. He shivers, and his whimpers are getting even louder now. I fucking love it. And I love having him in this position, being able to do whatever I want to his ass, and seeing his balls heavy between his splayed thighs, his monster cock hanging low and leaking so much there's a giant wet spot on the sheets. The amount of precum he makes is seriously one of the hottest things in the fucking world.

"Alex," he whines again.

He jolts when I grip his balls in my hand and tug. I

watch as his dick jerks and more precum leaks out of that gorgeous mushroom head. I cup his balls in my hand and roll them gently. He lets out a moan as he tosses his head back, his eyes closed. "Fuck, that's so good," he whimpers.

I hum and press a kiss to his backside while I continue fondling his balls, then tug again and get the same beautiful gasp as the first time, along with the fresh beads of precum.

"God, you're so damn sexy, baby," I rasp and he starts to move his hips, chasing his pleasure, humping the air. I grip his cock, and pull it back between his legs. A breath leaves him, and I slide my tongue over the head, moaning at the taste of his precum. Fuck, I'm addicted. I swirl my tongue around the head a couple of times, and he squirms, before I take the head in my mouth and suck.

"Mmmnnngg," he wails. "Fuck, that's good, darling."

His big powerful body is shaking as I hum and take him deeper, using my hand to stroke him as I do, before moving back up to the head of his cock and licking along the frenulum. He's moaning and begging as he thrusts his hips. "Alex. Please, I need your mouth on my hole, baby."

I pop off his cock and press a kiss to the tip before letting it go. Then I spread his cheeks and swipe my tongue over his fluttering hole. The effect is instantaneous. He bucks and whimpers, begging for more. "Shit," he says. "Don't stop."

I slide my tongue over his hole again, nice and slow, before moving down to his balls and licking all the way up to his taint, and then his hole, and he shakes, his cock bobbing and leaking as he moves his hips. I swipe my tongue over his hole several more times, before I delve inside. I hear him shout and feel his pretty pucker fluttering wildly against my tongue. "Oh, God," he moans. "Yes. Alex."

God, I can't get over how desperate and utterly wrecked

he sounds for me. I leave my tongue inside as long as I can, fluttering it and feeling his body tremble as he moans again and again. Then I'm pulling out and bringing my hand down on his ass.

He cries out, and I can't tell if it's in pain or pleasure until he says, "More," his voice broken and needy.

I slap the other cheek and my dick jerks as I watch his ass bounce and a red spot form on his golden skin. I repeat the gesture on the other cheek, moving back and forth, varying my swats so they don't land in the same place twice, and hearing his cries of pleasure echo off the walls of the bedroom. Jesus, he's driving me insane. I never thought I'd be rock hard spanking someone, but Bentley is everything. I can't get enough of his ass and his sexy as fuck noises.

"Fuck me," he cries, and I suck in a breath when I realize he's crying. "Fuck, I'm gonna come and I want you inside me. Please fuck me."

I reach around and slick my hand up with the precum that's sliding down his shaft and oozing onto the sheets, and spread it around his hole. I slide a condom on and add more of his precum, coating my dick in it, before I spread his cheeks and press inside him. I'm moaning the second I breach his hole, my eyes rolling back in my head at how fucking hot and tight he is, the way he chokes my dick. "Fuck, baby, so fucking good. Your ass is so fucking perfect."

He lets out a choked sob and I slide in a bit more. Reaching around to grip his dick, I stroke him slowly as I move farther inside him. "You like this?" I ask, and he nods as tears slide down his cheeks. "You like me inside you, baby? You like my cock splitting this pretty ass open?" He nods again. "You like my hand on your cock? Like me touching you?" I run my thumb over the tip of his cock as I speak and he shudders, nodding a third time. I gather his precum on my fingers and bring them to my mouth as I shove in a tiny bit more, and he gasps. I lick my fingers and moan, then move my hand back to his aching shaft, stroking it slowly again as I push in all the way and bottom out inside him. I press kisses to his shoulders and back. "Did you like me eating your ass?" I ask him, not moving just yet, even though I know he's desperate for me to fuck him.

"Yes," he breathes.

"And did you like being spanked by me?" Another kiss to his back.

"Yes," he says again.

"You want me to fuck you now, handsome? Want me to use my cock to make you feel good?"

"Shit, darling, please?" he begs, the tears coming again.

"You're so fucking pretty when you beg," I tell him, and his cock spasms in my grip, making me moan and press another kiss to his low back. Then, I move my hands to his hips and start to move, and he lets out a relieved sob.

Jesus I've never experienced sex like this before. Sex with Bentley is so much more intense than any sex I've had with a woman. It's electric and raw, and passionate, but there's also so much more intimacy involved, more vulnerability. I can't get over how open he is with me, how he responds to me, how he trusts me to take care of him, and it gets me harder as I move inside him.

This is the kind of sex I crave. The kind where it's not just a lust-filled physical attraction, but where you share a connection that has you feeling safe enough to bare your soul to the other person. The kind that makes you want to pleasure them the best you can, makes you ache for their satisfaction and enjoyment as much as your own, the kind of sex where, when it's done, you feel like you've experienced something beautiful together, and you know the person a bit better than you did before, using that knowledge to build a stronger, healthier relationship.

The sex can be animalistic and wild and fierce, of course, but even then it's because the person you're with is your safe place, your home, your shelter, and you know you can trust them to take care of you, to protect your heart and soul no matter what happens between the sheets. And that's what makes you want them so much. The connection you share, not just the mutual end goal of an incredible orgasm.

"Shit, cowboy," I pant as I move inside him, picking up my pace, my balls slapping against his ass over and over. My throat is constricting because I'm realizing, (yes, with my dick in his ass), that I'm falling so hard and fast for him, and I'm powerless to stop it. Not that I would even if I could. Because he's the best thing that's ever happened to me, and I want to be his forever, and for him to be mine.

"Alex," he sobs. "I'm so close. Tell me I'm pretty. Please?"

Oh, fuck. "You are, baby," I say, trying to keep the tears from falling at my incredibly ill-timed revelation of just how much Bentley means to me. "You're so fucking pretty. So goddamn gorgeous. So absolutely perfect. I can't get over how beautiful you are. One look at you and my heart fucking stops at how stunning you are. Now come for me, pretty baby."

Fuck, his body shudders and his hole clamps down on my cock as he releases spurt after spurt of his cum onto the sheets and pillow, and I'm shouting my release seconds later, pulsing inside him as I unload. He moves over a tad before he falls onto the mattress and I land on top of him, reaching over to swipe my fingers through his spunk and licking them clean with a moan. Fuck, I love the taste of him.

He's breathing heavily and I run my fingers through his hair and press a kiss to his shoulder blade.

"You okay?"

He nods, a sleepy smile on his face now. "Yeah, it was amazing. I definitely like rimming and spankings."

"I wasn't too hard with the spankings? I have to say I've never spanked anyone before but I loved it."

He hums. "You were great, darling. I have no complaints."

"I should get some lotion for your ass." I kiss his back and then pull out of him. As soon as I open the bedroom door Marble scrambles past me and jumps on the bed, then starts pawing at Bentley's hand. He laughs and starts to pet her as I make my way to the bathroom, remove the condom and toss it in the trash can, and then grab the lotion on the counter. Bentley is still petting my demanding feline when I return, only now she's on her back, purring like a slut while he rubs her belly.

"Thank you," he says softly as I rub the lotion into his reddened skin. He looks so peaceful it makes my chest ache with fondness.

"Of course. I was thinking though that we should probably have a safe word for you in case the spanking, or anything really, gets to be too much."

He hums. "How about Stacy?" he says, and I slap his ass, making him yelp and laugh. "Okay, how about Tux? I will remember that."

"Tux it is," I say, smiling at the mention of the huge, ridiculous penguin that still sits in the corner of Bentley's bedroom, reminding me daily how we met.

How on earth did I get lucky enough to find him?

Chapter Twenty-One

Bentley

"You're welcome," I tell Gloria one week later when she thanks me for "yet another wonderful massage."

"I have been getting massages twice a month for years and I've never had ones as good as yours. Those hands sure are strong." She grins at me and I flush.

"I'm glad you enjoyed it."

"Would have enjoyed it more if that handsome fellow who kissed you paid us another visit." She winks and I can't help laughing.

"I'm afraid the steamy side shows are over."

"Pity," she says. "You two a thing now?"

"We are." It's a bit personal but I don't mind, especially when her session got interrupted by Alex barging in on us and kissing me. Besides, I've been treating Gloria for months and she's become sort of a friend.

"Glad to hear it. You deserve someone special." She pats my arm and then waves at Peyton as she heads out the door. "See you in two weeks!"

I lift my hand in a goodbye gesture as she leaves and Peyton chuckles. "I think if you didn't have a boyfriend she'd be asking you out."

I shake my head and head back to the massage room to clean up, then take a bathroom break, before checking my phone. When I look at it I see I have a few messages from Alex. The Rock gif is first, followed by a *Supernatural* gif of Dean winking, and then a text.

Alex: How's my beautiful cowboy?

Shit, even reading it in a text makes me unbelievably horny, and my cock springs to life in my scrubs.

Me: I'm fine. How's my darling?

Alex: I'm damn near perfect, cowboy, but I could be better, if you know what I mean. Winky face emoji

Me: Lol

Alex: When is your next appointment?

Me: fifteen minutes

Alex: that's long enough

Me: for?

Alex: an orgasm

I suck in a breath. Okay, I wasn't expecting that.

Me: what?

Alex: get somewhere private and take that pretty cock out, baby

I bite my lip to stifle a moan as my dick jerks yet again. I close the door to my tiny office space, lock it, in case Peyton decides to come back here, and sit in my desk chair. Fuck, I can't believe I'm doing this. I've never actually sexted with someone before, or had an orgasm in public. I pull down my pants and briefs to my knees because I don't want them to get full of spunk, and when I do my dick bounces free, already half hard.

Me: Now what?

Alex: Are you hard for me, beautiful?

I groan as I suck in another breath, my dick lengthening even more at his endearment.

Me: almost, say something else

Alex: shit, baby, you want me to tell you that you're pretty? That your cock is complete and utter perfection, that your ass is a dream? Want me to tell you that I can't stop thinking about how wet you get for me and how pretty you are when you come? How sexy that O face is?

Me: fuck, I'm hard

Alex: show me baby

Me: uh, what?

Alex: take a picture of your cock and send it to me

Shit, I've never done that before either, but I find myself getting even harder at the idea of doing it for Alex. I stroke myself a couple of times to get more precum on my cock and it's oozing obscenely when I finally line my phone up and snap the picture

Alex: holy fucking shit, gorgeous, that's insanely hot. All that delicious precum. I wanna get my mouth on that perfect cock so bad

Me: You're making it hard to be quiet, darling

Alex: devil emoji. I'm jerking off to your picture baby

Me: can I see?

A few seconds later a video comes through and I open it immediately. Alex's groans and gasps of pleasure fill the room as I stare at him stroking his cock and my dick jerks once more, my ass hole fluttering, begging for that cock to fill it. He doesn't come on the video but it sounds like he's close, and I take my shaft in hand and stroke myself some more.

Me: Fuck, that's hot

Alex: It's all you baby. You do this to me. You make me so hard I can't fucking think straight

Me: send me a video of you coming and I'll send you one of me jerking off to it

Alex: I like how you think, cowboy

A minute later another video comes through, and once again Alex's moans and cries of pleasure fill the small space. I've made sure to turn the volume down so Peyton doesn't hear it as I watch, stroking myself as I do. It's so fucking sexy, my hand is soon covered in my precum and my balls are drawing up as I turn the video recorder on on my phone.

"Shit, cowboy, I'm gonna come," Alex whines. "So good, baby. Can't stop thinking about your pretty cock." Fuck, there's really something to be said for sexting, that's for sure. This is so damn erotic, hearing the noises he's making, the panting breaths, the pleasured whimpers and moans, seeing him touch himself and knowing it's to thoughts of me. I stroke myself fast and hard as I listen and watch that beautiful cock of his getting ready to ejaculate. He shouts his release and his spunk shoots out to cover his hand and cock, and pools on his abdomen. Seeing it has me biting my lips as I spray my own release, and as soon as I'm finished I send the video to Alex.

Alex: Damn, that's hot, baby. Now I just need the real thing

I chuckle

Me: You're insatiable

Alex: Guilty, smiley emoji. Hey, do you think it's still considered pebbling if we're sexting?

I laugh a little harder at that one.

Me: Not sure, but I kinda doubt it. It's about sending memes and gifs and messages that remind you of the person, or have some sort of significance or meaning to them, right? I don't think sexts count for that

Alex: your dick is very important and meaningful to me

Me: oh my

Alex: smiley emoji

Me: I gotta get cleaned up and get back to work, darling. Thanks for the orgasm

Alex: Kissy face emoji

I search for a penguin gif and send it before I set my phone down, and get back to work.

Alex

The following week, Bentley and I take a trip to the local farmer's market with Tommy and Pierre. It's open every Saturday and Sunday and it's a great place to shop for produce, meat, bread, and even has several small shops with things like jewelry, artwork, flowers, and more. I find a cactus that I decide I have to have, though I wonder if there's much point when I'm hardly in my apartment anymore. But when Bentley offers to get it for me and tells me I can move any plants I want to his place, his cheeks flushed as he does, I can't stop smiling. I do miss my plants, and it's hard to remember to water them when I'm not home. Fortunately, several of them thrive on neglect.

We stop by a shop that sells tea, and I get a combination of several different flavors, then pick up some coffee for Bentley from one of the shops that Tommy recommends. Pierre blushes beautifully and gives Tommy a kiss when Tommy tells us he has to go use the restroom but then comes back with a beautiful bouquet of flowers for his husband.

We eat lunch at the market, and when we find a donut stand we each pick one and gobble down the messy good-ness. We pick out some fruit and vegetables, and some meat for upcoming meals, and I tell Bentley he should open a stand here and sell all the amazing things he knits, which makes him blush and shake his head. "I can't interact with crowds of people all day," he tells me, which I already know, but it's fun to poke at him. "I can't imagine talking to strangers for hours. And I enjoy making things for gifts, not selling."

I squeeze his hand and press a kiss to his cheek. He started on another knitting project while we watch *Supernatural* together in the evenings, which we're on season four of now. Bentley was so excited because I finally got introduced to his favorite character, Castiel. I'm still not sure what I think of him, but Bentley says to just wait because I'll love him soon. He is funny with how little he understands about human slang and pop culture. I think one of the reasons Bentley likes him is because he's a little awkward, and it's endearing, but it also helps people who feel a little awkward themselves, or maybe don't understand social norms, feel seen.

Anyway, he's been working on a blanket for my parents for their upcoming anniversary, and I won't lie, I'm kinda jealous, because I want him to make one for me. I've been curling up in the blanket in his apartment that he made whenever I get the chance, and because he's him, he never asks if he can have it, just smiles at me and grabs a different one, even though the one he made is the only one big enough for his large frame and above average height. Still, though, it would be nice to have something that he made just for me, but I do know my parents will love theirs.

When we're finished at the market we head home and unload everything. I head to my place to put away some of the produce I bought, and then grab a couple of the plants that need more attention, along with a gift for Bentley that I purchased several days ago and was sitting on my doorstep when we got back, and bring them with me back to Bentley's. Marble is already there and I find her batting a toy across the living room when I enter.

"Honey, I'm home," I say, and Bentley pokes his head out of the kitchen, cheeks flushed. "What is it?" I ask.

"What do you mean?"

"You're looking at me weird."

"Nothing," he says, clearing his throat. "I uh...I was just wondering if you think...."

I step closer to him. "Yeah?"

He bites his lip, not meeting my gaze, hands in his pockets as he shuffles his feet. "You wouldn't want to move in with me, would you?"

I blink. Oh.

"I mean, you don't have to give up your apartment or anything, if you don't want to, but I thought, with as much time as you spend over here, maybe it would make sense, you know, to at least keep your groceries here, too, maybe move some more clothes over, and I could, uh," he clears his throat. "I could get you a key to my place and Marble's things could stay here."

I grin. "Yeah."

He looks up now, and his gaze meets mine. "Yeah?"

I step closer and kiss him. "Yeah, cowboy, I'll move in with you. Like you said, I practically already have. I'll keep my apartment, though, for now, anyway, cuz I don't think all of my stuff would fit in here with yours. I'd need space for all three of my bookshelves at least."

He grins.

"Here, open this and then I'll get some more of my things and we can make it semi-official."

He's beaming when he takes the small package from me and tears it open, only for his cheeks to turn bright pink when he pulls out the set of lacy panties I got for him to try. I slide my arm around his waist and he buries his face in my neck. "I found them on a website that caters specifically to men, so they should fit. And they have great reviews." His face is hot as he nuzzles in further to my neck, but I notice his dick is also hard, and I grin at how fucking adorable he is. "You wanna try them on?" He nods and I chuckle, taking his hand and pulling him into the bathroom.

"What if they look ridiculous?" he says, holding the pink pair in his hands, admiring the material, the other colors, light blue, purple, and black, sitting on the counter. God, just watching him touch them is getting me all hot and bothered.

"They won't," I croak out. "I promise. I'll go wait on the couch while you change."

He flushes again but shuts the door behind me as I leave. I'm so fucking hard and I haven't even seen them on him yet, but that ass is going to look incredible in those panties, I just know it.

When the door opens a moment later and Bentley steps out, that beautiful golden skin on display and his cock and balls nestled in the pretty lace panties, I nearly swallow my tongue. Goosebumps erupt over my entire body as a shiver races down my spine and my dick presses painfully against my zipper. It's a moment before I can even speak as I stare at him, so fucking pretty and absolutely perfect, my beautiful cowboy.

When I do speak it's just one word, and honestly I'm amazed I can even manage that. "Wow."

He blushes scarlet, but can't keep the smile off his face as he slowly makes his way over to me. My heart is jack hammering against my rib cage as I look at him. I can't believe this incredible man is mine.

"What do you think?" he asks, even doing a little turn for me so I can see his ass in them, too. The material is lace all around which means he's giving me a very enticing glimpse of his ass as well as his dick and balls.

"I think," I say slowly, "that we need to get you several more pairs."

He smiles wide and grips my hand in his, pulling me to the bedroom.

Chapter Twenty-Two

Bentley

*Alex: Hey, are you home? You wanna come down to the bar?
I miss your face. You don't have to come if you're super tired,
though, or if you're sick of people. But please come*

I chuckle. I've been to the bar several times since we
started dating, just to be able to see him in the evenings
because I miss him, too. I don't stay super long, but I'll have
some dinner while I'm there and it's fun to flirt with him
while he works, and steal kisses. I wasn't planning on going
tonight but I can.

*Me: Lol, I have to change first, and give Marble some
cuddles, but then I can come*

Alex: Yay! Kissy face emoji

I blush and smile like an idiot. It's been three months
since Alex and I started dating, and every day he makes me
feel like I'm special, valued, needed, and appreciated. Don't
get me wrong, he isn't perfect. He leaves his socks on the
floor more often than not, and he never puts the lid back on
the toothpaste, and he loads the dishwasher like a drunk
raccoon, and we've had our share of arguments about all

three of those things. Granted, I'm not perfect either. I like to leave the pantry door open after getting a snack, which drives him crazy, and I guess I have a tendency to use all the handsoap and not refill it. And Alex also thinks I'm a bit too particular about the dishwasher. Granted, neither of us realized these were flaws until the other person pointed them out. But we're managing. We've had to adjust, and communicate, and make room for the differences in living together and sharing the same space, but it's been worth it. The benefits have far outweighed the minor inconveniences.

I love that he comes home to me every night, that I get to wake up next to him every morning. I love that we make breakfast together on Sundays and Mondays when I'm off work and he doesn't go in until late. I love that he knows what creamer to buy for my coffee, and that his laundry is mixed in with mine, now.

I love that my sheets smell of both our scents. I love that Marble is just as much my cat now as his, and that he loves it that way, too. I love that the shower now houses both our body washes and shampoos, and that there's two razors on the bathroom counter. I love that the nightstand on his side of the bed is now piled high with books. I love that he leaves little notes for me on the coffee pot that say things like "Can't wait to kiss you" or "You make me happy."

I love that we have each other to talk to and confide in when we have a bad day, or celebrate with when the occasion arises. I love that I'm his, and he's mine, and that we've made this small apartment into our home.

He still has his place across the hall, though he's talked about starting to sell some things so he can officially move out.

I drop my keys on the counter and make my way to the bedroom, stripping out of my scrubs, taking a second to admire my ass in my pink panties. I've been wearing the ones he got me almost daily now, and Alex can't seem to get enough of them. I've even gotten a few more pairs in slightly different styles since he bought me the first ones. I never thought a pair of lace or silk panties could make me feel so damn sexy, but they do, and I love the way they feel, and the way my guy looks at me when I wear them. Alex has even requested I get some panties with holes cut out for easy access, or a thong with a strap we can move aside so I can wear them while he fucks me.

I slide into some jeans and a T-shirt and then sit on the sofa for a bit, with Marble curled up in the crook of my shoulder while I pet her. She purrs, rubbing her head against my cheek. She's so damn soft, and so boneless against me, it nearly pains me to let her go, but I do.

"Gotta go see your other daddy, princess," I tell her. "See you later." I press a kiss to her head and grab my keys and wallet before heading out the door.

When I arrive at the bar and walk in, I'm bombarded by the smell of vinyl, alcohol, and lemon cleaner, the sound of laughter and voices in conversation and the music blasting from the speakers. I see Alex at the bar and make my way over to him. As soon as he looks up and sees me, a smile lights up his face. The second I'm close he moves out from behind the bar and grips my shirt, tugging me to him and planting a filthy kiss on my lips that has my head spinning.

"Fuck, I missed you," he says over the ruckus. His voice is gravel, his eyes dark and his cheeks flushed. Fuck, he's close enough I can feel his erection pressed against me and it's lighting me up.

"Shit, darling," I rasp, gripping his hips.

"Alex, table five needs refills!" one of his coworkers yells, and he groans, then moves back to the bar to grab a tray full of drinks. He stops when he reaches me again.

"After I drop these off I'm taking my break. Meet me in

the stockroom." He kisses me and hurries off before I have a chance to respond.

Well, I best do as I'm told, I reckon, so I make my way down the hall and past the bathrooms towards the stockroom. I'm only in there for a second when the door opens and Alex bursts in, out of breath, before closing the door behind him.

"Wha–" the question I'm about to ask is silenced when he grips my cheeks and slams his lips against mine, backing me up against the wall as he ravages me.

"Fuck, I need you," he pants in between heated, hurried kisses.

Shit. I've never seen him like this before. This needy, this desperate. I think I like it.

"Fuck me," he begs. "Please baby, I need you to fuck me so fucking bad."

"Mmmm," I murmur as I kiss him back and he starts to undress me, tugging my shirt over my head before he slams me against the wall again and I grunt. His hands are everywhere, running up my chest, around my back, gripping my hair, my face as he ruts against me, his hard cock pressing into me again and again and making me moan. Then his hands move to the back of my pants, where they slide inside, and he sucks in a breath as he comes in contact with the silky fabric of my panties, and I feel his dick jerk against me as he grips my ass cheeks and squeezes.

"God, baby, please," he moans. "Can't stop thinking about you and this gorgeous body. Please fuck me, cowboy."

He's pressing his cock into me as he slides his hands inside the back of my panties now, moaning deep as he grips my bare ass cheeks. "So damn good." Fuck, I can feel his body vibrating against me and it's making me tremble.

"There's just one problem, darling," I say as he presses

kisses to my neck and jaw. "You got fucked the last time and I believe it's my turn to bottom."

His grip on my ass cheeks tightens and he humps me desperately. "No, please," he begs. "Please, baby, I swear I'll let you bottom five times straight if you just get that big, beautiful cock inside me right fucking now. I swear I'll die if you don't fuck me."

I chuckle even as I grip his hips to keep him pressed up against me. "Hmm, you feel awfully good," I tell him. I reach up and grip his throat and he whimpers as his dick jerks and he undulates his hips, drawing a filthy moan out of me. "Say it again, darling. Tell me how pretty my cock is, and I'll fuck your slutty little cunt until you're screaming for me." I tighten my grip on his throat, but not so much that he can't speak, and he shivers. He still hasn't stopped rutting against me and it's almost enough to drive me mad.

Every single word of praise makes my dick a little bit harder, makes me want him a little bit more. "Fuck, it's so perfect, baby. So damn beautiful. It's the prettiest cock in the world, and I want it inside me so damn bad."

I grip his throat a bit harder still and kiss him hard, before I pull away. "Strip," I tell him. "Show me that pussy." I don't think I've ever seen him undress so fast, his pants and underwear down at his ankles in record time and his shirt on the floor in a heap next to mine. I know this is risky. We could get caught, but somehow that makes it even more erotic, and being almost completely naked while we fuck in the back room of his workplace is really revving my engine.

"Hands on the wall and spread your legs for me," I tell him, as I undo my pants and slide them down. He obeys, and juts his ass out for me. God, it sure is pretty.

"Fuck, Bentley, please," he whines, shaking the taut globes.

"Shh," I coo, pressing against him from behind, my

panties still on, barely containing my erection, and soaked in my precum. I reach around and grip his throat again, my other hand on his abdomen as I move my hard dick against his ass and he lets out a noise that's somewhere between a wail and a gasp, making my dick even harder. "Feel what you do to me?" I rumble against his ear, making sure my precum gets on his cheeks and in his ass crack. "Feel how wet you make me, darling?"

"Yes." He trembles as tears slide down his cheeks. "Shit, baby, I'm a fucking mess. Please fuck me. I can't."

"Damn, darling, you're making me soak myself and I kinda like it. You keep crying like that I might come." I nibble on his neck as I grip his throat tighter and press him back against me, making him gasp.

"I reckon you want my cock inside your pussy right about now?"

He nods as much as he can with my hand around his throat. I rub my wet cock and panties against him a few more times just to see more of those perfect tears.

He nearly sobs in relief when I pull my panties down just enough for my cock to spring free, and release his throat so I can spread his cheeks, moving my dick around his hole, getting him nice and lubed up with my precum before I fuck him.

"Mmm, baby, your pussy feels so good against my dick," I murmur. "You gonna choke my cock with that pretty cunt?"

He nods furiously and juts his ass out more. I slide a finger inside him and he mewls, shaking as I grip his throat again. "Tell me it's mine," I growl in his ear, before sliding a second finger inside his tight heat.

He's so beside himself now I don't honestly know if he's registering my words until he says, "Yours."

I nibble his ear, and he sucks in a breath, pressing up on

his toes, allowing my fingers to slide even further inside him. His hands are against the wall, my hand gripping his throat, my fingers up his ass, and he's shaking for me. It's perfection, my beautiful Alex. "What is, darling?"

He sobs. "My pussy. It's yours, baby. It's all yours."

I slide a third finger in and he cries out when I peg his prostate. I can't fucking get enough and I do it again and again, just to hear him make those desperate sounds and feel his body shake against me.

"Bentley," he sobs, and I decide he's been tortured enough. I press a kiss to his shoulder as I slide my fingers out of him and slick them up with the precum oozing out of my dick. Then I cover his hole in it. I'm about to tear open the condom when he says, "Wait. I want you bare. Please?"

Fuck. "Are you sure?" I ask, my chest squeezing because I know what this means to him. He wants me. All of me. And my dick is throbbing even more now with that knowledge, desperate to be inside him.

He nods furiously. "Yes, yes, I want you, baby. No barriers. Please. Want to feel you and have you come inside me."

I drop the condom on the floor before gripping his chin and turning his head to the side. I plant a heated kiss on his lips and he whimpers. Then I'm coating my dick in my precum and lining myself up with his entrance.

His gasp of relief when I push inside is palpable. "Oh fuck, Bentley. Fuck you feel so good, baby. Don't stop."

I groan as I feel his tight channel squeezing my cock. God, it feels amazing.

"You're a fucking sadistic bastard, you know that?" he says, and I chuckle, pressing a kiss to his shoulder.

"I'm gonna fuck you so good you'll forgive me, darling."

"Get to it, then, cowboy." He still has tear tracks on his cheeks and my hand on his throat as I shove inside him to the hilt, letting out another deep moan.

"You feel heavenly, sweetheart," I rumble in his ear, his breaths heavy as my dick twitches inside him and I brush the tip of my nose along his ear, drawing a moan out of him.

"Fuck, so do you," he pants. "Show me what that pretty cock can do, cowboy." My chuckle is low and deep, and we're both moaning as I move inside him.

"God, yes," he gasps. My hand on his throat tightens as my other hand comes around to rest on his abdomen again and I use slow languid thrusts, feeling his hole clamp down around me, bringing me pleasure so exquisite I can't help but draw it out. He doesn't seem to mind, either, now that I'm inside him. His eyes are closed and he rests his head against my shoulder as I fuck him, every inch of his warm body pressed to mine.

"So fucking good, darling," I rumble as my dick spears him and he shakes. "Your cunt is so tight, baby. So good."

I work myself slow for a time before I feel the need to speed up, and start to piston myself faster, gradually picking up the pace, the sound of skin slapping skin filling the small room alongside Alex's whimpers and my harsh pants.

"Touch yourself, darling," I tell him as I move. "You're gonna make me come so hard, baby. Can't get enough of this pussy."

He starts to stroke his aching erection and we're both howling our releases seconds later, his hole clamping down on my cock as I shoot inside him, and then we're panting as we rest against the wall, my arms still around him and my dick still inside him.

"God, I needed that," he says, and I hum, pressing kisses to his sweat slick skin before I slowly pull out and watch as my jizz slides down his thighs. "Fuck, that's sexy. You want it?"

He nods, and I slide my fingers through the sticky mess, getting as much of it as I can before I bring them to his lips.

He laps up every last bit, moaning around my fingers, a blissed out look on his face as he swallows down my seed. Christ, I love watching him go feral for my spunk.

"Mmm, you taste good," he says. If I didn't know better I'd say he was drunk off my cock.

"You should get dressed," I tell him, handing him his shirt. He's still a little dazed but manages to get it on, then blinks at me as I start to pull his pants up after fixing my own.

"Thanks, babe," he says, a dopey grin on his face. I chuckle as I tuck him back into his underwear and fasten his pants.

"I loved coming inside you," I tell him, gripping his chin and pressing a kiss to his lips. "That was incredible. Thank you." I give him another kiss and he chases my lips, whimpering when I pull away, making me chuckle.

"You have to get back to work, darling," I remind him. He pouts and it makes me laugh. I press one last kiss to his lips. "Go on, now. I'll stay for a bit longer before I head home."

That makes him smile and he slaps my ass before he turns and heads back out to the bar.

Alex

"Okay, so that was a touchdown or a slam dunk?" I ask my brother as he and I, along with Pierre and Bentley, sit in the stands at a Boston Red Sox game at Fenway Park. I've never been a baseball person, and apparently neither has Bentley, but when Gloria gifted him with four tickets to a game I suggested we take Tommy and Pierre, because my brother is a long-time fan of the sport, whereas the three of us have never watched a game. We knew the batter hit the ball really far, and then everyone was up out of their seats cheering, so we did it too. Now we're yanking Tommy's chain by asking him questions that we know will drive him crazy, even though we already know the answers, or at least that the questions are ridiculous.

"Home run, you bird brain," he groans, and Pierre, Bentley and I all chuckle. I take a loud sip of my drink and Pierre lets out a belch that you would never think him capable of given his small size, making Bentley and I laugh as Tommy tries not to smirk.

"I have to pee," Pierre announces. "Be right back." He's dressed in white skinny jeans and a cropped Red Sox jersey that I'm pretty sure Tommy bought him, along with a Red Sox cap, and I'm noticing how many guys are staring at him as he makes his way up the stairs to the restroom.

"Pierre's catching a lot of eyes," I tell Tommy.

"Pierre always catches a lot of eyes," he retorts. His phone buzzes and he pulls it out, smiling as he reads the text.

"Who is it?" I ask, nudging his arm. I'm hoping it's Cyrus. Tommy has been pretty tight lipped about the older man since the dinner at Mom and Dad's, but I know my brother doesn't smile at text messages from just anyone.

As soon as the question is out of my mouth Tommy is scowling at me. I just laugh, then turn to my other side and press a kiss to Bentley's cheek because I can. He blushes and I grin, then stuff a handful of overpriced popcorn into my mouth.

"When is it halftime?" I ask, and Tommy scrubs a hand down his face, whispering something in Spanish that sounds like *Lord, give me patience.*

Bentley and I laugh, and Tommy looks at us. "You guys are asking bullshit questions on purpose aren't you?"

We laugh more.

"Assholes," he says, but there's a smirk playing at the corner of his mouth.

"I'm sorry, baby brother, we couldn't help it," I chuckle. "Tormenting you is really the only reason I'm here."

"Great," he mutters, just as Pierre returns to his seat.

"I'm here for the food," Bentley says, taking another bite out of his footlong hotdog.

"I'm here for the gorgeous men in tight pants," Pierre says, waving his hand in front of his face, and Tommy shakes his head, making us all laugh.

Chapter Twenty-Three

Alex

A couple of weeks later Bentley and I are on a date at the park. We've packed a picnic dinner, and are enjoying an evening showing of *Casablanca* as we sit on our blanket, surrounded by other couples also enjoying an evening out and a movie in the park.

It's in the mid sixties and we're wearing long sleeves and pants, as well as having applied mosquito repellent to our faces to keep the annoying little buggers away.

When I'm finished with my fried chicken I use one of the wipes we brought along to clean my hands off and then scoot closer to Bentley and grip his hand, linking our fingers together as I rest my head on his shoulder.

He smiles and presses a kiss to my hair as he squeezes my hand. My heart is bursting with so much fondness for this man, so much affection. So much love. Every day with him is a blessing, and I'm realizing more and more how much I want forever with him. If I'm being honest with myself I think I've loved him since before we started dating, but telling him that might have scared the shit out of him so

I haven't said anything yet. It's been a few months now, though, and I think I might have to say something soon or I'll go crazy.

I switch positions, lying down with my head in his lap, and he grins, running his fingers through my hair.

When I get woken by soft caresses against my cheek I realize I've fallen asleep and the movie is over. I blush, giving him a sheepish grin. "Sorry."

"I'm not offended," he tells me. "I have an idea."

"What?" I say, as he runs his fingers through my hair again and I stare up at him.

"We could go home, take a bath together, and then go to bed, or we can go home and take a bath together, and then you could fuck me while I wear the black thong I just got, and afterwards I'll give you a massage."

I shoot up, my energy somehow revived. "You have a thong?"

He nods, grinning mischievously.

"Fuck, yes, that option. Let's go." I scramble to my feet and he laughs as I hurriedly pack up our things.

We play with and pet Marble for a few minutes after we walk in the door, and then we move to the bathroom and strip down.

We touch, and caress, and kiss as we wait for the tub to fill up, and by the time we're stepping into the warm water I'm rock hard, and seeing Bentley's cock dripping with precum just makes me harder.

He settles against the back of the tub and I slide between his legs, my back to his front, resting my head on his shoulder as his arms come around me and we soak, letting the warmth ease our sore muscles and relax our bodies, breathing in the lavender scented bubble bath Bentley added.

I groan when his big strong hand reaches down to grip

my erection and he gives me a few slow pulls. "Mmmm, that's nice."

"I'll get you off if you think you can get hard for me again. I want this dick inside me when we're done in here." He presses kisses to my shoulder and ear, making me shiver as he continues to stroke me, slow and torturous. My eyes close and I spread my legs wider, my hand reaching up to slide around the back of his neck.

I nod and whimper as he uses his thumb to toy with my frenulum, making me buck up into him and gasp.

"Yes?" he says, on a husky chuckle, and I nod, unable to speak. Jesus this man is a menace in bed and fucking loves to torture me. He presses more soft, wet kisses to my heated skin as I thrust up into his hand, chasing my pleasure.

He doesn't say a word, just keeps moving his hand, twisting his wrist on each upstroke, rubbing his thumb over my slit, driving me wild. Then he's sliding his hand under my ass and slipping two fingers inside my hole, making me nearly shout as his other hand moves down to my balls and he rolls them in his hand, before tugging.

"Oh God," I gasp. "Oh fuck, Bentley." I'm being impaled by his fingers and encased by his incredible hands on both ends as he works me, bringing me untold pleasure, and my body is shaking as my balls draw up and he pegs my sweet spot over and over as he plays with my sack. "Fuck, I'm gonna come, baby," I whine.

When he squeezes my balls it's game over, and I shout my release as my cock pulses untouched into the warm, soapy water, my ass clenching around his fingers still inside me. Then I'm breathing heavily as he releases me and I settle against him, aftershocks of pleasure working through me as his arms wrap around me. I jolt and gasp when he runs his fingers down my over-sensitive cock and balls, purring into my ear. "You're so fucking pretty when you come, darling."

His words have another shiver running down my spine, and he cups my balls, just holding them gently now, while we sit, his aching cock pressed against my backside.

He nuzzles my neck with his nose and breathes me in, and for whatever reason I find his big hand cupping my balls to be incredibly erotic, and comforting at the same time, like he's telling me he's got me, and I'm safe, but also telling me I belong to him.

After a few more moments he starts to wash me off, and then I do the same to him, before we climb out. I shriek when he scoops me into his strong arms right after we've finished drying off and carries me to the bed, before tossing me on top of it. Fuck, that was hot.

"Okay, you should definitely do that more often," I tell him, and he chuckles as he climbs on the bed and hovers over me. He kisses me slow and languid, until I'm hard once more, and leaking onto my belly.

"Wait," I say. "You need your panties, and I have something for you, too."

He sits back and raises an eyebrow. "What?"

I grin and roll out of bed. "You'll see."

I make my way to the closet we now share and pull out a package that I then bring back to the bed with me as he opens the dresser drawer and pulls out a sheer black thong that has my mouth watering and my dick twitching. Fuck, watching him put it on is almost as sexy as watching him take them off.

When he turns and looks at me, his perfect cock straining against the material, a wet spot already forming, his long hair still damp and falling over his shoulders, those blue eyes fixed on me, I nearly lose the ability to speak.

"Get over here," I tell him, holding my arms out for him,

and beckoning to him, suddenly desperate with the need to touch, to feel, to hold.

He climbs on the bed once more and starts kissing me again as I fall down on my back and he hovers over me, his dick sliding against mine and making us both moan. We make out for a bit, dry humping each other, before he pulls back and stares down at me.

"You wanted to give me something?" he asks, and I blink, dazed from his kisses and the way his body feels against mine.

"Mmmm," I mumble, as I reach next to me and grab the package, handing it to him. He sits back and tears it open, grinning when he pulls out the cowboy hat I got him. He doesn't hesitate to place it on his head, and my body turns to mush when he looks at me with those long eyelashes fluttering, his bicep bulging and his leaking cock still covered in that sexy as fuck thong. Holy hell, what a sight.

"Shit, cowboy, you're gonna be the death of me," I murmur, making grabby hands at him to get him to come back to me. Fuck, I feel like my whole world is in those cornflower eyes and that bright smile.

He kneels between my splayed thighs and presses kisses to my cock and balls, making me suck in a breath. "I was thinking," he says, in between kisses and nuzzling me with his nose, "that you could rim me, and spank me, and then you can pick how you want to fuck me. On my back, or on all fours, or riding you."

I shiver and nod, and he pulls back. I almost whimper at the lack of attention to my cock and balls, but sit up as he gets into position on his hands and knees. Fuck, looking at him with his tight ass in the air, his cock and balls dangling between his legs, that thin strip of material between his cheeks, and that sexy as fuck hat on his head, has me feral for him, and I don't waste any time spreading his cheeks and sliding my tongue over his hole. I do it a few times with the strap from the thong still there, moaning at the taste of him and the way he thrusts his ass back, begging for more. We both love being rimmed, but it's one of Bentley's favorite things, along with the spankings and having his nipples played with, and I am more than happy to oblige.

Rimming him with his panties on is something we haven't done yet, but I am fucking loving it. It's like an extra tease to have the tiny barrier in the way, and he seems to really enjoy the feel of the material against his taint and hole when I use my tongue to press it against him. "God, you taste incredible," I murmur as I lick and suck and kiss and feast on his glorious ass, as he mewls and shakes underneath me. I think my favorite thing is pressing soft kisses to his pucker that have him trembling and gasping each and every time, his pretty little hole fluttering against my lips.

I don't slide my tongue inside him until he's a whining, whimpering mess and has tears sliding down his cheeks. We both get off on making the other person cry, and Bentley's tears are fucking perfection.

"You want my tongue, baby?" I ask, pressing kisses to his ass cheeks. "Want me to eat out this pretty pucker?"

He whimpers at my words and my cock jerks. "Please?"

"Hmm, since you asked so nicely," I say, then slide the string of his panties aside before spreading his cheeks wide and sliding my tongue into his hole as deep as I can get. He's shaking uncontrollably and saying my name over and over again as I move my tongue inside him. Fuck, he's delicious, and all mine.

I remove my tongue after several moments, before reaching around to grip his dick in his thong. "Fuck, yes, cowboy," I groan as I revel in the weight of his cock in my palm as his precum soaks my hand. "You're so fucking wet for me, baby. Let's see if I can get your pretty panties soaked before you even come."

I sit back on my heels and then raise my hand, bringing it down hard on his ass, and making him cry out. I bring it down again on the other cheek, and he whimpers even as he wiggles his ass, silently begging for more. I swat his ass hard again and again, making sure I vary the location to keep from hurting him too much, and his ass blooms a beautiful shade of red. His cheeks are streaked with tears, and I'm desperate to taste him again. Without warning I spread his cheeks again and spear my tongue inside, and he cries out.

"Alex," he chokes out as he squirms on my tongue.

"Fuck, I need you baby," I rasp, pulling out of him. I roll onto my back and pat my thighs, and he scrambles over, straddling me. His weight feels so perfect on top of me as he stares down at me with that hat and the sexy as fuck tears sliding down his cheeks. I reach up and wipe his cheeks, before bringing his lips to mine. As we kiss I slip my hand inside his thong and gather up as much of his precum as I can, then use it to slick up his pucker. His thong is almost dripping, it's so wet, and it's a sight to behold.

"You're so damn beautiful, baby," I tell him, then use more of his precum as lube to slick up my cock. I hold it up for him and he positions himself above me, then slowly lowers himself onto my erection as I hold the string of his thong aside. I fucking love that we use his precum as lube, especially when it's his turn to bottom. There's something insanely sexy about fucking him with his own juice.

Having no barrier between us when we fuck is incredible, and makes us both feel that much closer to each other. It's given us a deeper physical and emotional bond. I love coming inside Bentley and swallowing down my own cum when it slides out of his hole. And feeling him shoot his seed inside me is everything.

I gasp when I bottom out inside him in only seconds, and then grip his thick thighs as his hands rest on my chest. Fuck, why am I so overwhelmed all of a sudden at having him on top of me, taking my cock so well?

I move my hands to his face and stare at those beautiful blue orbs. I want so much to tell him how I feel, but I don't think now is the time. So instead I swallow and say, "Ride me, cowboy."

He chuckles softly and then starts to fuck himself on my cock, and it's the hottest thing I've ever experienced, all the power and strength, that raw masculinity, taut muscles coiling and rippling as he moves up and down on my shaft, his breaths getting faster, his eyes closing and his mouth parting, head tilting back ever so slightly, as pleasure consumes him. He's a vision to watch and I can't believe I get to be the one he shares himself with. I reach up and start to play with his nipples as he moves and I thrust up into him, and he moans, moving his hand to grip his hat, arms spreading to give me better access to his hardened nubs as if to say, "yes, please, more. Touch them more." I roll them in my fingers, pinch them, tug on them, and he moves faster, his dick bouncing up and down in his thong that is so fucking wet I can't see a dry spot on it.

"Give me your nipples, baby," I rasp. "Want my mouth on you."

He lowers his chest to my mouth and I swipe my tongue over the nubs, one after the other, moaning around them, before I suck them into my mouth and he cries out. I love how much pleasure he gets out of having me suck and lick on his nipples. His hands are braced on either side of me as I feast on the nubs, reaching one hand down to slide inside his thong, making him jerk and whimper. I gather more precum on my fingers and then move them down his crack as he squirms once again. When I reach his hole, I slide one finger inside, and moan as he sucks in a breath and I feel his hole clenching around the added intrusion, before he's relaxing once again and whimpering.

"More," he begs, and I don't know if he means my mouth on his nipples or my fingers inside him, but when he shoves his ass back and wiggles it, I take the hint and slide another finger inside. He rises, removing his nipples from my reach, and impaling himself on my cock and fingers, moaning so deliciously my dick jerks inside him.

"God, that's good," he says. "I'm gonna come, darling."

"Fuck, yes, cowboy, come in your pretty panties. You look so damn sexy riding my cock, baby. Love how hard you are, how fucking soaked you are. How good you feel around me. So fucking perfect, mi hermoso vaquero."

His eyes are closed and his hand is gripping the top of his hat as his body shudders and wave after wave of cum pulses out of his beautiful cock, soaking his thong and sliding down his legs and onto my belly as his hole clamps down on my cock and fingers, and I shout my own release, crying out his name as I do, my spunk filling him up. Fuck, I don't think I've ever seen anything so damn sexy in my life.

But my heart seizes when I see the fresh tears in Bentley's eyes as he looks at me, his chest heaving.

"Hey," I say, reaching up to cup his cheek. "What's wrong? Are you okay?"

He can't seem to speak as tears slide down his cheeks and he shakes his head. He bends down to kiss me even as he cries and it's so tender and filled with so much warmth it confuses the hell out of me.

"Bentley?" I ask again, when he pulls away. "Talk to me."

He opens his mouth but nothing comes out, and then he's pulling off of me, letting my dick and fingers slip free of his body, before he scrambles off the bed and hurries out of the room. My heart is jackhammering because I have no idea what's going on and I'm really starting to freak out now. Did I hurt him? Did I scare him? What the fuck is he doing?

I swallow and sit up when he comes back a second later holding his phone in one hand and typing something, my phone in his other hand. He finishes typing and then climbs back on the bed, still wearing his cum soaked thong and cowboy hat, my spunk sliding down his legs. He hands me my phone before he wipes tears from his eyes. What the fuck?

I take it, and see that I have a new message from him. I open it, and stare, tears starting to fill my eyes now too, as a smile spreads across my face and I let out a laugh. "Really?" I say, looking at him, and he nods, wiping more tears away.

"I love you, too, cowboy," I tell him, and he's kissing me again in a heartbeat.

Bentley

A week later, we're gathered at the community pool that is shared by the residents of the apartment complex, celebrating Isabella and Johnny's thirtieth wedding anniversary. There's love songs playing from portable speakers, balloons and gifts set up on one table, and heaps of delicious food arranged on another one. Scads of guests are escaping the July heat by cooling off in the pool and more people are visiting as they snack and drink. Isabella looks lovely in a red and yellow sundress and Johnny wears chino shorts and a white short sleeved button up. They haven't drifted from each other's sides once all evening and the party has been going for several hours already.

Alex has been introducing me to some of the other neighbors in the complex and we've enjoyed some time in the pool as well. Tommy is sitting at one of the tables with Pierre on his lap, feeding his husband food as if Pierre's a baby bird. Honestly it's kind of adorable, and they seem really happy now, which I love.

As the guests start to disperse and a slow song comes on the radio, Johnny takes his wife into his arms and begins to dance with her, and I don't think I've ever seen two people who are more in love.

"Hey," I hear, and turn to see Alex next to me, smiling. "They're pretty beautiful together, aren't they?"

I nod. "Dance with me?" I ask, and he smiles wider.

"Yeah, cowboy, I'll dance with you."

I take him in my arms right where we're standing and hold him close, and as I turn slowly, swaying to the music, I catch Isabella smiling at us.

My chest squeezes as Alex rests his head on my shoulder and sighs. I never could have imagined that moving to Boston to be near Peyton and start up my business would lead me here, into the arms of this incredible man and into the lives of these incredible people who have become more than a family to me.

"I can't breathe, cowboy," Alex says, when I press a kiss to his hair and squeeze him tightly against me.

"Hush," I murmur. "You're ruining the moment."

He laughs and plants a kiss on my jaw. "I love you," he says, and I look down at him.

"I love you, too, darling." He smiles and rests his head back on my shoulder. And when the song on the speakers changes to *Lover* by Taylor Swift, I start to sing along and Alex practically purrs as the words drift over his ear.

"Love when you sing," he murmurs.

Before the family parts for the evening, Isabella and Johnny open the gifts we got them. They both love the blanket I made for them and are thanking me profusely, telling me how wonderful it will look in their apartment and how talented I am, and how incredibly soft it is. When they open the gift that's from all four of us they are both in tears, staring at the oil painting we had done for them of one of their wedding photos.

By the time the party has ended and everything has been cleaned up it's nearly midnight, and I can't believe I lasted as long as I did, and even managed to enjoy myself the entire time. I am exhausted though.

Alex takes my hand and leads me home, and we shower together, before changing. Him into a fresh pair of briefs and me into my lacy purple panties. We climb into bed and Marble hops up, and nuzzles her head against my hand, demanding attention. We both pet her and she purrs before flopping down between us. We kiss a few times before we link hands and slowly drift to sleep.

Chapter Twenty-Four

Two months later

Bentley

"Ready?" I ask, holding my hand out to Alex. I told him to get dressed up somewhat and that I had a birthday surprise for him. My man is thirty today and we're celebrating by doing something I know he will love.

He smiles and takes my hand, and we head outside into the beautiful fall weather. He blushes when I open his door for him and slides inside.

The drive takes about fifteen minutes, and when I pull up outside a local regional theater and Alex sees the huge poster advertising this month's play, his mouth falls open.

"You're taking me to see *Little Women*?" he says.

"I'd like to," I tell him, and he smiles. "If you want to go with me. And I really hope you do because I already bought the tickets and there's no refunds."

He laughs and unbuckles, before sliding across the front seat to kiss me tenderly. "Yes, please," he says, sweetly, his hand cupping my cheek.

We climb out and walk into the theater hand in hand. There's people mingling in the lobby waiting for the show to start, but I see that several guests are in their seats already, so we make our way towards the open doors and I show the usher the tickets on my phone so they can scan them. They show us where to scan the barcode that will give us access to the program so we can follow along and learn about the actors and actresses as well as the theater.

It's not an overly large theater, but it's decent sized and very nice, and we have great seats, only a few rows back in the center.

Alex settles into his seat and immediately starts perusing his program. It's not long before the lights go down and the curtain goes up, and we're being transported into the 1860s. Alex can't stop smiling and I even catch him mouthing some of the lines as the play continues, which just makes me love him that much more, and I smile when he reaches over and takes my hand part way through, giving me that heart-stopping Alex smile.

It's an absolutely perfect performance and we stand and clap at the end when the cast members bow, before we make our way back to the lobby.

I tell Alex I need to use the restroom before we leave, and when I return, my shoulders tense and my jaw clenches, because who is talking to Alex, but Stacy.

"Wait, you're here with Bentley?" I hear her saying as I approach and slide my arm around Alex's waist. She blanches and her eyes flit from him to me and back again. "You guys are fucking each other?"

"Several times a week," Alex replies, a megawatt smirk on his face, and I can't help snorting at his absolutely perfect comment.

Stacy's date finds her then and she's still gaping at us when he tries to introduce himself and she grabs his hand, pulling him away.

We're both laughing as we make our way back to the Impala.

When we arrive home we change into lounge clothes, and order take out from Alex's favorite Chinese place. Then we sit on the sofa and I give him his present.

He has the most beautiful smile on his face when he unwraps the box and pulls out the blanket I knitted for him.

"You weren't exactly as subtle as you thought with those sad eyes and pouts when I showed you the one I was making for your parents," I tell him, and he laughs and blushes. "And I was actually working on this one at the same time, just not when you were home."

He pulls me in for a tender kiss. "I love it so much. Thank you."

"There's more."

He blinks, then digs inside the box and pulls out a very small sweater. "It's gorgeous, baby, but I don't think it's going to fit me," he says, holding it up to his chest. I laugh and smack his arm.

"It's for Marble, nincompoop," I tell him and he laughs. "If she'll wear it."

"Oh, she'll wear it," he says. "Maybe not happily but she will."

"Don't torture her," I say.

"Why not?" he asks, his eyes gleaming playfully.

I laugh and kiss him, and we cuddle on the sofa, and turn on *Supernatural*. It's not long though before touches turn to caresses and kisses turn to making out, and then we're disrobing and Alex is straddling my bare cock.

Tonight it's his turn to bottom since he's the birthday boy, even though he bottomed the last time, too. I gave him a hard time about it when he pushed me on my back and climbed on top of me, but one look with those gorgeous sapphire eyes and those pouty lips, and I knew I was going to give in.

I grip his thighs as he bounces on my cock, looking as beautiful as ever, both of us moaning at the exquisite pleasure of being joined this way, of our bodies being one. I want nothing more than to see him shooting his release all over me.

"Shit, baby, you feel so good," he whines. "Love your cock in my pussy so much."

I growl at his words, thrusting up into him. "Give me those pretty tits, baby," I demand, and he moans as his cock spasms at my words and he leans over so I can reach his nipples. I suck and moan around the nubs and his desperate whimpers tell me he's close. Especially once he starts panting my name over and over between murmured, "Oh fucks" and "Oh Gods." I love that he gets so turned on by me referring to his body parts the way I do. Seeing his body respond, his dick jerk, his eyes darken, his skin erupt in goosebumps, hearing the beautiful noises he makes, is intoxicating.

"Fuck, gonna come, Bentley," he wails, and then his dick is pulsing and spurting rope after rope of creamy liquid onto my chest as his hole clenches around me, making my own dick spasm and fill his perfect body.

He slides off of me and then proceeds to lick my dick like a popsicle, lapping up whatever cum he can, making me hiss and jerk as his tongue slides over the sensitive flesh. Then he's leaning over and licking my chest free of his spunk, before collapsing on top of me.

"Best birthday sex ever," he murmurs as my arms come around him. He yelps as Marble jumps up on top of his bare back and lies on him, and I laugh, kissing the top of his head.

Epilogue

Alex

"Oh, um, what are we doing here?" I ask, when Bentley pulls into a parking spot at *Johnny's* and parks the car. It's my birthday and he treated me to dinner at a restaurant I'd been wanting to try that turned out to be amazing, then told me he'd baked me a chocolate cake for dessert. But when we finished and he asked if I was ready to go I thought he meant home, so I'm kind of confused.

"What's—" I start, turning to face him, only to cut myself off when I see him holding up a penguin that looks like it's been knitted, no doubt by him, with a bow tie around it's neck, and my breath catches when I see what's dangling from the bow tie. A simple but gorgeous white gold ring.

"Oh my God," I say, as my eyes start to fill with tears and he smiles at me.

"I need to ask you something," he says, and I laugh as tears slide down my cheeks. "About a year and half ago I met this really amazing guy in kind of an unlikely way, and it turned out he was the best thing that ever happened to me. He told me once that penguins are the most romantic animals, and since our relationship started with a penguin, well I figure we should continue it with one, too." I have more tears spilling down my cheeks as he continues. "I don't consider myself a particularly intelligent person. I'm a simple guy. I may not know a whole lot. But I know I love you with every part of me." His eyes fill with tears and he clears his throat. "To borrow from Jane Austen's Mr. Darcy, 'You have bewitched me, body and soul, Alex Florez-Romano. And I wish from this day forth to never be parted from you.'" He takes another breath. "Will Alex marry Bentley?"

I'm full on ugly crying as I nod with tears of joy streaming down my cheeks. "Yes," I tell him. "Fuck yes, baby, you know I will." I grip his cheeks and smash the penguin between us as I give him a sloppy kiss. When we pull apart I grab a tissue from the middle console and wipe my face before I look at the ring again, itching to have it on my finger.

Bentley unties it from the ribbon it's attached to and takes my hand. We're both shaking as he slides the band around my ring finger and it settles into place. Holy shit. I'm getting married. To the best man I've ever known, my best friend. The ring fits perfectly and I can't stop staring at it.

"I love it," I tell him, "and I love you, cowboy. So fucking much."

"I love you, too," he says, and we kiss again.

"Did you make this?" I ask, taking the adorable penguin from him.

He grins. "I did."

"God, that's so sweet."

"Marble helped by attacking the yarn on several occasions and almost destroying it," he says, and I laugh. "Okay, now we have to go inside and do it all over again, because our family and friends are in there, and they're expecting a proposal. I didn't want to do it the first time in front of them and be a blubbering mess, so you have to give the ring back."

I laugh and slide it off, already hating being without it, but I figure I can make it a few more minutes.

I leave the penguin in the car and we head inside, greeted by my smiling family, who sing Happy Birthday to me, and then proceed to cut the cake. When I'm finished eating, Bentley kneels in front of me and everyone gasps and awws as he asks me to marry him yet again. Mom has tears in her eyes when I say yes, and she's the first to wrap me up in a warm hug after Bentley slides the ring on my finger for the second time. Even Tommy gives me and Bentley hugs and Pierre presses a kiss to each of our cheeks.

We get more hugs and kisses from friends and family. Peyton is there with a huge smile on her face, cheering the loudest of all, and there's even a picture of Bentley's Gram sitting on the table along with my presents, which I love, because it's like she's here with us.

We dance and laugh and eat, and I can't imagine a better birthday, or a better group of people to have around us as we celebrate the beginning of the rest of our lives.

I never would have expected that when I knocked on that apartment door a year and a half ago, and a gorgeous, shy man answered the door, it would lead us to where we are now.

But thank goodness life doesn't always turn out the way you expect.

The End

Thank you for reading Alex and Bentley's story. If you enjoyed it please consider leaving a review!

You can find the rest of my books, follow me on social media, and join my Facebook group here:
linktr.ee/felsnowauthor

About the Author

I live in sunny Florida with my family and enjoy reading and writing mm romance, watching Supernatural, and I believe that Starbucks is a form of self-care. Oh, and I also love penguins :)